I0601699

ISBN 978 1787233379

This book is dedicated to

Kenneth John Budd
1946 - 2013

Who showed me friendship in life
and courage and dignity in death.

The Moving Finger Writes

Colin Holcombe

6th August 1996

He had to hit her over the head three times with the spade before he could be sure she was dead and he had to be sure she was dead before he put her in the ground; he was no monster after all, he didn't want to bury her if she was still alive. After the final sickening blow with the spade, he sat on one of the cross beams that had supported the decking. He held his head in his hands weeping and wondering how it had all come to end in such a terrible way. It's not my fault, he kept telling himself, it's not my fault.

The affair, if you could call it that, had started only a couple of months earlier and had been largely at her instigation, at least, that's how it had been in the beginning. He should have resisted her advances of course, not only because he was her tutor; but because she was only sixteen and he was more than twice her age. But then, he was only a man after all, and he had the same needs and desires and weaknesses as any other man. Maybe he was more easily led than most; or maybe it was just something about her. The way she looked or the way she smelled maybe; something that had got under his skin. She *was* beautiful. She had the firm supple body of a sixteen year old with a pretty and delicate skin, and she had a sensual manner about her that was well beyond her years. How was he expected to resist her when she came on to him that way? As well as being beautiful, she was clever and intelligent; she loved music and the arts with a passion that matched his own.

That's what had started it all. The school had been staging a production of Shakespeare's Romeo and Juliet, and she had approached him after class, saying that a production of it was on at the Theatre Royal in Bath. She desperately wanted to see it but she had no one to take her. If only he'd had the strength of will to refuse her then, or the foresight to see where it would lead, she would still be alive now. She had told her parents that a school party was going to see the play. Somehow, she had managed to acquire two tickets. He supposed her father had provide the money, thinking that he was paying for a ticket for the play and school transport to get there, and she had somehow managed to purchase the tickets. He supposed that she was able to wrap her father around her little finger, like the daughters of so many doting parents.

The play had been a particularly good production, and she had genuinely enjoyed it, and he had enjoyed being with her and seeing her enjoy it. That night she had looked more like a sophisticated twenty five year old woman than a sixteen year old schoolgirl. The dress she'd worn for the occasion had obviously not been a cheap one and she had looked stunning in it. All dolled up to the nines for a night at the theatre she had attracted a great many admiring glances. He began to want her so badly that he told her stupid things. He told her that his marriage was on the verge of breaking up. Well, that part wasn't so wide of the mark but he also told her that he loved her and would leave his wife and marry her, that they would be together for the rest of their lives and she had believed him. It was all so romantic. Perhaps it had even been true when he'd said it. He knew, of course, that she didn't really love him; that it was just a silly schoolgirl crush and she would eventually come to her senses and realise that she really fancied boys of her own age. But it was a strange phenomenon that, despite the fact that he was twice their age some of the girls thought he was quite good looking, and girls had had crushes on him before. He had even succumbed a couple of times in the past, but he had never been this obsessed with any of the others. With Lucy, if he was honest with himself, he didn't care that it was just a crush on her part. He would have said or done anything to possess her. Reason took flight when he was with her. They had made love on three occasions now and she was like a drug to him, the more he had her, the more he wanted her. He felt like a teenager himself when they were together. He supposed it was a kind of madness. Either that or he was having an early mid-life crisis.

That evening, she had told her parents that she was going to the cinema with a girlfriend, Susan Cooper. Susie would always cover for her; they were as thick as thieves those two. In actual fact, they had gone to see a band that she liked at a place in town called, "The Cellar," in Weston-super-Mare. He had hated it. The band hadn't been too bad; three lads playing guitars and keyboard and a female vocalist who, judging by her performance that night, was destined for a successful solo career. But the club itself was brash and loud and crowded with lots of young people dancing and drinking far too much cheap alcohol. There were lots of places he would rather have taken her, but it was prudent to stay away from any of their usual haunts in case they bumped into somebody one of them knew. After the club he had brought her here to the house for coffee before dropping her off the usual short walk from her house in Clevedon. They both knew that the real reason for coming to the house was for sex rather than coffee and that part had gone well; even after they had consumed two bottles of wine between them. But then she had started on again about when he was going to tell his wife and her parents about them. She didn't like having to lie to them all the time about where she was going and who she was with. She knew her parents would object to the relationship of course, on the grounds of the age gap between them, let alone the fact that he was a married man but she was confident they would accept it when they realised how much they were in love with each other.

That was when they had their first, and as it turned out, only row. She started on about marriage again. He had heard it all before and it was beginning to get on his nerves. He told her they had to wait at least until he was single again, although what he really meant if he was honest with himself, was until he managed to get her out of his system. If he ever could that was. She had stayed on the bed crying and he had gone downstairs to make himself a black coffee. His head was spinning and he still had to drive her home. He drank his coffee alone in the kitchen, not wanting to return to the bedroom until the crying had stopped, but conscious of the fact that Lucy's parents would be getting worried about their daughter if he didn't get her home soon. It was all getting out of hand but he knew he couldn't end it yet, he still wanted her too much.

When he had gone back to the bedroom, he thought at first that she had just fallen asleep, but he was unable to rouse her.

He shouted at her, "Lucy!....Lucy wake up! You have to get dressed now....It's time to go." But there was no response.

He shook her by the shoulders, gently at first, but then more vigorously when that failed to bring her round. He even slapped her face, but there was still no response, *nothing*; it was as if she was dead. *Oh my*

God! He thought back to when they had been at the club, drinking. He'd had to pay a visit to the Gents, a most unpleasant experience he recalled; too small a room for the size of the venue, smelling of urine and God knows what else. It was filled with drunken youths waiting in line to pee into a totally inadequate number of urinals that were far too small for purpose and far too close together to be hygienic. He had briefly considered going into one of the three cubicles but just a quick glance inside one and the smell from it had changed his mind about that option, so he had waited his turn. On his return to Lucy in the bar, he had caught sight of her taking some tablets but he had naively just assumed they were medication or headache pills. It hadn't occurred to him that they could be anything else. *But what if they had been drugs of some kind?* Kids these days were always popping pills of some sort or another if you listened to the news. He had no idea whether she was in the habit of taking any, what did they call them, recreational drugs. *Oh Christ!* Could this really be happening to him?

The stupid cow must have had them with her, or perhaps somebody had sold them to her while he was doing his best to avoid being splashed by other people's urine in the toilets. What the hell was he supposed to do now? He caught hold of her wrist and felt for a pulse but he couldn't find one. What were the other tests? He couldn't think straight. His mind was refusing to function efficiently, partly because of the alcohol he had consumed and partly because he was beginning to panic. He watched her chest for a while to see if he could see it rising and falling but he couldn't be sure. He put his face up to her mouth but he could feel no trace of a breath. He put his ear to her chest to listen for her heartbeat, but was answered by only silence and her skin felt cold to the touch.

"Oh! Dear God!" He screamed out loud, *"She's dead! She's bloody well dead!"*

He kicked the side of the bed in frustration and began pacing the room, up and down, wringing his hands in despair, trying to think what to do.

Why had his wife chosen to go to some *damn* seminar that week of all weeks. If she hadn't gone, he would never have brought the girl here. Ha.... *the girl*....he was already beginning to distance himself from her. Lucy Penrose, that was here name, LP or **Vinyl** to her friends. Dear God, had she told any of them what she was doing tonight, or had she bragged to any of them about seeing him? He didn't think she had. She had always promised to be discreet but he couldn't be sure, she might have seen it as a way of forcing the issue, so that he had to come clean about their affair.

He stopped his pacing for a moment and looked at her lying motionless on the bed, praying for some kind of miraculous resurrection. Should he call an ambulance or the police, or both, he had no idea, and what would the consequences be? Well he would probably be arrested or something, *that's what!*

He didn't suppose there would be any real charges against him, why should there be? After all, he hadn't actually done anything wrong; well not illegal anyway. The girl was sixteen, so there was no problem with her age. She was his student however, and that made it look bad didn't it? So it could be argued that what he was doing was morally wrong, but no more than that.....*No more than that!*......What the hell was he thinking. His wife would certainly look on it as the last straw and divorce him. He would probably be kicked out of his teaching job and find it difficult to get another. And then there was certain to be an autopsy and drugs would be found in her system. What if the police then wanted to take things further? Suppose they thought *he* had given her the drugs? Maybe even that he was a drug dealer! *Or worse still!* Suppose they thought that he had administered some drug or other in order to have sex with her. Not only would he be arrested, he would be charged as a sex offender, a rapist of all things, and everyone knows how well they fare in prison. The more he thought about it, the less he liked the idea of calling anyone.

What was the alternative? He began pacing again; well...his wife wouldn't be home for another three days at least, so he had time on his side, and he was fairly sure that Lucy hadn't told anyone about him. He instinctively crossed his fingers at that one. Her parents thought she was at the cinema with a girl-friend, so if *he* didn't tell anyone what had happened, she would just be another missing girl who failed to come home after a night out. *Awful...yes....*but not his fault, he didn't see why *his* life should be ruined because she had been stupid and taken something with all that booze.

He wished he could turn back the clock and undo everything, but the words of Omar Khayyam filled his head; "The moving finger writes, and having writ moves on." Well, the bloody moving finger had written for him all right and no mistake. He was well and truly stuffed! And there *was* no going back, he could see that. He had to look to the future....his future.

He went back downstairs, opened the back door and went into the garden to get some air and clear his head so he could think. His instinct was to just take her body somewhere and dump it. *Idiot!* he thought to himself, that would just make things ten times worse. There would still be an autopsy when her body was found, and they would recover his DNA from her body somehow, as well as the drugs in her system. It would look to the police like a *rape and murder*! He'd end up spending the rest of his life in prison as a convicted rapist for sure. But there had to be some way out of his predicament, he just had to find it. He needed to make sure her body wasn't found. That was it, it was the only solution. He would have to find a way of concealing her body.

It was almost like daylight in the back garden. The moon was suspended in a bright cloudless sky. The well maintained back garden was both wide and long, wrapping itself around the sides of the house either side and joining the front garden, which, although only a quarter the size of the back, would still be considered large in comparison to most properties. The dining room had French doors opening out onto an area of decking at the back of the house. The decking extended some four metres out from the property and ran the whole width of it. It was a sun trap in the summer and he had enjoyed many a glass of fine wine and enjoyable conversation there with friends.

He could hardly believe that he was contemplating what was going through his mind. But it was almost as if he was operating in some kind of other dimension, completely detached from the reality of what had happened. He had little doubt that given enough time, he could take up part of the decking and dig a grave for the unfortunate Lucy, right here in the back garden, then cover it over and replace the decking without it appearing to have been touched.

There were some factors that made the plan more than workable. Firstly, the nearest neighbours were far enough away that none of the garden was overlooked. Secondly, the said decking had only been in place for a couple of years or so, maybe three, and the screw heads would still be easy to locate and easy to undo. Thirdly, there was a shed full of tools including two spades, a pickaxe, a chainsaw and various hand tools - everything he would need. And last but not least, his wife wouldn't be back for a few more days, providing him with plenty of time to accomplish the task.

He weighed up the options in his mind once again. Call the police and an ambulance to a dead girl and end up divorced, unemployed, disgraced and maybe even charged with something horrible and imprisoned.... or.... bury her in the garden and take his chances that she had not told anyone of their liaison. It was a no-brainer really. So, with great determination and the realisation that he couldn't have felt any real affection for poor Lucy after all, he opened the shed and selected the tools he would need for the job in hand, still operating in a kind of trance. The only tool not in the shed that he felt he would need, was a torch but he had a decent one in the car, so he retrieved that first.

Returning from the car, torch in hand, he weighed up his options. The decking ran the full width of the house and he remembered that there had been a patio area made of crazy paving outside the French-doors before the decking, but flowerbeds outside the kitchen window. He reasoned that the old flower beds would be easier to dig so he began unscrewing the decking below the kitchen window.

Removing the decking had proved to be even easier than he had supposed, but digging a large enough hole in between the decking support beams had proved to be anything but easy. He briefly contemplated cutting out one of the beams, but decided it would be too risky and too difficult to conceal. He was concerned that the decking might bounce a little in the place it had been and alert someone to the fact that something had changed. He had to use the pickaxe to loosen the compacted soil and large stones that were everywhere, and when he was a couple of feet down it became even harder. Once loosened, he had to dig out the soil and stones with the shovel and place it all on the tarpaulin he had spread out for the purpose. He was careful to keep the soil on the tarpaulin and avoid spilling too much elsewhere, so that he wouldn't have too much to clean up afterwards. He was conscious of the need to hide any signs of disturbance. It was a good two and a half hours of hard physical labour before he decided the hole was deep enough to conceal a body.

He had just thrown the last shovelful of soil unto the tarpaulin and was thinking of taking a much earned breather, *when Lucy appeared at the French-doors,* clutching her head and staggering drunkenly.

"I must have passed out," she said, slurring her words, "I couldn't find you....where had you gone?....what are you doing out here?"

He stared back at her with a mixture of bewilderment, incredulity, and a huge amount of relief. He dropped the shovel.

"Lucy! You're alive! Thank God!" he cried with genuine relief.

As she surveyed the scene, Lucy stared in confusion as her eyes slowly became accustomed to the moonlight. It looked for all the world as if he was digging a big hole under the decking. Why would he be digging a big hole in the garden in the middle of the night? It didn't make any sense to her. And why had he left her upstairs, passed out on the bed while he did it? Wasn't he concerned about her? And why was he so surprised to see her now? What was it he'd said? "Your alive....thank God."

Then it suddenly struck her like a physical blow......*"Oh my God!......you thought I was dead!....not just passed out,"* she began to put two and two together rapidly, *"and you were going to bury me in the garden! How could you? you bastard!"* she shouted in rage.

"No....Lucy....listen to me, it's not like that." he declared, holding out his arm and taking a step towards her.

Horror was etched on her face, *"Oh dear! she's dead...better bury her in the garden then...is that what you thought...you bastard!....you evil bastard.....Just wait till my mum and dad hear about this."* She continued to rant, *"First you screw their daughter, then you go to bury her in the garden! They'll ruin you for sure, they'll have you arrested!!! I'll tell the police you drugged me at the club, and that I woke up here....you'll go to prison for sure, you bastard....you evil bastard....you'll pay for this!!!"*

She turned back to go in doors, still only partially dressed from their earlier lovemaking.

He called out to her again, "**Lucy,**" then hurried after her. "Wait....it's not the way you think," he shouted, thinking to himself that in fact, that was exactly the way it was. He felt a little ashamed. But there was no going back now, that bloody moving finger had written with a vengeance this time and was moving on at a pace, faster than he could keep up.

She stumbled and fell as she entered the lounge area and he caught up with her, straddling her back and pinning her to the floor. She somehow managed to turn onto her back and tried to kick him off but he sat astride her waist and leaned forward, pinning her hands above her head. He wanted her to lie still so that he could talk some sense into her, make her listen to reason, but she was frightened of him now and angry; she fought like a tigress.

"Lucy!....Listen, let's talk about this," he pleaded, but she was in no state to be reasoned with.

He felt that she was getting her hands free so he leaned forward to apply more pressure on her wrists but in doing so, he inadvertently raised up off her waist a little and she somehow manage to bring her knee up, making painful contact with his crotch. He fell off her sideways, gasping in pain and holding his battered manhood, tears filling his eyes. Despite having been in a stupor earlier and her head pounding from all the tablets and drink she had consumed, Lucy was up off the floor in seconds. But she was unsure which way to run, she was disorientated and half naked in a strange house.

The brief hesitation cost her dear. As she started towards the door he managed to reach out and grab hold of her ankle, causing her to trip. She fell to the floor again and this time her head made heavy contact with it, rendering her unconscious for the second time that evening.

He stood up and surveyed the carnage around him, still in some pain. Luckily, nothing appeared to be broken, although the coffee table had been knocked over, sending a box of tissues and some magazines cascading to the floor. The biggest problem he faced, if you put aside the fact that Lucy now seemed intent on having him arrested and charged with drugging, kidnapping, and presumably raping her, was the mud that he had brought in on his shoes. He couldn't believe how calm he was now that Lucy's ranting had stopped and he was in control once again.

He took a moment to consider his options. It seemed to him that nothing had really changed since Lucy put in her unexpected appearance. Although Lucy was alive and not dead, he was still faced with the same alternatives as before. Lucy seemed determined to lie that he had drugged her and have him charged, out of pure spite. The only way he could see of saving himself from some serious jail time was to have her disappear. Ha! have her disappear. He couldn't even bring himself to think the word, *murder*, let alone carry out the action. But it was the only way, he had to go through with the burial!

Murder, that's what he was talking himself into, it wasn't going to be an accident, and it wasn't going to be just concealing a dead body anymore, it was going to be....all out....cold blooded....*murder*. The thing that truly shocked him to his core was the realisation that he would be able to do it. Of that there was no doubt in his mind. Who would have thought it? He was actually going to murder a young innocent girl....well....a fairly innocent girl...and bury her in the garden. He began to wonder, and not for the first time, whether he actually had any genuine feelings at all. Oh...how stupid....of course he had feelings. He loved music after all, didn't he? It was feelings for other people he lacked, he had no empathy for anyone......what did that make him? He wondered. Still...he could think about things like that another time. Right now there was work to be done.

How?....How was he going to kill a fellow human being? And a bright young girl at that, a young girl with her whole life before her; a girl that he had been intimate with only hours before. Best to make up his mind soon and do it while she was still unconscious. At least that would save her the trauma of it...and it would be easier for him as well. As he saw it, he could bash her over the head with something or he could strangle her, or he could stab her with a knife from the kitchen or even suffocate her. Once he started to think about it he realised there were lots of ways to kill someone. He coldly weighed up the options in his mind. If he started to strangle or suffocate her, she might come round during the process, and that would be unpleasant for both of them. If he stabbed her there would be lots of blood and he was anxious to avoid any mess. So he determined to drag her back into the garden and hit her over the head with the spade, and that....is what he did.

A while later he sat on the decking cross beam with his head in his hands. He stayed like that for some twenty minutes feeling sorry for himself, for the plight this girl had got him into. Finally he dragged Lucy's lifeless body across to the hole he had dug and laid her to rest. He had been unable to dig the make-shift grave long enough for the body to be stretched out completely, due to the spacing between the decking joists, and the fact that he had been reluctant to cut one. He had coped with digging underneath one of them, but it had been difficult and he didn't fancy going under another. So he had made the hole wider instead, enabling him to place her on her side and bend her knees up to her chin.

He pulled her head and shoulder up to one end of the grave as far as possible with some effort. He then took hold of her legs; those very same young legs that he had earlier stroked and kissed with such tenderness, and roughly pulled them up into a foetal position. Once that was done he stood above the grave and looked down on his handiwork with the critical, scrutinising eye of a builder or engineer examining his work, wondering if he had dug the grave deep enough. The truth was, he had no idea whether the grave was deep enough or not, but it was as deep as he could go in the circumstances and with the limited resources at his disposal. It would have to suffice.

He retrieved the remainder of her clothes and her handbag from the bedroom and deposited them alongside poor Lucy's body in the grave. Next, he placed all the large stones that he had laboriously dug out of the ground directly over the body, hoping that they would in some way help to keep it down and began filling in the grave. Once the body was out of sight he found it much easier to get on with the task in hand. He no longer had the feeling that she was watching him disapprovingly from the grave.

When the grave was fully filled in, he found that he still had a fair quantity of soil left over. It's one of those strange laws of nature that decrees that the earth you dig out of a hole, will never all fit back into it again, even if you don't bury anything. But he managed to spread it about, both under other parts of the decking and on the various flower beds and amongst the many shrubs. He then replaced the black weed barrier that he'd had to cut up and finally refitted the decking.

In the moonlight the job appeared to be perfect, but he realised that he would have to check it more scrupulously in daylight. There was also the inside of the house that had to be cleaned and restored to normal as well, so, as he was now incredibly tired, he resolved to call it a night and complete the clean-up jobs in the morning. After all, it was a Saturday and the schools had broken up for the summer. He would still have a few days before his wife's return, plenty of time to sort out anything he may have overlooked.

Exhausted, he took off his dirty clothes, showered, and went to bed in the guest room that he and Lucy had used for their ill-fated coupling.

That night, even with the burden of murder to keep him company, he slept soundly and dreamlessly, and rose in the morning to the sound of birds singing and sunlight streaming in through the unlined curtains. Sights and sounds, that Lucy Penrose would never experience again.

He felt well and decided to make himself some breakfast before resuming his clean-up operation. Once he had finished his coffee and cereal, that he had to have dry because there was no more milk in the fridge, he went back upstairs and tidied the guest room. The mud that he had walked in the previous evening had dried and vacuumed up easily, leaving no trace. He straightened the furniture and checked the house over from top to bottom to satisfy himself that all looked as it should do. The interior of the house taken care of, he ventured once more into the garden and was pleased to discover that there was very little left to do. A bit of tidying here and bit of sweeping there and all looked well. After the decking had been swept from end to end, it didn't present the slightest appearance of having been disturbed, sweeping it had actually deposited dirt and soil over the screw heads once again, so not even they would inform on him. He was very pleased with the outcome. He cleaned the tools he had used and returned them to the shed. All that remained now was to remove all possible trace of Lucy from his car....and his life.

Chapter 1

7th September 2013

Jack was thinking how lucky he was to be working in the open air on such a beautiful day. The conservatory firm he worked for was a national company and although strictly speaking, Jack was classed as self-employed, they supplied him with so much work that they were his only client. His partner, Ed, had often argued that they shouldn't put all their eggs in one basket and that they should try to get work from other sources as well.

"What if Nailbourne Conservatories go bust or something, we'd be right up the swannee," he'd argue.

He was right of course, but equally, they didn't want to turn down any work that Nailbourne Conservatories gave them, so they really didn't have time for any other customers. The only way to take on more work would be to take someone else on, an employee or two, and then there would be wages and national insurance to sort out. Would the extra work be worth the extra expense and hassle?

Which one of them would take on the additional administration work? and so the debate had become a sort of tradition between them. One arguing the case to take on a couple of employees and the other arguing against it, and the next they had the topic came up they had switched roles and were each arguing the opposite point of view. All this meant was that nothing was ever done to change things and life continued as it always had.

The job they were doing now was typical of the work they were given. A young couple in a nice three-bedroom, detached house with, it had to be said, an enormous garden, wanted a conservatory to sit in so they could enjoy the garden all year round To that end they had called in Nailbourne Conservatories. A salesman from Nailbourne had called out one evening and designed a conservatory for them on a laptop computer. The software not only allowed the designer to add in all the components that were necessary, but also priced everything, including the fitting charges, so the customer received a written quotation straight away, subject to a survey of course.

The young couple in question were Daniel

West and Rebecca Drake, and they had been living together for less than a year. Daniel was six feet tall, but weighing only eleven stone he looked a little slim for his height. He made guitars for a living and ran his own little music shop on the Gloucester Road, a busy thoroughfare leading out of Bristol centre. His shop kept a modest stock of guitars, violins and recorders and had a small workshop where he made guitars to order. He was slowly acquiring a reputation amongst professional musicians and had recently received a commission from a world-renowned guitarist and folk singer. He had inherited his house, "The Cedars," from his parents after they had gone to London for a couple of days and been killed in a car crash on their way home.

Rebecca Drake worked as a conference and events manager at a Holiday Inn near the centre of Bristol. She was five foot seven with dark hair, hazel eyes and a liking for fashionable clothes.

They had done a deal for the conservatory there and then, and now, six weeks later, survey completed and plans approved, Jack and Ed were digging the foundations.

Jack and Ed had met the couple only briefly the day before, when they had turned up to check out the property and unload some equipment ready for the next day's start. The pair had built conservatories for all sorts of people over the years, young and old, rich and not so rich. Some of them just let workmen get on with things and kept out of the way, not even offering a cup of tea or coffee, expecting them to have brought their own. these were the ones that often found something to complain about when the work was completed, in the hope they could screw some sort of compensation out of the company. Some people offered tea and even lunch on occasions but insisted on being there watching every hole dug and every screw inserted, and sometimes offered advice on how things could be done more efficiently. They were a real pain in the derrière.

This couple however were ideal clients. They had wanted to know what the plan of action was, left a phone number where they could be contacted if the need arose, showed Jack where the tea and biscuits were kept and even said there were a couple of cold beers in the fridge if they wanted. Neither Jack nor Ed would even think about drinking during the day when they were working, but it was a nice gesture that was greatly appreciated. It also meant that they would go that bit further to assure a clean tidy job. They seemed a really nice young couple.

Being a detached property had allowed them the luxury of getting a mini-digger around to the back of the house and it was in the cab of this digger that Jack was sitting, bare-chested to soak up the rays and collect some vitamin D, but with a peaked baseball cap to shield his eyes from the sun and cover what Ed referred to as his shiny spot.

Jack was very good at handling small plant and he always felt like a kid in a toyshop when they had occasion like this to use some. Ed was directing operations on the ground, indicating to Jack with hand signals exactly where he was to dig, and keeping a wary eye out for any unexpected drainage pipes, electricity cables, or as Ed was fond of saying, unexploded bombs.

If Jack ever did unearth a drain or cable....or an unexploded bomb, or indeed anything that required him to perform the digger driver's equivalent of an emergency stop, the pre-arranged signal was for Ed to stand perfectly upright with both hands raised straight up in the air and shout. *Stop!.. Stop!... Stop!...* at the top of his voice. Ed had spent a brief period in the Territorial Army and saw himself as officer material. At any rate, he was good at barking commands.

It was exactly that emergency stop scenario that now confronted Jack in his cab. As soon as he saw Ed's arms shoot aloft, he lifted the mechanical shovel well clear of the ground and switched off the engine so he could hear what Ed was raving about so excitedly.

Ed was shouting in an uncharacteristically excited manner, *"Jack!* Get down here...Look at this!...What do you make of it?"

Jack jumped down from the cab, half expecting Ed to point to some small fragment of pottery and declare that they had found a Roman Villa. Ed watched Time Team on the television as if it was a religion, and he was for ever stopping to examine tiny fragments of pottery or metal that he thought might turn out to be of national importance, but they had never found anything of any real value or interest.

Full of curiosity nevertheless, Jack looked down at where Ed was pointing with such excitement. At first, he didn't notice anything out of the ordinary, but then Ed jumped into the ditch and after scrabbling in the soil for a minute came up holding what looked like a *human skull* in his hands!

Jack almost jumped out of his skin, taken completely off guard by the bizarre find, "*Bloody hell!!*...Ed...is it real?"

"Looks pretty damn real to me," came the excited reply, "I wonder if it's Saxon or Roman or something?"

Oh! here we go, thought Jack, "Are you sure it's not just plastic or something? You know, it could be a stage prop, or from one of those skeletons they sell to medical students and doctors for training. Are there any other bits? It can't be real. It certainly can't be Saxon anyway, they would have found it when they built the house you idiot, so it's got to be after 1880."

"My God!...you're right....it could be quite recent," said Ed. "Look...I don't think I should go searching for any more bits. I think we should call the police. It seems to me if it wasn't real there would no point in anybody burying it....get on your mobile and dial 999."

"Why the police?" asked Jack, spreading his hands out in a gesture of exasperation. "It's probably a fake; and if it's not, it's bound to have been here for years. The police aren't going to be interested." Jack was now concerned that the find was going to hold them up on the job.

"Look," said Ed, "you're right that it's got to be more recent than the house, or it would have been found when they put the original foundations in wouldn't it? So I think we have to let the authorities know. We may have found a murder victim for all we know."

"How come, whenever we dig up a piece of pottery you think it's Roman or Saxon or something, but now we find a skeleton, you've come to the conclusion it points to some recent Jack the Ripper. Do you think the charming young couple that live here are serial killers or something and that they bury their victims in the garden?" asked Jack, shaking his head. "Are you absolutely sure it's real?"

Jack was reluctant to ring the police, not wanting to risk looking a fool for one thing and not wanting to be delayed for another. But he did as he was bid. After a brief conversation with a somewhat officious sounding woman while he paced back and forth, he asked Ed to jot down a telephone number. He seemed to Ed to be somewhat confused and not a little frustrated.

"She said it's not an emergency would you believe, so I have to ring the local cop shop; she gave me the number."

"Not an emergency! I thought finding a dead body buried in a garden would be a 999 job didn't you?"

"Yeah, but apparently, as nobody is in any danger at the moment, it's not. So we just have to ring the local nick and report it."

Jack rang the number he'd been given, and after spending some time trying to convince the person he was talking to that he hadn't just unearthed some animal bones, he was told that someone would call within the hour.

"They're going to send someone out in the next hour, and we have to sit still and wait." He said "we're not to touch anything. I knew this was going to delay us," replied Jack angrily.

"I still can't believe we couldn't just ring the emergency services," repeated Ed. "I thought the flying squad would be here in minutes, with a body being found."

"Well I suppose it's not as if the killer, if there was a killer, is still on site, is it? Or that the victim could still be saved by a paramedic. Whoever that is, or rather was, if it's real, they're way past being resuscitated."

"Yeah, I suppose you're right, but I think we ought to call the owners of the house to let them know we've found a body in their garden, don't you. And Nailbourne Conservatories, to let them know we've been delayed and why. If we get held up too long we'll have to move on to the next job, or our schedule is going to be right up the creek."

"Do you think we'll be interviewed on television or anything?" asked Ed. "It's bound to make the local news."

"Maybe...I wonder if they would pay for an interview. At least that would recoup some of the money we're going to lose. But do you think the publicity of finding a body, if it is a body, will be good publicity or bad?"

"Don't they say that all publicity is good publicity?"

"Yeah that's right, we might get a big influx of work and have to take someone on."

"Oh!....Don't start."

Whilst waiting for the police to arrive, Jack and Ed made their phone calls and settled down in the garden with a cup of tea and Ed's paper. The sun was shining so Ed took his shirt off as well and sat with his partner, who never wore a shirt when he was working unless it was raining or below freezing.   The pair of them relaxed and soaked up the sun. The skull, which they now saw was badly damaged at the back, possibly by Jack's mechanical shovel, sat on top of Ed's tool box next to Jack's feet, looking like a rather dirty theatre prop from a Shakespeare play.

Ed placed the puzzle page from his newspaper in front of it so it looked as if the skull was reading, but Jack was less than impressed by his partners attempt at humour.

"For God's sake Ed, have a little respect. That was a human being once," now fully convinced of the skull's authenticity having seen it up close, "somebody's son or daughter. It's not a bloody toy!"

"You're right," agreed Ed, suitably admonished, as he removed the offending paper.

When Rebecca Drake received the call from Ed telling her that they had found a body in her garden, her blood ran cold. She was convinced it had to be the work of Craig Harper. During last year's summer, she and her family had been targeted by a pair of extremely violent men who had twice tried to kill her father. She called her partner, Daniel West, and told him of the phone call between bouts of crying. They both agreed to leave work and return home to find out exactly what was going on, but not before calling Detective Inspector Paul Manley, who had become a family friend during the dreadful business of that summer.

Inspector Paul Manley was thirty-three years old, a shade over six feet tall and now married to Margaret Manley, nee Collins, who worked for

Rebecca's father Richard Drake. Rebecca and Margaret were more like sisters than friends and Richard's wife Elizabeth looked on Margaret as a second daughter. So it had been natural for Rebecca to think of calling Paul straight away, it was the same as calling family.

The first person to turn up at the house, after Daniel and Rebecca, was a young constable by the name of Brian Huntley. Jack showed him the skull. At first, he didn't appear to know what to do, but instructed Jack and Ed to wait in the house while he called in for instructions. However, before he had time to make the call the home owners Daniel and Rebecca turned up, demanding to be told exactly what was going on.

Constable Huntley was endeavouring to calm down the obviously distraught woman, explain thing to her partner and answer the endless train of questions from the builders when the door-bell rang again. This time it was more police who turned up and they took over, somewhat to the relief of constable Huntley.

The tall, plain clothed officer introduced himself to the constable as Detective Inspector Paul Manley, and explained to him that the householders, Daniel and Rebecca, had called him when they heard of the grim discovery. There was another constable with him whom he introduced as Constable June Kelly.

June Kelly was also a familiar figure to Rebecca and Daniel, and greeted them as friends, "Hello Rebecca...Daniel...Paul tells me a body has been found in your garden....how awful for you both."

Constable Brian Huntley was relieved to have a more senior man take over and explained to Paul that he hadn't yet had a chance to actually do anything other than view the discovery in the garden.

"I was just about to call in and get some advice," he explained.

"That's all right," said Paul, realising the young officer was pleased to have assistance, "I'll take over if you like." He then instructed Constable Kelly to take statements from Ed and Jack while he had a look at what exactly had been found.

Paul called for **SOCO** or Scene of Crime Officers as soon as he had satisfied himself of the skulls authenticity, then called his DCI to let him know what had happened.

After they had given their statements to June Kelly, Ed and Jack were told that they could go.

"It's going to be some time before you can re-commence your work on the conservatory, I'm afraid," said Paul sympathetically.

"This is going to screw our schedule up and no mistake," grumbled Ed as they prepared to leave, "and what about all our gear in the garden? When can we pick that up?"

"I sorry," replied Paul, "but you will have to leave everything as it is at the moment, until SOCO have finished at least. I'll let you know as soon as you can have your tools from the garden."

"Inspector, we need those things in order to earn a living, what about the mini-digger? That's hired and is costing us money every day."

"I'm sorry, but I don't think it will be more than a day or two, SOCO will examine everything and I'll tell them how important to you the tools of your trade are, and they will be released to you as soon as humanly possible, I can't promise any more than that, I'm sorry."

"But why do you need them? We only arrived on scene yesterday and that thing's been in the ground a lot longer than that, even I can tell."

"SOCO will want to examine the treads and the shovel from the digger to see if they have picked anything up, and actually, I'd like you to leave your boots as well. I promise you can have them back ASAP."

"Our boots! Oh come on inspector; what can you possibly want our boots for!"

"I'm sorry...But you've both been trampling over a potential crime scene. Have you no other shoes with you?"

"Yeah, in the van," said Ed, realising the futility of arguing, and submitting to Paul's request.

After they had removed their boots, the unhappy pair thanked the Inspector, realising that he could do no more, and left the property, intent on using their unexpected spare time to clear up their yard and bring their paperwork up to date. Neither of them were men to just sit around doing nothing.

As they left, Jack could be heard saying, "Saxon! How the hell could you possibly have thought it was Saxon?" and June and Paul grinned at each other, frowning and shrugging their shoulders.

June let SOCO into the property just as Richard and Elizabeth Drake turned up, and the house soon filled with people in white overalls. Paul sat in the lounge with Rebecca, Daniel and Rebecca's parents. He explained what was happening while June filled SOCO in with events and they commenced their work.

"Is it anything to do with Craig Harper?" Rebecca asked, clearly upset.

For the first time, Paul realised just why Rebecca was so emotional. Craig had gone missing and to all intents and purposes had escaped abroad, but now that a body had turned up it was natural for her to assume that it was something to do with him.

"Rebecca, listen to me, I can assure you with one hundred present certainty that you will not be hearing from Craig Harper again, trust me on that…. please."

Rebecca was pleased to hear it but puzzled. Her father assured her of the same thing with just as much conviction, but she didn't see how they could be so certain.

Paul turned to Daniel, not wanting to be drawn on the subject of Craig Harper any further and said, "I have to ask you Daniel, have you any knowledge of the body in the garden? Any idea who it could be? Or how it got there?"

"None at all Paul, it's a complete shock. The body must have been there since before Dad bought the house. Maybe it's hundreds of years old or something?"

"I'm sorry Daniel, but even if it was somehow missed when they built the house, it would definitely have been found when the decking was installed. When did your father buy the house?"

"I think I was two years old when we moved in, so it must have been in 1986."

"And the decking, was that there when you all moved in?"

"No, I can remember my dad fitting that, I helped him by fetching and carrying things for him as he worked, so I must have been about seven or eight years old, say around 1992, something like that. I can't see him getting his seven year old son to help if he was disposing of a body, can you? I assume that's what you were thinking?"

"I know this must be hard for you Daniel, but these are the sort of questions that are going to be asked. Hopefully, we can establish that the body was buried before your parents moved in, although, if you say your dad installed the decking, that seems unlikely. I have to warn you Daniel, that if the body turns out to be contemporary with your parent's occupation of the house, your Dad is going to be the prime suspect."

Rebecca chipped in, "Paul!...You can't possibly think that Daniel's parents had anything to do with burying a body. It must have been there when they moved in."

"Look, I'm sorry Rebecca, but the fact that I am a friend is going to rule me out of the investigation anyway, so it doesn't really matter what I think. But anyone is capable of killing in the right circumstances Rebecca. Let's not get too wrapped up in speculation until we know when the body was put in the ground and who it is, because there maybe the possibility that the body has only been there since Daniels parents died."

"What!!....you're accusing Daniel now!"

"Of course not, Rebecca....we all know Daniel didn't kill anyone, or bury anybody, but everything depends on how long it's been in the ground and I'm not going to be running things remember." Paul reach out and took Rebecca's hand. "I'm just trying to prepare you for what's going to come, I'm sorry."

"No I'm sorry Paul, I didn't mean to snap at you, I'm just a bit on edge," said Rebecca as she reached over and kissed him reassuringly on the cheek.

"Let me see what SOCO are up to," said Paul, anxious to change the way the conversation was going.

Paul spoke to the head of the SOCO team from the French-doors so as not to encroach on the garden while the team was working there. He was informed that they had already begun unearthing the rest of the body, that appeared to be all there, and that they would want the house cleared so that they could establish whether or not it was the scene of the murder itself.

"How do you know it's a murder?" asked Paul, "it could have been an accident or suicide or even a natural death that someone tried to cover up."

"Because it looks as if someone bashed the victim's head in several times with a large blunt object," was the reply. "We're going to be some time going over the house and grounds, it would be better if you got everyone out now. Which rooms have you been in?"

"Just the lounge, dining room and hall, but tell me, how do you know the damage to the skull wasn't caused when it was uncovered by the digger?"

"I can't be one hundred percent certain at the moment, not until the skull can be examined in more detail, but the damage doesn't look fresh, and there seems to be some soil clinging to the edges of the fracture and even inside the skull, it would have been much easier if the builders hadn't moved it. But there you are Inspector, that's why you need us, isn't it?"

"I don't suppose you would like to speculate on how long the body's been in the ground?"

"Difficult to say at the moment Inspector, we haven't even got it all out of the ground yet! You have to give us a chance to do our thing. All I can say at the moment is that I don't think it's been there more than say...fifty years, but it's certainly been more than five......Any help?"

"Not really."

"Then leave us to get on Inspector, I'll let you know what we find as soon as we find it. Have your lot done much tramping about over our crime scene?"

Paul explained that he had been in the house on several occasions prior to that day because he was a family friend and that after he had arrived with Constable Kelly, he had gone into the garden, but no further than where the end of where the decking had been.

"I've got the boots the workmen were wearing and explained that you will need to examine the digger, but they're obviously anxious to have their tools back as soon as possible," he continued, "and apparently the digger is on hire."

"All things come to those who wait Inspector. We'll be as quick as we can with the workmen's things. I appreciate they need their tools, but if it's a murder, and I can't really see it being anything else, we need to be thorough."

Paul returned to Rebecca and Daniel, "You're going to have to move out for a while I'm afraid. Why don't the two of you stay at your parents', Rebecca, until things are concluded here," he said looking at Richard and Elizabeth questioningly.

"Now that's a brilliant idea," said Elizabeth, pleased at the thought of them staying for a while.

Both Daniel and Rebecca agreed that it was the best solution to their present plight, Rebecca saw enough of hotels with her job so was reluctant to stay in one as a guest.

Paul tried his best to reassure them, "I'll let you know who will be running the investigation as soon as I know myself, and I'll call back in to see you at your parents' house after work."

"You and Daniel can stay with us as long as you like Rebecca, our house is still your home, you know that," Richard said, secretly just as pleased as Elizabeth at the prospect of having his daughter stay for a while.

It would be nice to have Rebecca back home for a while and he found Daniel good company as well, they had struck up a good friendship since he and Rebecca had been together.

"Thanks Dad, if Paul is calling in after work to update us all, why don't you bring Margaret home with you after you close the shop and we can all eat together."

"Sounds like a plan to me," said Richard.

After sorting out arrangements with her Mum and Dad, Rebecca and Daniel collected what they were allowed to take with them, which amounted to little more than a toothbrush and change of underwear, and after saying their goodbyes, set off for her parents' house with Elizabeth. Richard returned to his antique shop, where Margaret was busy working and anxious to hear what had been happening.

Despite the upheaval Rebecca was now quite upbeat about the whole thing. It would be nice to spend a few days at her parents' house, and she still had lots of belongings there that she needed to go through. Daniel was not as happy about the situation however, even though he got on well with Rebecca's Mum and Dad. He was concerned that his Dad would be blamed for the body that had been found and he was unable to defend himself. Daniel was determined to fight his father's corner for him.

On his return to the station, Paul brought his DCI, Detective Inspector Blake, known to one and all as "Blakey," after the bus inspector in the sixties sit com "On the Buses," up to date with events.

"Well....do you intend to get personally involved in your all cases Paul?" he asked, referring to the fact that he Paul had met the Drakes and his wife Margaret during his last murder enquiry.

"I take it that I'm not going to be involved in this one though sir?"

"No Paul, I'm sorry, but you are far too close to this one from the start, and Roy Darnley hasn't got too much on his plate at the moment, I propose giving it to him."

"Roy's a good man sir, he gets results, and I'll pass on what little I have to him."

Just as Paul had finished speaking there was a knock at the door and Roy Darnley entered.

"You wanted to see me Sir?" he enquired. Then, seeing Paul, held out his hand to him, "Paul, nice to see you."

After a round of hand shaking, the three men sat at the DCI's antique mahogany desk and Chief Inspector Blake and Inspector Roy Darnley listened with interest as Paul told them what he knew of Daniel and Rebecca and Daniel's parents, and the mysterious skeleton in the garden.

"Would you have any objection to keeping me in the loop as to how things pan out?" asked Paul, "I promise not to interfere or get in your way at all."

Roy Darnley considered the request for a moment and replied, "Let me get a handle on things first Paul, we don't even know how long this body's has been in the ground yet. If it turns out to be that long that we can rule out Daniel and his father as possible suspects, then I see no problem. But no promises Paul."

"That's fair enough, I appreciate your position Roy," said Paul, as he shook his colleague's hand for a second time.

Paul Manley and Roy Darnley knew each other by reputation and had chatted on occasion in the canteen and at various police socials but had never actually worked together. Roy was an experienced Inspector with a good reputation in the job. Paul was the new boy who had been lucky with the jobs that had come his way and was fast getting a reputation as a man who gets things done. Roy Darnley was going to be cautious in his dealings with Paul until he knew him well enough to form his own opinion.

The meeting over, Roy Darnley went off to get his team together and set up the incident room for a new case. The large open-plan room had a desk and computer for each member of his team, countless phone lines, and its very own mini-kitchen area with micro-wave oven and the all-important coffee making facilities. Roy's office was separated off from the main room with a glass topped partition. There were three large, free standing notice boards and two enormous fixed white boards for displaying information and photographs. Inspector Darnley cleared these of all traces of the previous case they had been used for and pinned up the small amount of information he had relating to the new one, which amounted to a photo of the back of Daniel and Rebecca's house and a photo of each of them that Paul had just given him. The boards would fill up quickly once SOCO supplied them with their findings and interviews began. Paul entered the room and stood looking at them, feeling very strange at seeing pictures of people he was close to on an incident room board.

"Any idea how long it's going to be before we get an ID on the girl?" he asked.

"May not be too long actually," answered Roy, not wanting to be rude but wishing Paul would stay away until he could get his head round the case, "the SOCO boys have found a handbag buried with the body; it's not in very good condition but there are contents, and the lab is hopeful of getting some ID from it. We should know pretty soon. When we do have an ID, it should tell us how long she has been in the ground. I'll want to interview your Daniel as soon as," he finished, trying desperately to look busy.

"Of course, I'll let you get on. If there's any way I can be of assistance, you let me know," said Paul, realising that he was in the way.

"I'm sure we'll manage Paul. I know you are going to be anxious to be kept informed," he said, picking up some papers from the desk in front of him and arranging them into a neat pile. "If I get any information that I feel I can let you have, I will, but you have to just let us get on with it Paul."

Paul turned and left the room, allowing the door to swing shut behind him He had a mountain of paperwork waiting for him in his own office, but his mind was elsewhere.

* * * * * * * * * * *

Elizabeth opened her front door with a warming smile and let Rebecca and Daniel into the house, receiving a kiss from them both. She was over the moon that things were going well between her daughter and Daniel, both she and Richard liked him a great deal and felt he was the perfect partner for her.

Rebecca was grateful that she still had some of her clothes at her parents', as they had been allowed to remove only one change of clothing from their home. Daniel was not so lucky, but Rebecca told him that he needed to buy some new trousers and underwear anyway, and Elizabeth said that, as he was about the same build as her husband, he could use some of his shirts. She also said that she was sure Paul would pick up some stuff from the house tomorrow or the next day for them, if he could clear it with SOCO and Roy Darnley.

Richard returned home a little later with Margaret, as Rebecca had suggested and the two girls hugged as if they hadn't seen each other for years. When Paul arrived some time after, they were all ears for any information. However, he was not as forthcoming as they had hoped, although this was, in part, due to the fact that there was very little to tell.

"All I can say to you at the moment is that the man you will be dealing with is Inspector Roy Darnley," he said, taking up residence on one of the settees. "He's a good man and I'm sure he'll manage to get to the bottom of things." The others followed his example and sat down. "Now I haven't actually known any of you, including my darling wife here, for all that long, so I have lots of questions myself, although," continued Paul, "because of the circumstances of our meeting I do feel I know you all very well. There are a great many things I don't know, especially about you, Daniel," he continued, looking at Daniel and smiling to reassure him, "so I would like you to tell me about your parents and their friends. Everything you can remember."

"Does all this mean that you think the body was buried when my parents were in residence?" asked Daniel with a look of sadness on his face.

"Not officially, the **SOCO** team won't be finished at the house for some days, but the man in charge has now said it looks initially to him as if the body was buried between ten and twenty five years ago. I'm sorry, Daniel, but if that is confirmed, it *will* make your father the prime suspect, there's no way round it. The body was found in his garden and was buried at a time when he was in residence there. You told me that your dad bought the house in 1986 and that the decking was put in place around 1992. Now speaking purely as a detective, my first thought would be that the decking was put there to help conceal the grave in some way, and that is certainly what people will assume."

"My dad would never have killed anyone Paul, unless maybe to protect me or Mum from someone. But even then he would never have tried to conceal the body. And is it right that it was a woman?"

Paul nodded.

"Dad was old school; he was always very protective of women, it simply wasn't him Paul, there's no way."

"OK, but that means that we have to work on the premise that somebody else, maybe a family friend, or maybe, but I think less likely, a stranger killed the woman, and then somehow managed to bury the body in your garden without your parents knowledge. I have to say that it is difficult to understand how they could have done it, or indeed, and possibly more importantly, *why* they would have done it. Why take the risk of burying a body in the garden of somebody else's house? Was there ever a time when your parents had people staying at the house? Or was there a time when they left the property unattended for days on end?"

"Well, Dad was self-employed and Mum was a school teacher so we often went away on holidays for two, three, sometimes even four weeks at a time.

Someone could have easily gained access to the grounds and buried a body in the garden on one of those occasions."

"That's true, Daniel, although the question still remains to be answered why someone would choose to dispose of a body in your garden? I would think that it was much more difficult to conceal the burial of a body in a cultivated garden, rather than out in the country somewhere. Especially the garden of a house that is occupied. And how did they know the house was empty? Where did your Mum teach? and what did your Father do?"

"Mum taught at a primary school in Bristol, and Dad was a self-employed music teacher."

"Where did he teach?"

"Sometimes there at the house, but often he would go to the pupil's home, and I think he ran an evening class at Clevedon Comprehensive."

"What instruments did he teach?"

"Piano and guitar. Most of the pupils that came to the house would have been learning piano, but the home visits and the evening class were mostly guitar, I think." Daniel appeared to be lost in his thought for a moment, "It was wonderful to hear him play," he continued, "he was very talented. He could easily have had a successful career playing but he just loved to teach."

"What were the circumstances of your parent's death Daniel and when was it exactly."

Daniel sat back on the large sofa and composed himself for a minute, bracing himself to talk about events that he still found distressing. He'd had a very close and loving relationship with both his parents and he was still angered by the senseless manner of their death, and the seemingly casual way it had been dealt with by those in authority.

He began, "Mum and Dad had been in London for a long weekend, in 2003, you know the sort of thing, a west end show, tea at The Ritz, the normal touristy things people do in London. They were driving back on the old A4 because Dad hated the motorways. Ironically he always referred to them as death traps. Well they were driving through one of the little villages, I can't even remember its name at the moment, somewhere between Hungerford and Marlborough. Anyway, it was a thirty miles per hour speed limit through the centre, and a man.....well a boy really, he was only seventeen, pulled out to overtake a car going the other way and would have hit them head on. My dad swerved to avoid him and apparently lost control when his nearside wheel hit the kurb and they drove into a stone wall. Dad loved old cars, and he was driving an old Ford Consul 375; no **ABS** brakes, no air bags, and the addition of the seat belts didn't save them. They both died in hospital from their injuries.

Well it turns out that the seventeen year old, who failed to stop at the scene and was arrested much later, had failed his driving test, so he had no insurance or licence or anything. He shouldn't have been driving at all. The police who attended the scene said that from the skid marks and the impact damage it looked as if my dad was doing about thirty eight miles per hour, so he was held partially responsible for the accident, even though eye witnesses said they had seen the other car earlier, speeding in the village. He was fined £400 and banned from driving for a year. *What a joke!* How can you ban someone from driving who's not allowed to drive anyway? It doesn't make any sense. I'm sorry Paul, but it makes me so angry when

I think about it. That man....or boy, whatever you think he is, killed my parents. He got away with it virtually unpunished and showed no remorse, and I'll bet he's passed his test now and is out there driving somewhere, putting other people at risk."

Daniel looked at them all, feeling a little embarrassed at having been so emotional and Rebecca put her arm around him.

Everyone sat in silence listening to Daniel's story, sympathising, and afterwards they just sat quietly until Paul broke the tension by saying, "Let's leave it there for now Daniel. But Roy Darnley is going to want to interview you and he'll want you to make a full statement about what you remember from when your parents were here. It would be helpful if you could compile a list of family friends and times when the property was empty because of holidays and the like. Did either of your parents keep a diary?"

"No, nothing like that."

"That's a shame; have you still got any of your dad's appointment books? Or even dated receipts for lessons would be a help. Anything you can find or remember will be helpful, especially if it places them away from the house for a period of time. Even if it's not the time of the murder, it set a precedent and shows that there were time the house was empty. When they have a times frame for the murder; they'll want to account for your Dad's movements."

"I'm not sure what I can put my hands on, Paul, but there is a lot of dad's stuff still in the loft that I have been meaning to go through, I'll start tomorrow if I can have access to the house."

"I don't think Roy will let you do that, his team will want to go through it all themselves."

"Oh yeah of course, but the trouble is that they'll want to look for anything incriminating, while I want to try and find something to clear him."

"I'm sorry Daniel. But Roy's team will be looking for clues as to what happened. Whether they incriminate or clear your Dad, they'll just want the truth. Anyway, that's about all we can do until we have identified the body and know what time frame we're looking at. As for access to the house, I'll have a word with Roy and see if you and Rebecca can bring away some more clothing. But I doubt he'll let you have anything else until his team have been through it. I wouldn't if I was running things. The house is a possible crime scene and it could be some time before you're allowed back."

"I see."

Rebecca put a comforting hand on Daniel's shoulder and said with conviction, "Don't worry Daniel, we all know your Dad didn't do it, so there is no way the police are going to find otherwise, isn't that right Paul?" she said, looking in Paul's direction for confirmation of her statement.

"Let's wait and see what they find out about the body first, shall we. Because I'm sorry to say that the problem is, although we're all sure nobody will be able to prove Daniel's father is guilty, unless we can find out who did, he will always be the prime suspect."

Rebecca put her arms around Daniel and gave him a hug, saying, "Well, if the police fail to find out who killed the poor girl, *we will*, won't we Paul?"

"Well......I......Look, Roy Darnley's a good man, if anybody can get to the bottom of things, he can, so let's give him a chance shall we."

Elizabeth broke the somewhat sullen mood by announcing, "Well I'm sorry, but I haven't prepared anything for dinner, so I suggest we get a takeaway delivered, if everyone is OK with that?"

Chapter 2

Inspector Roy Darnley sat at his desk having just got off the phone to Daniel West, and arranged for him to come in to be interviewed at eleven-o'clock. He was just about to ask someone to fetch him a fresh cup of coffee, when Sergeant Julia White entered the incident room and approached his desk carrying what he hoped was the post mortem report on their victim.

"Is that what I hope it is Sergeant?" he asked, looking up as she reached his desk.

"Well, Sir, if you mean is it confirmation that you are this week's lottery winner then I'm afraid not Guv. But if you mean, is it the PM report on our body under the decking, then partly. It's not complete, but they have identified the body and the cause of death." Inspector Darnley got up from his desk and indicated that Julia should follow him into the main room.

"Perhaps you'd like to bring us all up to date then Julia," he said, clapping his hand to attract everybody's attention and indicating the large white noticeboard containing the scant information they had so far. "Listen up everyone," he shouted and clapped his hands again to make sure everyone was listening.

Julia stood in front of the board and eyed the faces before her. Detective Constable Clive Pascoe and her Inspector were the only friendly faces to be seen. The other six men and one woman on the team all seemed to resent her a bit. She could only suppose that it was her age that they resented, because at twenty nine, she was younger than any of them. Well, as far as she was concerned that was their problem not hers. She had decided on a career in the police before leaving secondary school and she had made a bloody good start, so she wasn't going to let her unpopularity get her down. If her colleagues didn't like her then they would just have to deal with it. She could.

Julia began, "We now know that the body found under the decking at the West's house, The Cedars, is that of Lucy Penrose who went missing on the 6th August 1996, aged sixteen. It looks as if the cause of death was several blows to the back of her head with a large flat object. The pathologist speculated that a garden spade would fit the bill but he couldn't be sure. It could just as easily have been a piece of the decking itself. Forensics are still checking all the tools and the decking to try and identify the weapon. Lucy's handbag was recovered from the grave, along with this tie-pin." Julia pinned a photograph of a tie-pin, and also a post-mortem photograph of Lucy Penrose's remains, on the board and continued. "It's solid gold, and is the representation of a section of a music stave with two notes on it. Lucy wasn't wearing a tie, so there is a good chance it belonged to her killer."

Roy Darnley took over, and Julia did well to conceal her annoyance, "Now I want everybody back here in two hours from now," he announced. "That should be enough time to locate all the relevant files on our victim Lucy Penrose and her disappearance. Philip, can you get everyone started on that?"

"Will do Guv." replied Constable Phillip Strange, "Do you want me to act as office manager on this one?"

"You seem to enjoy the role Philip and you performed well last time, so why not?" Roy looked around the room to make sure he still had everyone's attention, "Right...listen up....Philip is going to be office manager again on this one, so co-ordinate everything you do through him. Make sure he knows what you're working on and what you're doing at all times. I don't want anything missed and I don't want any work duplicated." He clapped his hand together; this time in a gesture of haste, "Come on then...chop...chop."

Two hours later the team were gathered once again, and everyone was engaged in reading the assembled files to familiarise themselves with the disappearance of Lucy Penrose sixteen years earlier.

Sometime later, after draining the last of his coffee from a rather less than spotless mug, and slamming it down hard on the desk a couple of times to get everyone's attention, Roy Darnley, said loudly, "Right then.....listen up everyone.....in 1996 the house where Lucy Penrose was found was owned and occupied by Jacob and Florence West, the parents of Daniel West, who was twelve at the time and is now the present occupant with his partner Rebecca Drake. Just in case there is anyone here who doesn't know already, Daniel West and Rebecca Drake are good friends of Inspector Paul Manley, so tread carefully in that respect.

"We don't regard either of them as suspects though, do we Guv?" asked Constable Mary Prescott.

"Well hardly Mary! Daniel wouldn't have been long out of short trousers when Lucy went missing and I don't think he would have arranged to have foundations dug there.   However.... interestingly enough, our Mr Jacob West, was a self-employed music teacher, who ran a night-school class at Clevedon Comprehensive, where Lucy went to school. So that, together with the music related tie-pin, and the fact that he was occupying the house where her body was found, obviously makes *him* our prime suspect. Now Jacob and Florence West were both killed in a car crash in 2003, but we still need to put a good case together against him in order to satisfy ourselves that no one else was involved in poor Lucy's death. He may have had an accomplice, or it's possible that someone else killed her and Jacob just helped to dispose of the body. It is also possible, though in my opinion unlikely, that Jacob had nothing at all to do with Lucy's death or burial. Either way, let's make sure we do a thorough job. I don't want any loose ends. I don't need to tell you that when the press get hold of this they are going to want to know why the original investigation didn't find Lucy or her killer at the time. Now unfortunately, not only is it proving difficult to locate any of the original team, the senior officer has since died and most of his team have retired and moved away. To make matters worse there was some kind of flood at the storage facility where the Lucy Penrose files were kept, a burst water pipe or something, and approximately a third of the boxes of files are affected. Now some of the documents in those boxes are virtually illegible, but others are only partially damaged so we need to go through them all, even if that batch of files looks hopeless. If we can salvage one page, or even half a page from a file it may prove to be the all-important piece of the jig-saw...so be thorough."

"Yeah....no making papier-mache puppets," said Clive Pascoe, eliciting a few laughs. They stopped quickly however when everyone saw that their inspector was somewhat less than amused.

Constable Philip Strange suddenly announced from the corner of his desk, where he had been sitting devouring a banana, "A friend of mine runs an antiquarian book stall Guv. and he's always going on about this great book restorer who does work for him occasionally. I could let him have a look at any illegible documents that look important."

"How are we going to know the document is important if it's illegible," asked Peter Evens, smiling.

Philip grinned back at him, "Well, *parts* of an important document might be illegible, mightn't they?"

"Where do you want us to start Guv?" asked Julia, stopping the exchange before Roy could become even less amused.

"Well Julia...I'd like you to take Peter with you and go to Lucy's school. See how many of the staff from back then are still working there, see if any of them remember Jacob West and if they do.... what he was like? Was he more than friendly with any of the girls? Check the school records. Find out what night of the week Jacob took his night-school class and who attended. You know what to ask. I'll take Mary with me to inform Lucy's parents that we have found their daughter's body. Have you got their address?"

Julia passed him a piece of paper from her desk, "John and Felicity Penrose sold their house in 1998 and moved to the country, Guv. However, the people they sold it to are still there, and they gave me the Penrose's new address, The Old Mill, Almondsbury. It's only half an hour away."

"Thanks...you and Peter get off to the school, speak to everyone you can, and see if you can get addresses and contact numbers for any staff that were there at the time but have moved on."

"OK Guv."

Julia was pleased with her assignment. Checking out the school staff was an important part of the investigation, whereas informing parents that their child's body had been discovered was something she would willingly forego. Not because she found it particularly distressing, as she knew many of her colleagues did but because it was simply boring. You had to waste ages pretending to be sympathetic and hand out tissue after tissue to sobbing relatives instead of just getting on with the investigation. She rummaged through the file containing the names and addresses of Lucy's family and friends and other contacts, and finally located the address and phone number of the school.

Roy continued, "Clive, you've been going through the statements that were taken at the time. Did they interview Jacob West when Lucy went missing?"

"I haven't seen his name in connection to the case at all, Guv. He's not listed with the teachers at Clevedon Comprehensive, not being an actual member of staff, I suppose. But he must have been interviewed. My guess is that it's among the files that are too badly damaged to read. Perhaps the school still have records from when he was there though. They would have had to pay him somehow, so perhaps the day he worked is mentioned on an invoice or receipt or something."

"Julia, did you get that," asked Roy.

"I'll ask when I'm there Guv."

Roy again looked at Clive Pascoe, "What about Lucy? Anything to suggest she went to these classes?"

"Nothing here about her attending classes outside school hours, but I'll check into it Guv."

"That's OK, I'll check with her parents when I'm there, see if she had lessons outside school hours. Now listen up people....we need to go through all the paperwork from the original investigation, and look at it with fresh eyes now that we have a prime suspect and know where poor Lucy ended up. We need to find out if Lucy had guitar or piano lessons, even if she didn't go to the night-school, she could still have been having private tuition. She must have had some kind of contact with Jacob West. Let's find that connection, it has to be there."

Sergeant Julia White walked up to Inspector Darnley's desk and sat on the side of it with one foot still on the floor and the other dangling in mid-air. "I've been thinking Guv," she said "that tie-pin looks pretty unique to me, I'll bet it was specially made for someone. I'll obviously ask at the school if anyone remembers a pin like it, but it might also be an idea to release a copy of it to the newspapers nationwide to see if anyone recognises it."

"Good thought, Julia, get Philip to sort it out will you? It shouldn't be too late to get it in tomorrow mornings papers if he's quick"

"OK, Guv," she turned to get Peter and headed off for Lucy's old school, but Roy called after her.

"I don't care how long it takes at the school, Julia, even if you have to go back, but make sure you get everything, yeah."

Julia nodded to signal that she understood, gestured to Peter Evans to follow her and left the office with him in tow.

Roy Darnley had a last look around to make sure everyone was busy and shouted across to Phillip, "Phillip...get a number for your book restorer chappy will you?...you never know."

He then left with Mary Prescott to break the news to Felicity and John Penrose that their beloved daughter was now just a pile of bones on a mortuary table. Breaking bad news of that sort was not something Roy Darnley had ever gotten used to, especially when it involved children. He was a family man himself, with two grown-up daughters of his own, he couldn't begin to imagine how much pain and suffering he would have to endure if anything ever happened to one of them. Even though, finally knowing for certain that their daughter was dead would bring some amount of closure to Lucy's parents, the news was going to tear open wounds of the worst kind.

* * * * * * * * * *

Constable Mary Prescott rang the bell of The Old Mill as her Inspector braced himself for the task ahead. From the name of the property, she had expected a large converted building set in its own grounds, but in reality it was no more than a 1930's semi with an extension over the garage. The name seemed incongruous.

The door was opened by John Penrose, who looked to be at least ten years older than his 56 years. He looked from Mary Prescott to Roy Darnley and back again as they introduced themselves before having to clutch hold of the door-frame for support. It was clear from the way the small amount of colour he had in his face drained away that he knew exactly what the appearance of two police officers at his door meant.

"You'd better come in," he said sadly, stepping aside.

He led them into the front room where his wife, Felicity, who looked even older, despite being two years his junior, was sitting staring at the screen of a television that had obviously been designed for a room twice the size. She looked round as they entered and burst into tears at the sight of them.

John pointed to the settee and said, "Please sit down Inspector...Constable," as he went to comfort his wife, "Where did you find her...I take it that's why you're here."

"I'm so sorry," said Roy, as the couple joined hands to hear the news they had been expecting for sixteen years.

"We've discovered Lucy's body buried in the garden of a house that belonged, at the time, to Jacob and Florence West. Do the names mean anything to you?"

"Jacob West. The name sounds familiar," said John Penrose sitting next to his wife and holding her firmly to give what support he could, though in need of it himself.

Felicity reached her hand across and grasped her husband's upper arm, "Lucy had piano lessons with a Mr West..... I think his name was Jacob," she said, losing her fight to control the tears and burying her face in her husband's chest.

"I'm sorry," apologised Inspector Darnley again, "Was that at the school, or did Lucy visit his house?"

"Oh no, Inspector," said Felicity, re-emerging from her husband's embrace, "We had our own piano....Mr West came to our house, where we were living....when....when....Lucy."

Mrs Penrose got up and walked over to a hexagonal table that stood in the bay-window covered with a black lace cloth. She picked up one of several photo-frames that were arranged on it and brought it over to the seated officers, handing it to Mary Prescott.

The picture was of Lucy, sitting at an old upright piano, obviously in the act of playing but turning to smile at whoever was taking the photograph.

"She was very pretty, Mrs Penrose, it must have been awful, not knowing what happened to Lucy all these years. I'm so sorry," Mary said, standing and leading Mrs Penrose back to her husband's side.

She sat next to her husband again, clutching the photograph she had just shown to Mary. "You're very kind...both of you.....how did our Lucy die?" she asked, the fear etched on her face.

Roy Darnley looked Mrs Penrose in the face, summoning up the most sincere expression he could raise, and said solemnly, "It would seem that Lucy was struck on the head with some force......she wouldn't have known anything about it......she would have died very quickly.....she wouldn't have suffered at all....I can promise you that."

He deliberately made no mention of the fact that they had no idea what led up to Lucy being killed. The truth was that they had no idea what Lucy may have suffered before she died.

There was a great gasp of relief from Felicity and she stared back at Roy Darnley with gratitude. "Thank you Inspector, it helps a little, knowing that she didn't suffer," she said, looking to her husband for confirmation that he felt the same. He smiled back at his wife but Roy could tell there was another question lurking behind the sad eyes, that he was reluctant to ask.

"Have you arrested, West," asked Mr Penrose, instead of the question tearing at his insides.

"Mr and Mrs West were both killed in a car crash in 2003."

"I see. So he won't be paying the price for what he did."

His wife put her hand on his arm again and said, "God must have been watching, John, and called him to account for what he did."

"Even though Mr West is our prime suspect," continued Roy, "we have to tie up any loose ends, make sure we haven't missed anything. We still have to gather evidence against him, so do you mind if I ask you one or two more questions?"

"No, of course not Inspector," answered John, "what did you want to know?"

"Did Lucy have a boy-friend at the time, do you know?"

"We thought she might have been seeing someone but we never knew for sure."

"What about a best friend?"

"Oh yes....she had lots of friends," cut in Felicity, "but I suppose she was closest to Susan Cooper. We used to think they were like sisters."

"Are you still in contact with this Susan Cooper?"

"We still exchange Christmas cards, that sort of thing. Susan is married with two little girls now.....she still lives locally....I've got her address if you'd like it."

It was plain from the look of anguish on her face as she spoke of her daughter's friend, that Felicity was thinking that her dear Lucy should also be grown up with a family now.

"Yes....please, that would be useful. And if you could make a list of her other friends for us, people she socialised with, other children, or adults. But not right now. Take some time to think and call me when you've done it. I'll arrange to pick it up."

"You're sure that it was this Jacob West, her piano teacher that killed her, are you Inspector." Asked John Penrose, close to tears himself now.

"I'll be honest with you Mr Penrose, it's early days....we've only just found Lucy, so we have to investigate all the possibilities. But Mr West knew her and she was found buried in his garden, so it's most likely he was her killer."

Felicity Penrose stood up and returned the photograph to its place on the little table, whispering, "We've found you now, my darling;" and kissing it gently before putting it down.

While his wife was at the table John Penrose took the opportunity to ask the question he had been reluctant to ask before. He steeled himself and whispered, while indicating with his hands that his wife needn't hear the answer, "Why did he kill her Inspector?......did he?...... you know....was she?

"We don't know, Mr Penrose, I'm sorry, it's been too long."

Mr Penrose turned away, fighting to control the anger that was surfacing in him, then turned back. "Thank you for not upsetting my wife more than you needed to Inspector. I'll get Susan's number and address for you. She knew Lucy as well as anyone, they were like sisters. Susan's an only child as well, you see."

"Thank you," said Roy, with a lump in his throat.

Mr Penrose fetched Susan's details and the Inspector and Mary Prescott said their farewells and left the grieving couple to their tears......all sixteen years-worth.

* * * * * * * * * * * *

Clevedon Comprehensive was now Clevedon Academy but although its name and status had moved on, the buildings that comprised it appeared to have been left behind in a kind of sixties time warp. The main building was a large rectangular box, three stories tall with large metal framed windows separated by similar sized coloured panels of alternating orange and green. One or two other buildings, which had been erected at a later date in order to manage the increasing school age population of Clevedon, looked slightly less run-down, but, although contrasting strongly with the original building, still lacked any architectural elegance and were also in need of some maintenance.

Sergeant Julia White and Constable Peter Evans drove up to the front gates of the school and drew to a halt beside the automated entry console that, unlike the buildings, looked brand new. Julia, who hated to be driven anywhere by anyone, reached her arm out of the driver's window and pressed the large green button, which instruction number two on the console had requested her to do. Instruction number one had been to, "Stop Here."

Well that's helpful she thought, the wording is so small on the console, that you can actually only read instruction one once you've complied with it. She was just about to convey this information to Peter, when a rather immature sounding female voice enquired over the intercom.

"Good morning. What is the nature of your visit to Clevedon Academy today?"

"Sergeant White and Constable Evans, Avon and Somerset Constabulary. We'd like to speak to the headmaster please," said Julia a trifle sharply.

"The **Head Tutor** is Mrs Henshaw," said the voice, obviously annoyed that Julia had assumed the person in charge would be a man, "may I tell her the reason for your visit?"

"No.....I'd prefer to do that myself," replied Julia, a little amused and in one of her moods where she loved to wind people up.

"Mrs Henshaw normally likes me to ascertain the reason for any visit if no appointment has been made," the voice insisted.

"*Oh, does she?* Well this time she's going to be disappointed, isn't she? Now we're here on official police business so just open the gates and let us in will you," said Julia, with as much authority in her voice as she could muster whilst trying not to laugh.

"*Well!*" was the final word Julia heard over the intercom, but it was followed by a definite metallic click, and the large double gates began parting.

"Why do you do that?" asked Peter, also slightly amused if he was honest.

"Do what?"

"You know what.....try to wind people up."

"I didn't know I did."

Facing them as they drove through the gates was a large and singularly impressive sign indicating that parents and other visitors should use the car-park to the right of the main building, staff should use the staff car-park at the rear of the Academy and that any deliveries should be conducted before 8.30 am. or after 4.30 pm. Monday to Thursday. Julia drove up to the front of the building and parked outside the main entrance, ignoring the sideways, questioning glance from Peter in the passenger seat.

As they got out of the car a somewhat plump lady, who looked about fifteen, but who was probably in her late twenties, came hurriedly through the main entrance doors, waving her arms and announcing excitedly. "Excuse me...you can't park there, you'll have to go to the main car-park....no-one parks there."

Julia recognised the voice as the same one from the intercom and replied, "Oh, I'm sorry about that, but it's done now isn't it, I'm sure it won't hurt for a little while, especially as you say no-one else parks there. Has Mrs Henshaw been informed that we're here?"

The plump lady was quite obviously angry at Julia's choice of parking spot, but said only, "I'll show you to her office. But I warn you, she's very busy."

"A warning. Oh dear, is she terribly dangerous when she's busy then, have you fallen foul of her wrath many times?"

The plump lady looked away rather than reply and showed them the rest of the way to the Head Tutor's office in silence, knocked rather reverently on the door and waited patiently for permission to enter which was given with a rather sharp, "Come."

Plump, as Julia would now always refer to her, poked her head into the office and announced, "Sergeant White and Constable Evans to see you Mrs Henshaw. Shall I show them in?"

"Well if they're just outside with you, Megan, I imagine they could find their own way from there.... but yes...that would seem to be the logical next move."

"Very well, you can go in" said Megan, and added to Mrs Henshaw. "They parked outside the main entrance."

"Heavens!....whatever next," said a smiling Mrs Henshaw, as Julia and Peter finally entered the hallowed domain of the Head Tutor. "Sergeant...Constable, please sit down," she said, standing to shake their hands across her desk, "can I offer you some tea or coffee perhaps?"

Julia wasn't normally one to accept refreshments when conducting enquiries, but she supposed, correctly as it turned out, that Plump would be dispatched to fetch any such, so she replied, "Oh that's very kind of you," and turning to the now rather alarmed Megan continued, "tea, milk one sugar for me..... Peter?"

Peter wanted no part of the exchange and declined any refreshment, so Mrs Henshaw indicated to Megan that she should get the tea for Julia, and that she herself would have her usual coffee.

Julia beamed at Plump as she left the room and called after her, "Thank you Megan."

Mrs Henshaw smiled at Julia and said, "You really mustn't be too hard on Megan. I know she's a little pompous and a stickler for the rules, but if there's anybody that I really don't want to see she's an absolute God-send. My name is Rachel by the way. Now, what exactly can I do for you, Sergeant? I do hope you're not here to arrest one of my students."

"No, nothing like that......Can I ask you....Rachel, were you here in 1996 ?"

"Yes...as a matter of fact I was, but only as a lowly English teacher then. I was made deputy head in 2001 and became Head Tutor in 2003, when the existing head retired. Bit of a stick-in-the-mud as far as schools are concerned, I'm afraid, but I can't bring myself to leave Clevedon, it's so beautiful here."

"Well that's good news for us as it turns out, Rachel. Do you remember the disappearance of Lucy Penrose?

"Oh my God!....Yes, of course....is that why you're here? After all this time, have you found her?"

"We've found her body...yes. Did you know her then?"

"Oh yes...Lucy was in my class...in...well it must have been 95, the year before she went missing. Found her body you say?....That's sad, I'd always hoped she'd run off or eloped or something and was alive and well. She was a lovely girl, very bright, good at most subjects in fact, as I remember.....Oh, she would have done so well in life....Gone a long way if she'd wanted...It was such a tragedy. What happened to her?"

"Was there anybody you suspected might have been involved in her disappearance at the time?"

"No, no-one, it was an awful time for the school you understand with all the publicity and everything, as well as coping with the tragedy of it, but there was no-one at the school who anybody ever suspected of being involved. We all thought that it must be some stranger, unless she had just run away for some unfathomable reason. As I remember she had a good relationship with her parents. Forgive me, but the police didn't seem to have a clue at the time."

"That's all right, Rachel. Do you remember a Jacob West?"

"Jacob West....yes, I met him a few times. He used to teach music here in the evenings. A nice man as I remember. I was tempted to enquire about lessons myself. I've always wanted to play an instrument. I so admire those who do. Don't tell me he had anything to do with young Lucy's disappearance! I remember I rather liked him.....Oh no! surely not Jacob."

"Did Lucy have any contact with him, do you know?"

"Lucy was very musical....Now let me think." Rachel Henshaw put her right hand to her mouth in the pose of someone deep in thought and continued, "Wait...now, Jacob taught guitar here at the school....and Lucy was learning piano....so no, I don't think they would have met......unless....oh now wait a minute, Jacob taught piano as well if I remember correctly, so he may have been her tutor...just not here at the school....if you see what I mean."

There was a knock at the door and Megan entered with the tea and coffee. She put the tray down on the small table beside Rachel's desk and withdrew from the room quickly, presumable not wanting to be put in the position of having to actually hand the cup to Julia.

"Do you think you could compile a list of Lucy's friends and any staff that were here at the time? Is there anyone, besides yourself, that is still here, from Lucy's time at the school?

Rachel thought for a moment and replied, "No...it's just me I think. Everyone else from back then has moved on, or retied, or died of course. A lot can happen in sixteen years Sergeant, but I will do my best to compile those lists for you, and if you leave me a number I'll call you when it's done, or if I think of anything else."

"Do you remember whether Lucy had a boyfriend at all?"

"I don't remember there being one, but staff wouldn't necessarily have known anyway. But I would be surprised if there wasn't one actually, she was a very attractive girl and very popular."

"One more thing. Cast your mind back......can you remember anybody wearing a distinctive tie-pin at all back then? A gold music stave with diamond notes.

"Good Lord no.....it sounds expensive. Staff certainly wouldn't have worn anything like that, it would be too easy for it to go missing."

"Thank you Rachel, you've been very helpful." Julia stood and offered her hand, which was shaken warmly a second time, as was Constable Evan's.

"Can you find your own way out?" asked a smiling Head Tutor, "or would you like me to get Megan to show you?"

Julia grinned back, "I'm sure we'll manage. Give me a ring when you've compiled the lists and I'll arrange to pick them up. It would be helpful if you could do it ASAP."

"I'll start now," said Mrs Henshaw, smiling, "but you're very naughty Sergeant."

Julia looked at Rachel questioningly and Rachel replied, "You didn't even touch your tea."

Julia and Peter slipped out of the room and closed the door quietly behind them.

Chapter 3

14, White Tree Drive, Long Ashton, was a large five bedroomed house with a curved gravel drive leading up to a double garage and annex. It formed part of an exclusive little enclave of only a dozen houses on the outskirts of what had once been an idyllic old village that had seen its fair share of development and was now tagged on to the south of Bristol.

Having parked his car a short walk away from the house, he made sure the husband's car was gone before walking up the gravel drive to the front door. Unsure of how his re-appearance after so long would be received, he rang the bell and waited anxiously for it to be answered, looking around nervously to see if he was under surveillance from any nosey neighbours.

He had looked out an old coat from his wardrobe, one that he hadn't worn for years and that could quite easily be discarded, and he had purchased and donned a baseball cap, something he would never contemplate wearing under normal circumstances. He was confident that if anyone took any notice of him, the description they would give later would resemble him in height only, if that even.   Eye-witnesses were notoriously unreliable.

When she opened the door, she fully expected to be confronted by some unemployed yobbo trying to sell dusters and brushes of some sort, so it took her a few minutes to realise who it was.

"Oh my God!......what the hell brings you here......I was hoping I'd seen the last of you years ago....and what's happened to you for God's sake, you look like a tramp," she said, eyeing him up and down and smirking.

"It's nice to see you again, as well, Alice. How are you doing?....Can I come in? There's something I need to speak to you about."

"What on earth could we possibly need to speak to each other about after so long? And why did you have to call?   Couldn't you have phoned or written? Why did you have to subject me to a meeting?"

"Well, I see you still keep your tongue nice and sharp. And you'll never find out why I'm here unless you let me in......will you?"

She stared at him for a moment, trying to make up her mind whether to let him into her house or not. Instinct was telling her to shut the door in his face, but in the end, curiosity got the better of her and she stood aside to allow him to enter.

He'd never been in the house before and he now found himself standing in a large entrance hall with four doors leading off it and a rather grand staircase leading up to a half-landing that featured a very impressive, modern, stained glass window depicting a large exotic bird in flight. The window flooded the hall and stairs with copious amounts of daylight that arrived in shafts of various hues, depending on what part of the window they had come through.

"Very nice," he commented, "hubby's done well for you both. Where is he, by the way? Gone to work already?"

"As if it's any of your business."

She opened one of the doors on the right of the hall and led him through into a lounge that could easily have accommodated four full-size snooker tables, and indicated that he could sit. There was a four-seater settee and two, two-seater ones for him to choose from but he said his business wouldn't take long and he preferred to stand.

She shrugged her shoulders. She was curious to know what he was doing there, but the shorter the visit the better as far as she was concerned.

"A cup of tea wouldn't go amiss," he said, "my throat's a bit on the dry side."

"I thought you weren't going to sit because your business wouldn't take long," she said, somewhat angrily, but relented and turned towards the kitchen door.

Earlier in the day he had located a length of lead flashing in his shed, that had been left over from some building work he'd had done. He'd selected one of his thicker socks, rolled the lead like a Swiss-roll and inserted it into the sock, making a short, but very lethal, cosh. He had the home-made cosh tucked into the waistband of his trousers at his back under the coat, and he now withdrew it as she turned her back.....brought it up over his head..... and then crashing down onto the back of her head with considerable force as she made for her kitchen.

She emitted what amounted to no more than a faint sigh as she crashed to the floor, bouncing sideways as her right arm made contact with the side of one of the two-seater settees. She lay where she fell, with blood spilling from the back of her head onto the pale brown carpet, making an obscene, irregularly shaped stain.

He instinctively looked around towards the front window to make sure his murderous actions had not been witnessed by a passer-by or peeping-tom, and them calmly walked over and drew the curtains together completely shutting off the outside world.

He knelt down and felt for a pulse but he couldn't find one. However, past experience had taught him to make sure, so he used the cosh twice more as she lay there unmoving. He had to be certain she was dead. He didn't want to make that mistake again. Getting up, he headed for the kitchen which turned out to be just as impressive as the rest of the house he'd seen. There was a large conservatory on the back of the house that spanned the lounge and half of the kitchen, but the back door led directly into the garden. The door was of hardwood with a solid panel at the bottom but six small glazed panels at the top. Just to the left of the door, at eye level, were several small hooks on a board that proudly proclaimed it was a souvenir from Brighton. The silly cow never did have any taste, he thought as he looked at it. There were two sets of keys hanging from the hooks and one key on its own.   He removed the single key having rightly assumed it fitted the back door and inserted it into the lock. Opening the door just far enough to reach through to the outside, he smashed the glass panel nearest to the lock with the cosh, having first removed the now bloody sock. He closed the door again and as far as he was concerned it looked as if someone had smashed the glass in the door and then reached through and turned the key that was in the lock to let themselves in.

He re-traced his steps back into the lounge and looked about the room. It was perfect. Hubby was obviously a bit of a collector and on the wall opposite the kitchen door there was a tall display cabinet full of silverware. There were several tankards and jugs of various sizes together with some candlesticks, boxes and a variety of other items that all looked, to his untrained eye, to be solid silver. The door of the cabinet was locked and the key was nowhere to be seen, so the cosh was once again put to good use, smashing this glass as well. He stared at the contents for a moment, whilst making up his mind how best to transport them, then returned to the kitchen and searched the cupboards until he found a carrier bag. He realised straight away that it was not going to be big enough or strong enough for the amount of silver in the cabinet. He would have to take it all in order to make the burglary look genuine so he searched the house for something that would be more up to the task. He found what he was looking for as he opened the cupboard under the stairs and located an assortment of cases. Having selected a medium sized suitcase, he proceeded to fill it with the entire contents of the display cabinet and placed it near the front door ready for his departure. He then commenced a thorough search the whole house once again, from top to bottom.

No cupboard or drawer was left undisturbed until he located what he was looking for. In one of the guestrooms, tucked away on the top shelf of a bookcase full of romantic fiction, were several photograph albums of various sizes and ages. He quickly took the albums down and threw them onto the king-size bed. He then took his time, going through them meticulously page by page. In the middle of the fourth album he found what he was looking for, ripped them from the page and pushed them into his coat pocket before continuing to look through the remaining albums, to make doubly sure there were no similarly incriminating photographs.

Job done, he looked about him as he left. The place certainly looked as if it had been burgled alright. He was pleased with the way things had gone. Carrying the case of silver, he cautiously opened the front door and looked up and down the street. All was quiet. Nearly every driveway was empty and the street deserted, so he slipped out of the house, closed the door behind him and strolled off to where he had parked his car some streets away. He passed one or two people on route; a man walking his dog, three young teenagers who were either skiving off school, or on their way to the job centre and a young mum pushing a pram. But none of them seemed to take any interest in him. He was amazed at just how relaxed he felt. After all, not only was he currently in possession of valuable stolen property, but he had just carried out a cold blooded and calculated murder. He wasn't proud of the things he had been forced to do but he was impressed with the cool manor in which he had carried them out. He had nerves of steel.

As he approached his car, he noticed a small park on the other side of the road that had eluded his attention before. There were modern railings running along the top of a small dwarf-wall and you could still see the remains of the original Victorian railing where they had been cut off during the second world war, to be used in in some obscure way in the fight against the Nazis. On the other side of the railings, some fifty or sixty yards from where he stood, was a park-keeper's hut, green and unobtrusive, alongside which were three large plastic waste bins. Two of the bins were also green in colour, but not a dark green like the hut, which somehow blended in with the park environment, but a vivid lime green that stood out from their surroundings like a belisha beacon. He assumed they were intended for grass-cuttings and other organic waste from maintaining the park. The third bin was black in colour and had its lid open as if currently in use. This would most probable be for the litter the general public left behind on their visits to the park. It only took him a split-second to make his decision. He walked past his car, crossed the road to where the inviting bin was located and with a brief look around to make sure nobody was watching, he tossed the case of silver over the railings and into the gaping jaws of the bin. There was a bit of a clatter as the case fell onto the rubbish and cans of indeterminate origin that already resided within the confines of the bin.

Confident that his actions had not been observed, he returned to his car and drove home. As he steered the car though the normal hustle and bustle of workday traffic back to his house, he took the time to study his emotions once again. He had just killed a woman in cold blood for the second time in his life, and the only thing he felt was a little anxiety, anxiety that he might be discovered, that he might have to face the consequences of what he had done. He felt no remorse. After all, he reasoned, both times he had been forced to take the action he had out of self-preservation. It hadn't really been his fault; it was almost a kind of self-defence.

Once home he put the clothes he'd been wearing into a bin bag, along with the cosh he had spent so much time making, and took them to his local council tip, where they ended up in the compactor, never to be seen again. Life could once again return to normal.

* * * * * * * * * * * * * * * *

Paul Manley was sitting at his desk trying to clear his in-tray and downing the last dregs of his third cup of coffee of the day, when Sergeant Reginald Evans poked his head round the open door and announced, a little excitedly -

"We've got a shout Guv......burglary gone wrong by the sound of it....woman dead at the scene, SOCO should be there before we are, and the Prime Minister is already there."

The Prime Minister that Reg was referring to was Constable John Major, a recent addition to the team, but one who had fitted in well and everybody liked. John enjoyed being a detective constable and was a good one, so he had little ambition to progress further.   At fifty years of age and a lifetime of experience in the job, he was a valuable asset.

June Kelly met them in the car park. "What's the address Reg?" she enquired, starting the engine.

"14, White Tree Drive, Long Ashton," replied Reg opening the front passenger door for his Inspector and then jumping into the back seat.

When they arrived at the house SOCO were already busy and one of the team supplied the new arrivals with over-shoes to wear, before Constable John Major showed them over the scene.

They followed him from the large entrance hall, where they all stopped to admire the impressive staircase with its stained-glass window, into the lounge, where the victim's body lay crumpled on the floor just as it had fallen.

"What was the victim's name?" asked Paul, staring at the lifeless body.

"Alice Bridgeman aged 53, Guv. Married to John Bridgeman. We're trying to locate him now. The neighbours say he goes to work early," informed John Major.

"Who found the body?"

"Cleaning lady. She let herself in with a key after not getting a reply. She said she was surprised when she saw the curtains were still closed. Apparently Mrs Bridgeman is always up and about early."

"Where is she now?"

"In with a neighbour being comforted, Guv. Do you want to speak to her now?"

Paul stopped looking down at the unfortunate Mrs Bridgeman. "No that can wait, show me the rest of the house first."

They followed John Major into the extensive kitchen.

"It doesn't look as if the Bridgeman's were short of a bob or two. I certainly couldn't afford a house like this," said Paul, admiring the surrounding.

"The burglar seems to have come in through here Guv," said John, pointing towards the back door. "The key must have been left in the lock so he was able to break a pane of glass and reach through to open it."

"It was probably the sound of the glass breaking that brought Mrs Bridgeman to investigate," offered Reg.

"Yeah....but the only thing is.....it looks from the way she has fallen as if she was heading for the kitchen and was struck from behind. So if she was coming to investigate the breaking glass.....how did her killer get behind her?" queried John.

Paul stared at the key in the lock of the back door, and then at the keys hanging on the hooks to its left, and turning to June said, "Why do think she left the key in the lock, when they're obviously in the habit of hanging their keys on those hooks?"

"Maybe she'd just been out in the garden, Guv." offered June.

"What's she got on her feet?"

June went back to the lounge, and announced on her return, "She's wearing her slippers, Guv, and the bottoms look pretty clean. She hasn't been outside in them and I don't see any shoes anywhere nearby."

"No shoes in here either..... and....." Paul looked quizzically at the glass on the floor.

"And what Guv?" asked Reg. wondering what

had caught his inspector's attention.

"Have SOCO been in here yet?"

"Not yet Guv......why?" asked John.

"The glass is in the wrong place," he stated, looking at the broken shards on the kitchen floor.

"How do you mean, the wrong place, Guv?" asked June, "It's on the inside. The glass was obviously smashed from the outside."

"Yeah...but look how close it is to the closed door. The door has a draught strip at the bottom so it's in close contact with the floor tiles. If the person who smashed the glass was outside when he did it, then he would have had to open the door at least two-thirds of the way in order to come inside, and that would have pushed the broken glass across the floor further into the room than it is, I'm sure."

"Blimey!!....I think you could be right Guv," said June, cursing herself for not having spotted the fact herself. She had aspirations to be an inspector herself one day and told herself that if she was ever going to achieve it, she would have to become just as observant as her inspector, whom she admired a great deal.

"John, go and ask SOCO if they mind us

opening the door fully, and if they have no objection June, I want you to go around to the back garden and come in the back door.....Actually," he paused, and then said "no....better get SOCO to photograph and do their bit inside here first, before we go disturbing things, and then June can go around and come in the back door."

"Will do Guv," said John, leaving the room.

Well over an hour elapsed before SOCO finished in the kitchen and they took the last photograph as June Kelly arrived outside the back door as Paul had requested. As soon as they were done, Paul gestured that she should enter as anyone would normally. As June pushed the door open enough to allow her to enter the room, the broken glass on the floor was pushed aside as they expected.

"Whoever broke that glass, never came in that way, unless they only opened the door sufficient to squeeze through, and I can't think of a single reason why they would do that, can you Constable?"

"No Guv, I can't."

"So why would a burglar try to make it look as if he came in the back door, when he didn't?"

"He obviously doesn't want us to know how he actually got in, Guv."

"Yeah, exactly.....what if she knew him....and she let him in. Or what if he was already in the house. Have they located the victim's husband yet?"

Reg. had just returned to the kitchen and answered the question, "The prime minister's just gone to fetch him, Guv. He should be here soon."

"Why has John gone to fetch him?"

"He was really upset on the phone apparently Guv. It didn't sound as if he was in any condition to drive."

"OK....where does he work?"

"Don't know Guv. John got his work number out of their address book and just told me he would fetch him and that he shouldn't be more than twenty minutes, so it can't be far away."

"Get John to take him straight to the station. We'll interview him there, no need for him to see any of this. That is of course, assuming he hasn't already seen it."

"You fancy the husband for it then Guv?"

Paul shrugged his shoulders, "We have to look at him first. I don't think this was a stranger. Speak to the neighbours.....if it wasn't a happy marriage they'll know."

The divisional doctor put his head round the kitchen door and looked at Paul questioningly. "I've finished everything I can do here Inspector, so we'll take the body to the mortuary now, if that's OK with you?"

"Cause of death?" asked Paul.

"At the moment it looks like several blows to the back of the head with something very heavy. Whatever it was, it did a lot of damage."

"Any sign of it?" Paul asked of nobody in particular.

"SOCO haven't found a murder weapon yet," volunteered June

"Any idea what it could have been Doc?" queried Paul

"If we were playing Cluedo, Inspector, I'd say it was the lead pipe. But I don't think a single piece of pipe would have been heavy enough. More like a bag of lead pipes. A truncheon would have done it, maybe, but there was definitely more than one blow. Whoever it was, they wanted to make damn certain she was dead."

"Time of death?"

"Not that long ago. I'll let you know more as soon as I've got an accurate time, but for now, all I can say is that it was sometime earlier this morning."

"How early this morning?"

"Not that early....so I think it would have been after the husband left for work in my opinion....but I can't be certain at this time, so don't hold me to it. Is that what you wanted me to guess at?

"Thanks Doc. You can take the body now."

"Prime minister's just rung to say he'll be at the station in ten minutes with John Bridgeman Guv," interrupted Reg, phone in hand.

"OK, I think we've done all we can here. June can drive me back. I'd like you to stay a bit longer though Reg. Make sure they leave no stone unturned looking for a murder weapon. Something very heavy according to the doc, possibly a truncheon of some sort. If it's not in the house he may have got rid of it locally. Make sure all the waste bins get checked, you know the drill. Do we know what was taken?"

"According to Mrs Presley next door John Bridgeman had a collection of antique silver in the showcase," said Reg, indicating the damaged cabinet, "and Alice Bridgeman, our victim, always wore nice jewellery. And that's a bit odd actually Guv."

"What's a bit odd, Reg?"

"Well her jewel box and contents are still on her dressing table and although the box was open, it doesn't appear that the contents have been touched, even though the room itself has been ransacked. The burglar wasn't interrupted upstairs so how come he didn't take the jewellery? I think he was looking for something specific Guv and that reinforces your idea that she knew her killer. It certainly doesn't smell like a normal burglary to me."

"Those are my feelings as well Reg. But it obviously wasn't the silver he was specifically looking for. He wouldn't have needed to ransack the place to find that. It was on display for heaven's sake. It seems more likely to me that the whole burglary was staged to stop us thinking the murder was premeditated. OK, as soon as you're finished here, start checking the local fences and pawn brokers. See if anyone has tried to sell a collection of antique silver this morning, and when we've got a list of the stolen items, get it circulated as soon as."

Paul took one last look around and said, "Come on June, get me back to the station. Let's see what our Mr Bridgeman has to say for himself."

As soon as he was back at the station Paul selected Constable Peter Creek to help him interview John Bridgeman. Peter was another recent addition to the team but from what Paul had gleaned from his old DCI, he was good at interviews.

It was a rather haggard looking John Bridgeman who lifted his head out of his hands and looked somewhat pleadingly at Paul and Peter as they entered the interview room.

The two policemen sat opposite the victim's husband and watched him closely, "I'm sorry for your loss Mr Bridgeman, but we have to ask you some questions, some of which may be painful. If you're not up to it now we can do it later," Paul said, as he and

Peter both took notepads from their pockets and placed them on the table in front of them.

Paul had been studying the man closely since entering the room and his distress seemed both deep and genuine. But it also looked as if the burglary had been staged to cover up the murder, and in nine cases out of ten when a woman is murdered, it's the husband or boyfriend who are responsible, and he'd seen some pretty good actors in his time.

"What time did you leave for work this morning?" asked Peter, starting the ball rolling.

"About seven o'clock as usual," came a somewhat hesitant reply.

"What is it you do, exactly?" asked Peter again.

"I own and run a little kitchen company, Bridgeman Designer Kitchens. We design and install fitted kitchens and bedrooms, mostly top end stuff. We predominantly import from Germany and Italy but I also have contact with some specialist cabinet makers in this country for completely bespoke kitchens. We do fitted wardrobes as well but it's a small part of the business."

"Your shop is only twenty minutes from your house by car," stated Peter, "why did you leave so early this morning?"

"Why?.....Oh my God!" John Bridgeman put his hand up to his mouth in horror, "what time did it happen?...I should have been there! Shouldn't I? If only I hadn't left so early....Alice might still be alive."

"Or you might both be dead now," said Paul, who thought for a moment that the man was actually going to cry, but he brought himself under control. "Why did you leave when you did?" asked Paul, repeating Peter's question.

"I always leave early...always have. It's a habit as much as anything, although it allows me to get the previous days paperwork sorted before I open shop at nine. What time did it happen?"

"We're not sure yet but it's possible that whoever was responsible was watching the house, waiting for you to leave. Did your wife have any enemies that you know of?"

"No! Good Lord no, everyone liked Alice. She didn't have an enemy in the world."

"And what about you?....Do you have any enemies?"

"No."

"Have either you or Alice had any run-ins or disputes with anyone lately? Family, neighbours, disgruntled customers perhaps?"

"No! Nothing like that Inspector.....I thought my wife interrupted a burglar."

"We're looking at all sorts of scenarios at the moment **Mr Bridgeman**. Would your wife ever let anyone into the house that she didn't know well?"

"No, Alice was particularly careful about that sort of thing, even if someone had identification on them she would most likely ring to check them out."

"You and Alice were both married before. Is that right?"

"Yes....my first wife died....Julia....she had leukaemia. Alice divorced her first husband in 1997 or 98, something like that."

"Did she still have any contact with him?"

"No...It was a clean break. They sold the house and split the proceeds and as far as I know there has been no contact since. I don't think we even have an address for him."

"What's his name? We'll need to speak to him."

"George....George Edwards........He was a teacher I believe, well they both were, he and Alice. Different schools though, I think, but that's all I know about him really Inspector. Alice never really spoke about him, not to me anyway."

"What did Alice do, John? Did she still teach?"

"She was a primary school teacher for most of her life before she met me but she gave up full time work when we got married in 2002. Now she just does a bit of.......*did*.....a bit of supply teaching."

"And your marriage was all right?....No problems between the two of you?" probed Peter.

"No! we were happy.....both of us."

"I'm sorry to ask you Mr Bridgeman, but were you....or have you....been seeing anyone else since you married Alice?"

"No of course not!....I told you...we were both very happy."

"You never suspected that Alice might be seeing someone?"

"No!"

"Thank you John," Paul said. Then he looked at Peter to see if he had anything else to ask.

"Just one small thing, John. Was Alice ever likely to leave the key in the back door when it was locked," asked Paul.

"No, I don't think so. As I said, she was very security conscious. Why do you ask? Was the key in the lock when she was killed?"

"It looks that way."

"The key for the back door is always hung on a hook in the kitchen. I know it was there when I left this morning because I locked up before we went to bed last night and neither of us had reason to open the door this morning, not before I left anyway, and I can't think of any reason Alice would have gone into the garden after I left. It's not a wash day so there were no clothes to hang out. Oh.....It's today our cleaning lady calls. Mary....was she the one who found Alice?"

Paul nodded in response and John Bridgeman said, "I'll have to speak to her....see how she is. It will have been a shock for her and I don't think she's very strong emotionally.   Alice pulled her up about something once, something quite trivial, and the poor woman went to pieces."

"OK John, I think we can leave it there for now but I would like to speak to you again soon and I'd like you to compile a list of Alice's friends for us, anyone she spent time with. Did she have any hobbies or go to any clubs, play sport,....that sort of thing?....And of course anything else that you think we ought to know......Can you do that for us, John?"

"Yes of course....Can I go to the house now?"

Paul considered the request for a moment and replied, "Peter will take you there to pick up a change of clothes but you won't be able to stay there I'm afraid as it's a crime scene. Where will you stay?"

"There's a flat that I let out over the shop. It's between tenants at the moment so I can stay there."

"That's fine. Peter will take you there after you've picked up a change of clothes."

They led John Bridgeman down to the car park and seated him in a police car so that Peter could take him, first to his house and then to the flat over his shop.

When he was in the car, Paul pulled Peter to one side and said, "When you get to the flat go in with him and have a discreet look around. He gave the impression that it's normally let out but see if there are any signs he's stayed there before. It could be a convenient little love-nest if our Mr Bridgeman has got a piece on the side."

"You think maybe he's having an affair? The wife found out and they had an almighty row?"

"Actually, no, I don't think that but let's check it anyway...yeah."

Paul watched the car pull away and wondered if his instincts about John Bridgeman could be wrong.....After all....nine times out of ten it's the husband or boyfriend and that's big odds.

When Paul returned to his office he arranged for John Campbell to check out John Bridgeman's version of events. "See if anyone can place him at the shop when he says he was there, will you? Find out what his normal routine is. If he has been using the flat over the shop for any liaisons the neighbours are sure to know. Neighbours always do."

Paul then turned to Derrick Price. "Derrick, I want you to check on the victim's life See if she was at it on the sly with anyone. Ask the neighbours if they've ever seen Alice let anyone into the house after her husband's gone to work. She knew her killer, I'm sure of that."

* * * * * * * * * * * * * *

The team were in the middle of their morning briefing when the phone rang on Reg's desk and, after the briefest of conversations, he announced loudly.

"SOCO have just been in touch Guv. They say that there's a faint trace of the victim's blood on some of the glass fragments from the back door. They said it looks as if he used the same thing to smash the glass as he did to hit her over the head, which means you were definitely right about him not coming in that way, because he'd already killed the victim before breaking the glass."

"So she did let her killer in. That means that either she knew him, or he was someone you would normally let into your house." He turned to June.

"Who would you let into your house June?"

"Well, *you* obviously Guv." joked June, "meter reader possibly, doctor if I'd called one, milkman for a cup of tea maybe, a salesman of some sort if he was expected, or some big hunky Hollywood actor, I wish."

"Could Mrs Bridgeman have been having an affair?" Paul looked over at Derrick and asked, "Derrick, any news on that front?"

"Doesn't seem like it Guv. I've spoken to the neighbours and local shop keepers. They all say she was squeaky clean, no hint of an affair or any kind of scandal."

"What about Mr Bridgeman?"

John Campbell replied, "I spoke to all the people that were likely to be about at that time of the morning, Guv, and they all confirm that he is normally in work at the time he said. Also, two of them confirmed that they saw his car there that day at the usual time. They also confirmed that a young couple were staying in the flat until recently. If the autopsy confirms the time of death, then the husband has an alibi that looks pretty good, Guv."

"OK, but double check it for me John. If the

witnesses only saw his car, then it's just possible that he got somebody else to drive it to his shop that morning, or maybe left it over-night and got a taxi. Let's not leave any loose ends."

"I'll double check, Guv."

"OK...June, get an address for the ex-husband, what was his name....George something?"

"George Edwards, Guv. Already done, 172 Riverbank Road, Sand Bay. Nice day for a trip to the seaside actually, Guv. Shall I bring my cosy?" asked June grinning.

"Only if you'll feel comfortable wearing it whilst driving my car June, and where are you going to keep your warrant card?"

"Yeah....or your handcuffs?" asked Reg, who'd been listening.

"Give it a miss then, shall I Guv. Do you want me to ring and see if he's in?"

Paul thought for a moment before replying, "Tempting, as it's a bit of a drive, but I think not. Let's surprise him shall we? Catch him off guard a bit. I don't want him thinking up the answer to questions before we get there. If he's not at home, then we can have an ice-cream and chat to the neighbours about him until he gets back.”

An hour and ten minutes later, June parked Paul’s Ford Mondeo outside 172 Riverbank Road and they both admired the house.

“Looks like he’s done well for himself,” said Paul, admiring the detached four bedroomed house and the new Toyota Avensis that was parked on the drive. “Looks as if our man is in anyway, June. I wonder what he teaches?”

“How to make money by the look of it, Guv.”

They walked up the path to the front door and rang the bell. The door was opened a couple of minutes later, by a man in his early to mid-fifties, about six foot tall, balding only slightly and looking relaxed and cheerful.

“Yes...what can I do for you,” he asked, looking curiously from one to the other as they showed him their warrant cards and introduced themselves.

"Inspector Paul Manley and Constable June Kelly....do you mind if we come in and chat for a minute?"

George Edwards stood to one side and ushered his unexpected guests into the lounge. "What exactly would you like to chat to me about, Inspector? I hope I haven't inadvertently broken the law in some way."

Paul pointed to the red leather settee and chairs that dominated an otherwise bland room, "I think we should all sit down, if you don't mind," he said.

"Yes of course....please take a seat, both of you.....Can I get you anything? Tea, coffee, or a cold drink perhaps?"

Paul and June both declined refreshments and all three of them took up positions on the leather three piece suite.

"It's concerning your first wife, Alice," said Paul, trying to gauge the man's reaction, but not really observing any.

"First wife!........*only* wife, Inspector. Alice and I divorced in 1998 and I never re-married. Once bitten, twice shy, as they say. Although I believe she did get married again. We haven't had any contact at all since the month or so following the divorce, when we were dividing things up you understand, although most of that had already been done by then.   It wasn't a happy time for either of us Inspector and we were both anxious to get on with our new, separate lives. What's happened Inspector?   Is Alice in some kind of trouble?"

"Why would you think that? Was Alice often in trouble when you were together?"

"No...not at all, it's just not every day the police arrive to discuss her, so I naturally assumed that either she is in some kind of trouble, or she's had an accident of some kind.   Is that it?   Has Alice been in an accident?"

"Alice is dead," said Paul bluntly, again looking for any tell-tale sign of emotion and seeing none.

"Oh....I see. Well I'm sorry to hear it of course Inspector, truly I am, but really, I don't know what to say to you. Alice was part of another life. I don't think she has entered my thoughts for years. I'm sorry she's dead Inspector.....but there's no grief in me for her, I'm ashamed to say. Do you find that shocking?"

"So if you've had no contact with her all these years you wouldn't be able to help us locate any friends at all, or know if there are any relatives we could contact?"

"No Inspector, I'm afraid not, both her parents are dead and she was an only child."

"I'm sorry to have to ask this but why did you and Alice divorce?"

"Oh, nothing spectacular, Inspector. We just grew apart and started arguing all the time, row after row about nothing in particular I'm afraid, until in the end we both agreed we'd be happier splitting up. It was all fairly amicable when it came to it. We were both reasonable people, Inspector, and there were no children to worry about. It was all quite easy. After all, we both wanted the same thing......Not to see each other again basically."

"During the years you and Alice were together was there ever any confrontation, or disagreement between Alice and anyone else? A friend or neighbour maybe?

"No... Again, I'm sorry Inspector but I thought she might have re-married as I said. Isn't she still with her husband? Can't he help you?"

"Yes, and he is doing of course, but it's best to get as much information as possible from as many different sources as possible. I'm sure you can appreciate that. I know you say that there hasn't been any contact between you, but are there still any joint assets at all? Another property, for instance, a holiday home or anything? An outstanding debt perhaps?"

"As I told you Inspector, everything we owned was split down the middle when we divorced. There is absolutely nothing to connect us at all. Not property, not money, not family, nothing."

"Can you remember the last time you spoke to Alice?"

"Neither when it was, nor what was said Inspector, other than it was probably in 1998 or 99. No later than that certainly and it was probably about the proceeds from the sale of our house, but I'm guessing about that."

"Well, thank you for making that clear. There is one thing that I find puzzling however."

"Oh....and what's that Inspector?"

"Well...... we've been talking about your ex-wife for a while now.......and you still haven't asked me how she died. I find that a little surprising."

"I see......yes, I suppose you might think that.....but as I've said to you Inspector, Alice was part of another life.....a life that I just have no interest in any more. To put it bluntly, I don't care how Alice died. I'm sorry if that shocks you but it's just the way it is."

"I'm a policeman, Mr Edwards.....nothing shocks me anymore. Thank you for your candour."

Paul looked around the room they were in. It was tastefully decorated and very neat and tidy. George Edwards was house-proud and, although the red suite contrasted with the rest of the room, it wasn't out of place and showed style. He stood up and walked over the fireplace above which was a picture of an eighteenth century naval battle featuring a three masted battleship in full sail with cannons blazing. Paul knew nothing about art but he instinctively looked at the signature to see if he recognised it. He didn't know the artist but did note that it was a limited edition, number four of twelve, so it didn't come cheap.

"You've obviously done well for yourself

George," Paul remarked, "What is it you teach? You are a teacher aren't you?"

"That's right, I'm a retired geography teacher, Inspector, but I was left some money after my divorce from Alice and I made some good investments with it. I've been lucky."

"Can you tell me where you were yesterday morning, say between 6am. and 10 am?"

"That's easy. I was here, having breakfast, and then doing a little gardening. Alone I'm afraid, so no one to corroborate my alibi, if alibi I need?"

"Well I think that's all for now, but we may need to speak to you again, and here is my card, just in case you suddenly remember something you think might be of interest."

George Edwards showed them to the door and they said their farewells.

As they were driving back to Bristol, June asked, "Well, what do you make of Mr Edwards, Guv? Bit of a cold fish if you ask me."

"I didn't get the impression he was hiding anything though, June. Quite the contrary in fact. But look into his finances for me anyway will you? You're good at that sort of thing. See if he really was left some money and find out what the good investments were he made. Confirm that there is no outstanding financial tie between him and his ex-wife. Maybe something that the new husband is unaware of. If she was due any money from the inheritance or the investments, and was chasing it, that could be a motive for murder."

"I'll get onto it straight away when we get back, Guv. And he still didn't ask how she died, did he?"

"No June, he didn't."

"If it was an ex-husband of mine I'd want to know.   I wouldn't be able to contain my curiosity....would you?"

"No."

Chapter 4

Michael Tucker had been a pawn-broker all his life. He had grown up in a pawn-brokers shop and gone into the family business as soon as he left school. He had been in partnership with his father and elder brother until his father's death, when his brother decided to up stakes and move to Spain, taking his half of the business with him. So now Michael just ran the one little shop, but business was quite good. A recession might be bad news for a lot of people but pawn-brokers normally got by.

Yesterday had ended on a high. A young drug addict who called himself Sid brought in a suitcase full of silver.

"What'll you give me for that lot?" he enquired, lifting a rather expensive looking suitcase onto a table in the middle of the shop and pacing about nervously.

Michael opened the panel in the grill over his counter that allowed larger objects to be passed through and said, "Put it up here, I'll have a look."

He hadn't been hopeful. The lad had brought stuff in before, normally ornaments and household stuff that he had nicked from somewhere, but a couple of times he had brought in watches and the odd bit of jewellery that Michael had made a few bob out of. He'd assumed that the suitcase, which was a good quality leather one, would be worth more than the contents. Household junk was what Michael expected to see, but when he looked in the case he couldn't believe his eyes.

He quickly transferred the suitcase to his back office and had a quick look through the extensive array of silver objects.

"Hey! Where are you going with it?" asked Sid excitedly, almost climbing over the counter, until he saw that Michael was just going through the contents of the case on his desk.

Every single piece looked to be solid silver and good quality. Not a single piece of silver-plate amongst it. Where the hell had Sid managed to get hold of stuff like that?

"How the hell did you get hold of this lot Sid? You haven't done anything really stupid have you?.....That's all got to be as hot as hell. Don't you go bringing the police to my door."

Sid was leaning through the grill straining to see what was happening in the office. "I swear to God Mike, I don't know where it come from. I was just sitting in the park, by the keeper's hut, and somebody just chucked it away...right in the rubbish bin....over the railings it come.......Even I can see that's good stuff......Gotta be worth a fortune innit....How much you gimme?"

"How much do you think it's worth Sid?"

"I dunno.....You tell me....You're the expert right, but don't try and rip me off man......It's gotta be a grand at least, yeah?" said Sid, hopefully, never having seen a thousand pounds in his whole life.

"Are you saying you want a thousand pounds for it? Is that what you're saying?"

"Yeah...yeah I am. It's worth a lot more than that...I aint stupid.....but yeah....I guess it's hot......but you got connections right?.....You can sell it on?"

"Yeah, I can sell it on all right but it won't be easy Sid. It'll have to go abroad, all of it. I can't sell in this country, the police will be circulating lists. A clever lad like you knows that. The thing that worries me is, what are you going to do with a thousand pounds? You and I both know that you could kill yourself with that kind of money."

"So....what do you care? It's my money I can spend it how I want."

"I don't want your death on my conscience Sid. Why don't we agree that I'll pay you the thousand pounds for it, but not all at once.....Let me give it to you twenty five quid at a time.....We'll keep a tally......That way you get the money and you get to stay alive and enjoy it as well."

Sid knew that Michael was right. If he had that kind of money all in one go he would probably end up dead. "How do I know you'll let me have it all?" he asked, worried he was going to lose out somehow.

"You know me Sid. We've had dealings before and I've got a reputation to maintain. You can trust me. It's better than ending up dead in the gutter. And where would you keep that kind of money anyway....It would get stolen and you would probably get knifed for it or worse. Where are you staying these days? Is it somewhere the money will be safe? Look on me as a kind of bank and you can withdraw money when you want it without the worry of it being stolen."

Sid knew that everything Michael had said was true. The only place he could keep the money even half safe was in his underpants and that wouldn't guarantee its safety.

"OK......twenty five quid at a time......but I swear if you try and cheat me, I'll cut you, so help me I will. I'm gonna keep a note of how much I've 'ad."

Michael handed over twenty five pounds to Sid and watched him leave the shop with a spring in his step, thinking, bloody typical...I do my good Samaritan bit and stop him killing himself and he threatens to cut me.

Michael was a contradiction, a pawn-broker with a heart. Sure, he did a lot of illegal deals, bought from some quite nasty people sometimes, but if someone was in genuine need he didn't mind paying a bit over the odds now and again. He enjoyed helping people. It made him feel good about himself. Something his brother had never understood. Although Sid was a drug addict and a complete waste of space, Michael was genuinely concerned about him and had no intention of cheating him out of his thousand pounds. Why should he? From what he'd seen of the stuff in Sid's case it was worth a small fortune.

* * * * * * * * * * * * * *

Two days after Sid's visit to his shop, Michael was still marvelling at the pieces he had brought in. Whoever had put the little collection together had certainly known their stuff. Even the least desirable piece was solid Georgian silver in good condition with clearly discernible hall marks. Michael thought there was probably thirty or forty grand's worth in total for him, even if he had to pass it on at a fraction of its true value. He was worried about where it had come from, but as excited as hell about how much he was going to make out of it.

Today, however, he was destined to be a very disappointed man indeed. He was about to get into trouble because he'd been careless. He had been examining a particularly nice tankard that was one of the items from Sid's suitcase. He thought that he recognised the makers mark but he needed his book of silver marks to make sure and realised that he had left it in the main shop, so he opened the grill and flap in the counter and entered the shop to retrieve it, leaving both the grill and the flap up.

No sooner had he reached the book than the shop door opened and in walked two plain clothes police officers. He could spot the police a mile off, so he immediately made to return to his office, but seeing the anxious look on his face, one of the men beat him to the counter flap and blocked his path.

"Hello Michael," said Constable Derrick Price, "how's business....good? This is my colleague, Constable Campbell. Do you mind if we have a look around?"

Before Michael had a chance to say, "That's private in there," Derrick had walked to the office door and looked in. Michael's heart sank.

Spotting the tankard on Michael's desk, Derrick exclaimed, "Wow! That looks nice Michael.....Can I have a closer look?"

Michael knew the game was up as he saw Derrick take a type written list out of his pocket. "Well as a matter of fact," he said cheerfully, ignoring the growing hollow feeling in the pit of his stomach, "I was just about to ring you lot about that. You've saved me a phone call," he said, cursing his own stupidity and crying inwardly as he saw a small fortune disappearing before his eyes.

"Oh yeah, just about to do your upright citizen bit were you, and call us to say that you've just bought some naughty?"

"*Yes* as a matter of fact, I was," he replied earnestly.

"Well go on then.....show us the stuff."

Michael reluctantly returned to his office and showed them the contents of the suitcase he had purchased from Sid. They only had to check the first few items on their list to realise that they had recovered John Bridgeman's silver collection.

"I think you'd better shut up shop for the day and come with us Michael. Our Inspector is going to want a word or two with you about this," said Derrick smiling.

"I swear to God, I was just about to check the hallmarks on the stuff before ringing you, to make sure it was as good as it looked so I didn't waste your time."

"I know you were Michael. Why don't we put it all back in the case to carry......Do you have a coat?" asked Derrick, turning the sign on the shop door from open to closed.

Michael had little option but to admit that he had bought the silver from Sid, suspecting that it was stolen, though not where from or under what circumstances, and he continued to argue that he had been about to call the police when the constables had called in, arguing that he hadn't know for certain that it was stolen until he'd had a chance to examine it more closely. Michael had no idea where Sid was staying but Constable John Major had had dealings with Sid in the past, and it wasn't very long before inquiries had him located at a derelict block of flats, that was being used as a squat.

John explained to Paul, "One of my informants tells me that Sid has been seen going in and out of the old flats in Barton Street. They're due to be demolished sometime next year and squatters have moved in big time.”

“You know the flats John, how many men should we take to make sure we don’t lose him?”

“The whole place is a warren Guv. And it’s not self-contained little units anymore apparently. I’m told the squatters have knocked holes through from one flat to another so as to give themselves plenty of escape routes if they should ever be raided. There’s a lot of drug dealing goes on. One of my mates had occasion to go in there a while back and he reckoned they must have had heavy equipment in there to make some of the holes.”

“Christ! You make it sound as if we’re going to need an army just to arrest one man. The DCI’s not going to be very happy, let alone the Chief Constable.”

“We could always make it worth their while Guv.”

“How do you mean, John?”

“Well Guv. Ninety nine percent of the squatters there are going to be on drugs, and twenty percent are going to be dealing on some scale or another, so if we have to go in heavy handed anyway, why not grab a few dealers while we're at it? If we bag a few it'll look good on the figures and keep the Chief Constable happy."

Paul picked up his phone, "Yeah...maybe. I'll run it by the DCI, see what he thinks."

Three hours later, Paul's team turned up outside Barton flats in two cars, followed by a further four police cars and five large riot vans. Three full of personnel and two ready to transport any prisoners. The posse of police had approached the building without using their sirens in an attempt to catch the occupants as much by surprise as possible, and now officers with bolt-croppers were opening the large corrugated gates that represented the only vehicle access to the one time car-park that surrounded the flats. The whole of the building and its grounds had been enclosed by a seven foot high solid wooden fence, covered in notices declaring that the property was scheduled for demolition and was unsafe. Several holes had been made in different areas of the fencing by the squatters, to serve as ingress and egress to the property and uniformed officers were now stationed at each.

When the large gates were opened, Paul's team, together with his **DCI**, the police cars and four of the five vans entered the car park and a hoard of both plain-clothed and uniformed officers swarmed out and entered the building. The remaining transit van parked across the now open gates and men also poured from that. There had been unconfirmed reports of firearms being seen at the site in the past, so an armed response team went in first.

Paul, June and John Major positioned themselves close to the vehicles waiting to transport prisoners so that John could identify Sid when he was brought out. From where they were positioned they had a clear view of anybody being brought out of the front entrance. They also had an unrestricted view down the right hand side of the flats, along which, anyone exiting the rear entrance would be conveyed to the waiting vans. The rest of Paul's team had entered the building with instructions to help out where needed but had all been given descriptions of Sid.

The building itself had a rectangular footprint and consisted of twenty-five self-contained flats facing front and rear on each of four floors, making a total of two hundred flats in total. There were two exterior staircases on each façade of the building, running up to open terraces on each floor where the windows and doors of all the flats had been either bricked up or boarded over. Warning signs had been erected at various spots declaring the building to be unsafe, mimicking the ones on the outer fence, but this had only been done with a view to discouraging squatters. A ploy that had failed miserably. There were no windows at all on either side of the building, because the inside of this area was mostly taken up by the lift shafts and the internal staircases, the two lift shafts being situated centrally with a stairway on either side. The daylight for the stairs was supplied by windows facing to the front and rear of the building.

When the flats had been in use the lawns and gardens that surrounded them had been regularly maintained but now they had become a jungle that was quickly encroaching over the large car parking areas, and the tarmac was slowly breaking up and allowing various plants, including trees in some places, to push through in their relentless search for sunlight.

Inside the building the lift doors had been secured to prevent access. However, on a couple of the floors the doors had been broken open and a multitude of rubbish, domestic appliances and the carcasses of at least two dogs had been thrown down the shafts. The smell from the lift shafts was everywhere. The police began clearing the building floor by floor ascending the stairs with armed response going ahead of the others, but it soon became apparent that holes had been made, not only through the walls separating the flats, effectively linking each flat with the one next door, but at some point on each storey a hole had been made through the reinforced concrete floor so that occupants could drop through to the floor below, so the whole operation became a melee of bodies running this way and that in disarray. Fortunately the officer in overall charge had been foresighted enough to make sure that there were enough police positioned at the various exits to mop up any squatters who slipped through.

* * * * * * * * * * * *

The sleek black Mercedes pulled in and parked

approximately a quarter of the way down Barton Street facing west. Both sides of the street were bordered with high chipboard fences painted green and sporting notices stating the land had been purchased for development by Brunel Housing Ltd. Back in the 1930s there were three bedroomed Victorian terraced houses on both sides of the road. The houses to the left of the black Mercedes had been demolished only three months earlier by Brunel Housing six and a half years after the last occupants had left, in order to stop the constant demands that they be put to use. The terraced houses on the right, together with the houses that backed onto them, had largely been demolished in less than a few minutes, one night in January 1941 by the German Luftwaffe. The rest of that entire block had been pulled down a couple of weeks later when it was decided it was dangerous to leave them standing, and the area remained a bomb-site until, in the nineteen sixties, two more complete blocks of houses were also demolished and Barton Flats, built on the site. Now it was the turn of Barton Flats themselves to be pulled down and the site re-developed.

The two men who were sitting in the black

Mercedes were on the payroll of some rather unpleasant people in London, and some of the drugs that these people distributed were sold in Bristol through a supply chain of dealers, some big-time, handling thousands of pounds worth at a time and some small. One of the smaller dealers had started doing a little business on the side for himself, trying to work his way up the pecking order, and the two men had been sent to show him the error of his ways. The car had been parked for no more than five minutes when a head poked out of one of several holes that had been cut in the fencing surrounding the Flats. The owner of the head beckoned to the men in the Mercedes who now exited the car and followed him into the precincts of Barton Flats through the hole in the fence.

The two men from the Mercedes were easily distinguishable from the third man by the way they dressed. The occupants of the Mercedes being attired in expensive hand-made suits, whereas the third man was wearing dirty jeans and a baggy jumper that also doubled as his night-time sleeping attire.

"He's on the second floor," said baggy jumper

nervously, being quite scared of his two visitors.

"Take us to him," replied the Mercedes passenger, with an air of authority that baggy jumper would have been foolish to ignore.

Baggy jumper led the two men down the side of the building towards a collection of domestic wheelie-bins.

"Where are we going?" asked Mercedes driver, "why aren't we going in through the main entrance?"

"The doors are chained shut in case the pigs come calling," he replied. "They'll make a lot of noise cutting those chains off and it'll give us a chance to get out or at least stash some gear before they get in. Follow me."

Baggie jumper moved a couple of the bins to one side disclosing the fact that, concealed behind them, there was a large hole cut in the outer wall of the building and led into one of the stairwells.

"Up here," he said, as the men followed him through the wall and up two flights of stairs to the second floor. When the flats had been in use anyone exiting the stairwell and wishing to call at one of the flats would have found themselves on a kind of large enclosed landing, from which they would have had to exit through double doors onto an external walkway running the entire length of the building and onto which the front doors of the flats opened. Now, however, most of the windows and doors accessed from the walkway were boarded over or bricked up, except for those few where the window boards had been taken down to allow in daylight, and where at least two doors on each level had been completely removed.

Baggie jumper once again indicated that the men should follow him through a hole in the wall, this time leading from the enclosed landing into the end flat. The flat had a distinct odour of urine and stale air and there was a semi-conscious man lying in one corner on a bed of cardboard and one dirty blanket. They were led through three more rooms, until, in the fifth, they found the man they were looking for.

When they first entered the room the man in question assumed they were other squatters passing through but, when he saw how they were dressed, he realised that they had come for him and he made a dive for the hole in the opposite wall in order to escape. Unfortunately for him his move had been anticipated and Mercedes driver grabbed his ankles and pulled him back into the room where he turned and sat with his back against the wall staring at the new arrivals and shaking with fear.

Baggie jumper wasn't keen to see what was going to happen next and said, "You don't need me anymore...I'm off...Have you got my money?"

Mercedes passenger took a brown envelope out of his inside coat pocket and dropped it at Baggie jumper's feet. He stooped to pick it up warily and took off in the direction they had come.

The man on the floor eyed his visitors with suspicion, his knees pulled up to his chest and his arms half raised in anticipation of a blow. He was going to get a beating for sure but he had no idea how severe it would be. He could only pray that he wouldn't suffer any permanent damage.

"I'm sorry all right," he pleaded, "it won't happen again...I promise.....You don't have to do this.......Please."

Mercedes driver and Mercedes passenger both removed automatic pistols from inside their coats and cocked the weapons, "Put your hands behind your head and cross your legs," said driver.

Oh! Jesus were they going to shoot him?.....He expected a beating...Not this!

The man on the floor crossed his legs as requested and put his hands behind his head, "***Please!!!!***" he shouted again.

The two strangers pointed their weapons and the seated man instinctively put one arm out in front of himself as if this motion alone would be enough to fend off the bullets, but the gesture was woefully inadequate. Both men fired one after the other in quick succession and the man on the floor screamed in both shock and agony as both his kneecaps exploded with the impact of the bullets.

When the echoes of the gunfire and died down the two men became aware of noise, both outside and inside the building. The room they were in was one of those that had the boarding removed from the windows so Mercedes driver walked over to it and looked out.

"Christ!" he exclaimed, "the place is swarming with bloody coppers...where the hell did they came from?......let's go!"

They quickly ran back to the end room which they had entered through the hole from the landing and they were just about to exit the same way when they heard noises from that very landing. Realising that police were entering the landing from the stairwell, they returned to the scene of the shooting, looking about them for another escape route.

"This way," said driver, who, peering through to the next room on again, had noticed a hole in the floor.

They quickly entered the room and stood either side of the hole looking down to the room below, which looked and sounded empty. One end of a length of knotted rope had been secured around the middle of an iron bar that had been placed across the doorway. The other end of the rope dangled down through the hole in the floor.

The two men took it in turns to lower themselves, quickly and quietly, through the hole in the floor to find themselves in the kitchen of the flat below. This room also had a hole in the floor, but here there was no rope to aid descent and make an easy escape route. They stayed quiet and listened for a moment. The police seemed to be making themselves scarce.

"What the hell are they up to? One minute they're coming for us mob handed, next it's like they've cleared off. What's going on?" asked passenger.

"I don't think they're here for us," replied driver, "I think we've been unlucky enough to get caught up in a raid on the squat."

"So where have they all gone?"

"I'll wager our shots scared them off, but we haven't got long. They'll be back with armed backup any minute. We'd better get out quick."

They had to act quickly so, despite the fact that there was no rope they lowered themselves through the hole in the floor one at a time and dropped to the flat below. Driver managed it with no difficulty but passenger twisted his ankle on landing and proceeded to follow his companion with difficulty out of the flats through the hole in the outer wall once again.

Outside Barton Flats, something about the side of the building they could see had been troubling Paul but he couldn't work out what it was. There was definitely something, but he couldn't quite put his finger on it.

"Do either of you have one of those floor plans they were handing out?" he enquired of his colleagues.

"No Guv," replied John, turning his head to peer into the van behind them, "but there's one on the dashboard in there if you want it."

Paul turned to look where John was indicating and sure enough, sitting on the dashboard in front of the steering wheel, was one of the photocopied floor plans that had been handed out so that officers could familiarise themselves with the layout of the flats before they entered. Paul walked around to the driver's side of the van and got in. He sat behind the steering wheel and studied the plan.

The floor plan showed the layout of the entire site, including the grounds, and clearly shown on the plan at the rear of the property, was a walled-in area that had been labelled, "Waste Disposal Enclosure." It had obviously been the place where the waste bins for the flats had been stored ready for a weekly collection. Paul had a mental picture of the bins in his mind, large green or black plastic affairs on wheels with convex lids and requiring specialised vehicles to empty them. Suddenly he realised, that's what had been bothering him. About a quarter of the way down the side wall of the flats from where Paul was, were several wheelie bins, but not the large industrial type that he visualised the flats would have had when they were occupied. These were the smaller, common household bins. They were completely incongruous to the surroundings. Where had they come from? he wondered, and what were they doing there? Were they hiding something that was against the wall?

Paul's train of thought was suddenly shaken by the unmistakable sound of *gunfire* coming from inside the flats. Two shots in quick succession. Pandemonium broke out in all quarters and many officers could be seen running for cover and shouting warnings to colleagues. John and June ran to the other side of the van Paul was sitting in for cover. Paul looked once again down the side of the building where there were now two uniformed officers escorting a struggling youth in cuffs, heading towards the vans.

Both the officers and their prisoner froze at the sound of the shots, not knowing whether to continue the way they were heading or return the way they had come. Consequently they did neither and remained where they were. After a few minutes of inactivity they decided to continue heading for the vans and recommenced their journey. All of a sudden a man emerged from behind the wheelie bins that Paul had been having such a problem with. At first Paul thought that he must have been hiding there all along, but he soon realised that he had just exited the building somehow and was looking to get away.

He was brandishing a gun and, seeing the uniformed officers coming towards him and not too distant, he pointed his gun in their direction and pulled the trigger. There was a horrendous bang as he fired, and one of the uniformed officers slumped to the ground. His colleague let go of the arm of their prisoner and bravely knelt beside the fallen officer, despite the gunman firing again, thankfully missing his target the second time.

Paul watched the events unfold before him in slow motion whilst instinctively turning the ignition key and starting the van's engine. As he did so another man, also armed, emerged from behind the same bins. This second man, however, appeared to be limping. While all this had been happening two unarmed police officers, one male and one female, who had hurriedly exited from the front of the building, rounded the front corner making for the perceived safety of the vehicles, but inadvertently exposing themselves to the two gunmen, who now pointed their weapons in their direction. All four froze, looking like the living statues that inhabit many a city centre, the gunmen with weapons held in outstretched arms and the two officers caught mid-stride.

Paul put the van into gear and accelerated towards the gunmen, who, hearing his approach, now swung their guns towards him. They had time enough to fire one shot apiece before Paul reached them and for a split second, when the windshield of the van exploded over him, Paul thought he had been hit. Recovering his composure he quickly steered towards the first gunman and the van struck him a glancing blow knocking him to the ground. Then, pulling the steering wheel sharply left, he was able to steer it towards the second man, who now threw down his weapon and jumped clear, just in time, as Paul brought the van to a screeching halt and jumped out.

John Major and June Kelly, who had both run after Paul in the van, and the two officers who had so narrowly escaped being shot at, pounced on the second gunman before he could recover and Paul ran from the van towards the first gunman who still lay prone on the ground, anxious to discover the fate of the man he had deliberately run down. Pleased to find that he was still breathing, Paul kicked the gun out of the man's reach before cuffing his injured prisoner.

June, who was first to reach him, grabbed hold of the second man and cuffed his hands behind his back. With the gunmen safely in custody the area began filling with officers again and it was discovered that the gunmen had exited the building by way of a hole that had been made through the outer wall of the flats and concealed from view by the placement of wheelie bins.

* * * * * * * * * * * * * * * * *

With the operation at Barton Flats concluded, everyone was waiting to hear the news from the hospital, not least Paul who was anxious to hear the fate of two patients. Detective Chief Inspector William Blake stood up now that Paul had assembled everyone and quieted them down.

"I know you are all anxious to hear about Constable Reece," he began, "and I'm happy to be able to report that he was not seriously wounded. Apparently the bullet went straight through the side of his chest, albeit glancing off and breaking a rib in the process, but he should make a full recovery according to the doctors. He wanted me to pass on the message that, if any of you are thinking of visiting him, either in hospital or while he is convalescing at home, you need to take something liquid and alcoholic with you. Whiskey preferred apparently. No fruit. Now I didn't think to take anything in when I visited and he was still in casualty then anyway, so I've put a couple of bottles on one side for when he gets out."

Once the news of Constable Reece's condition had been delivered, there was a tangible lightening of the atmosphere in the room and DCI Blake continued. "The two gunmen that we encountered at the flats are in custody as you will all be aware, one in the cells here and the other chained to a hospital bed, where I am sure you all hope he is in a great deal of pain."

There were several cries off, "Hear! Hear," but Paul enquired further, "Sir, as the one who ran him down, I would like to know the extent of his injuries. He's not likely to die or anything is he?"

"No Paul, not that it would be any great loss if you ask me. Apart from a rather nasty break to one arm and a broken ankle he got away with cuts and bruises, which is far less than he deserves, but for God's sake don't quote me. The bloody press are swarming all over the place. Having said that however, the press do seem to be quite supportive of our actions for a change."

"Who are the gunmen, Sir? And what were they doing in a squat?" asked June, articulating the question that was on all their lips, "From their clothes they didn't look short of a bob or two."

"Carl Jenkins and William Filer. It would seem our friends were down from London, looking for, and it would seem, finding someone that they had obviously traced to the squat. Why they were after him we don't know yet. We haven't had a chance to speak to him properly, he seems to be in quite a bad way. He was shot in both knees, so he obviously upset somebody a great deal. The Met are keen to get their hands on our shooters so we shall be sending them home soon. It looks as if they are responsible for at least three drug related killings in London over the past two years. It was just bad timing for them that they were in the building when we turned up. Anyway, the Chief Constable is very pleased. Not only did we nab a couple of London's most wanted, but we bagged six dealers of our own, one of whom was a reasonably big fish it seems, according to the drug squad anyway. It was bad timing for him as well being in there when we turned up. He must have been there supplying some of his dealers because when we located his car, we recovered drugs worth at least a hundred and forty grand. The drug squad think he could be the missing link in a supply chain they've been monitoring for a while, so we seem to be in everyone's good books for a change. So well done everyone, especially you Paul, I believe the Chief Constable is putting your name forward for a commendation. These guys don't seem to mind shooting police officers so if you hadn't taken the action you did we may well have had other officers down."

"Well done Guv," said June, to a round of applause from the room.

Paul turned to face everyone with a big grin on his face and said in a posh voice, "I'd just like to take this opportunity........"

Paul's attempt at a speech was cut short when he was bombarded with a deluge of paper cups and screwed up paper, together with cat-calls and laughter.

"*Right!*" said the DCI, holding up his hand to settle everyone down again, "don't let it all go to your heads. There's plenty more to be getting on with. Paul, I understand you managed to get your man in the end as well. A good result all round."

"Yes Sir, thank you, we're just off to chat to him now."

"Do you think he killed Alice Bridgeman?"

"I've got an open mind at the moment, Sir. He did sell the silver collection that was stolen from the murder scene, but I'm convinced Alice knew her killer and let him in. I can't see how a woman like that would know someone like this Sid, although she was a teacher, and presumably Sid went to school somewhere, at least for some of the time. I'll see what he has to say for himself, and let you know."

"Would you like me to sit in on the interview with you?"

"It's your case Sir, I'd be pleased to have you conduct the interview," said Paul, a little miffed at the idea.

"Who were you going to take in with you, Reg?"

"Actually, I thought a gentle touch might get us further, I was going to take June with me."

"You rate her as an officer don't you?"

"I know she's inexperienced, Sir, but she's got the inquiring mind of a good detective, and she didn't hesitate to get stuck in with the gunman today. Did you know it was June that put the cuffs on him?"

"Yes...Reg told me. He rates her as well apparently. You and June go ahead and do the interview Paul. Let me know how it goes."

"Thank you Sir."

Sid had been slumped in the chair in the interview room feeling very sorry for himself indeed, and when Paul and June entered the room he began to rant.

"I'll cut that bastard's head off for grassing me up....I swear I will......He owes me a grand.......no matter what happens to the bloody gear...he still owes me for it!!! That's right ain't it?.....the deal was done before you lot took it....so he still owes me for it....right?"

"Calm down, Sid," said June, exchanging amused glances with Paul, "you'll give yourself a hernia. Just sit and calm down. We've got a few questions for you, that's all."

"Give myself a what?.....what questions? I aint done nothing wrong. Someone got shot yeah....well I didn't have no gun on me.....you knows that right.....was it a copper got shot?"

"Please....Sid....just calm down," said June.

"But I ain't done nothing wrong!!"

"You call beating a woman to death and stealing her husband's silver, nothing wrong, do you Sid.....Sid what by the way?" asked Paul.

"What you talking about? *I never killed no woman!* I wasn't the one with the gun. What the hell's that bastard been telling you. I found that silver, *it's mine!*" cried Sid.

"Of course you did Sid, you were walking along the road and there it was, just lying there in the street. The judge is going to believe that, no trouble, you'll be OK......Oh no – hang on a minute – what about the dead woman?....You didn't just find her did you Sid....no.....You hit her over the head until she died."

Sid was a bit more focused now, trying to think, suddenly realising how serious the situation was. He stared at Paul and June across the table with his hand up to his head, the fingers spread out across his forehead.

Sid tried to sort things out in his head, "This is all about me finding that silver yeah? You know I had nothing to do with no shooting at the squat right?" All the time he was speaking Sid was looking for any sign that they believed him, "Look, I swear to God I found that silver. I was sat in the park, by the park keeper's hut, and suddenly this suitcase comes over the fence and lands in the bin. There was no woman nor nothing, I swear, unless it was a woman what threw it. But if it was I didn't see her, right? Just the case with all that silver in it, flying over the fence, like I said. Well, if whoever slung it over the fence didn't want it, I figured I could have it. What's wrong with that? Michael's still got to give me my money, right? I found the stuff, so it's mine, yeah?"

"Did you see who threw the case over the fence?"

"No!...I didn't see no one. Not a woman and not a man. I just heard this big crash as it landed in the bin....right next to me man. Hang on a mo....I did hear a car door slam....soon after, and a car drive away, that's summit to go on innit?"

"Did you see the car?"

"No I didn't see it....I just heard it drive off."

"That's not a lot to go on then, Sid, innit?" said Paul, mimicking Sid.

"I'm doing my best for you man, you knows I didn't kill no woman right? You believe that yeah?"

"We don't *know* anything, Sid, other than the fact that you were in possession of the silver that was stolen from the house where a woman was killed! You've got to give us more to go on than that."

Sid looked scared, "You gotta believe me, I swear to God I was sat in the park and it just come sailing over the railing. I didn't steal it and I didn't kill no woman, honest to God man...I swear."

Paul and June got up, "Well I think that's all for now Sid, but we'll be speaking again soon."

Sid stood up expectantly, "I can go now then; yeah?"

"You can go now then...*Nah.* You'll be staying with us for a while Sid. We've got to check your story out."

"Oh man! I aint done nothing wrong...I keeps telling you....I just wants me money from that bastard that grassed me up."

Outside the interview room June asked, "You don't think he had anything to do with it, do you Guv?"

"Not in a million years, June, no, I think he was telling us exactly what happened. He was sitting in the park and whoever killed Mrs Bridgeman and staged the robbery, threw the silver over the fence to get rid of it. It's just as he said, innit."

June smiled, "What now then Guv?"

"That's a good question June. I don't like Sid for it and I can't see any reason, at the moment, to suspect the ex-husband, or for that matter, the new husband, although he's still our prime suspect. But whoever it was, she knew him and she let him in. You've still got to look into the first husband's finances and we're checking more deeply into Bridgeman, but I'm sure that was genuine anguish he was suffering. I really can't see it being him. It's time to speak to anyone else that knew Alice, either as Alice Edwards or Alice Bridgeman. Let's get to know our victim a little more thoroughly. I also think house to house enquiries along the road facing the park would be worthwhile. Someone may have seen Sid's mysterious car drive off, or even someone tossing a suitcase over the railings. You never know; we could get lucky."

When Paul and June returned to the incident room Reg was on the phone and called over, "Guv, I've got John Bridgeman on the line. He wants to know if he can go back to his house to pick up some more clothes and things. What shall I say?”

Paul thought for a moment and replied, “Make sure someone goes with him. Or better still, *you* go with him. But he’s not to go into any of the downstairs rooms, only upstairs, and I want you to give me a list of everything he takes. See if you think there could be another reason he wants to go there.”

“OK Guv.”

* * * * * * * * * * * * * *

He drove slowly past the entrance to The Cedars looking closely for any sign of life. It was the third time that he had driven by that week but on both the previous occasions there had been a police van parked outside, indicating that they were not yet finished investigating the murder scene itself.

It was a relatively quiet country road except for sound of birds singing in the nearby birch trees. There was a wide grass verge either side of the road, rather than pavement, and the residential properties that lined it were large and far between. Today there was no van outside so he pulled onto the grass verge some way past the house and walked back followed by a curious squirrel; both of them keeping a watchful eye out for any sign of activity or danger.

Seeing the house again brought memories flooding back, most of them good, but not all. He once again made sure there was nobody about, either walking or driving past, before he hopped over the driveway gates and walked swiftly to the house. He knew the property well and was familiar with the large kitchen window at the side of the house. If it hadn't been changed, he was confident he could open it and gain access to the house that way.

He took the pallet knife that he had brought for the purpose and inserted it between the bottom of the window and the window sill. The casement was hinged at the top and opened out. On the inside, at the bottom of the window was a simple pivoted handle with a blade that slotted into a metal receiving plate on the frame below. He looked through the glass to see the end of his pallet knife protruding inside to the right of the handle blade and as he knocked it to the left with his hand it took the blade with it, releasing it from the receiving plate and allowing him to pull the window open. He had noticed some bamboo bean poles propped against the fence to his left and he now opened the window to its full extent and used two of these poles to prop the window open. Next to the bean poles there was also an old wooden crate that he now tested to make sure it would support his weight. Assured that it wasn't going to break beneath him, he now placed it below the window to stand on, just as calmly as if he was performing some household chore rather than breaking into a crime scene.

He was just about to heave himself up through the open window when he was overcome with a strange compulsion to view the back of the house. Having no idea why he was doing so, he walked to the back of the property and surveyed the scene before him. The whole of the decking had been removed, not just the top planking but the support joists as well, and there were still sections of the ground tapped off and markers placed where items of interest had been removed for examination.

The events of sixteen years ago came flooding back as if they had happened yesterday. He stared at the grave site and was transfixed by what he saw. *The body of Lucy Penrose materialized slowly before his eyes.* She was lying in the grave with her legs pulled up to her chest just as he had left her all those years before. *He was unable to tear his eyes away and he recoiled in horror as she turned her head towards him accusingly and called his name.*

"This can't be!" he cried aloud, his heart now pounding in his chest. He was a rational man. He knew there were no such things as ghosts. If there had been, Lucy would surely have visited him long ago to point her accusing finger and frighten him half to death. No....this was all in his head he knew, but the knowledge didn't stop his heart from beating faster than if he had been running to the top of Kilimanjaro, or the cold sweat from trickling down his neck.

When he next looked at the grave she was gone. All trace of her had been removed by the police and the grave was empty once more. He wished he had never come. The chances of finding what he was looking for where pretty remote, if indeed it still existed at all.

A few minutes ago he had been as calm and collected as if he had been relaxing in his garden at home. Now his hands were shaking and he kept looking behind him to reassure himself that Lucy wasn't watching his every move. He returned to the window and climbed in with some difficulty, managing to dislodge the bean poles and bringing the window crashing down painfully on his ankle. Irrationally, he looked back to make sure it wasn't Lucy that had dislodged them. The sooner he could be away from this accursed place the better.

He searched the house from top to bottom but failed to find what he was looking for; either it no longer existed or it was in the hands of the police, in which case his fate was in the lap of the Gods. It might be looked at and discounted as being of any interest, or it might be examined in detail and recognised as the damning evidence it was. Only time would tell.

He allowed the window to drop shut behind him but was unable to relocate the handle. Leaving the window unlocked; he returned the crate and the beanpoles to their former home, grateful to be leaving at last. He was still struggling to banish the apparition of Lucy in the grave from his mind; it had seemed so real. Once home he needed a stiff drink to stop his hands from shaking. All the time he had been in the house it had felt as if Lucy was accompanying him in his search. But in the morning, with the arrival of a new day, he was himself again; even managing to sing alone with the radio as he made his breakfast.

Chapter 5

Roy Darnley sat on the edge of a table facing the team and downed the last of his coffee before asking of everyone present, "What have you got for me? I hope it's lots."

Julia was the first to speak. "We've interviewed all the staff who were working at Lucy's school while she was there, all except two that is, and they're both dead now, but fortunately we do have their original statements on file undamaged. But no one stands out Guv."

Phillip spoke up next, "Bad news from me I'm afraid Guv. One of the files we had trouble reading looks as if it was the interview with Jacob West. It would have been really helpful to have it restored but my restorer chappy said he thinks it's beyond saving."

"Right....It looks as if we're back to square one then. Mary, contact Daniel West. I know he never believed his father was guilty and was trying to prove it. See if he's come up with anything that we've missed. The rest of you keep digging, follow up any leads you have. Julia and I are going to interview Susan Cooper, Lucy's best friend, see if she remembers anything new."

Susan Cooper had married at twenty one to a boy she had gone to school with, Simon Winters. They had two children, a boy aged eight and a girl of six. Simon worked as a self-employed plumber and was doing quite well, which accounted for the nice little three bedroomed semi-detached house that they had managed to obtain a mortgage on.

"Lucy and I were best friends back then, Inspector. We had no secrets from each other," said Susan, brushing a hair away from her face and trying to stay composed while remembering the loss of her friend.

"Did Lucy have a boyfriend or were there any boys that wanted to be and Lucy rejected?" asked Roy.

"There were lots of boys that wanted to be Lucy's boyfriend and she did date a few. I gave a list of them to the police at the time but they were all nice lads

Inspector. I dated a few of them myself. We were only young back then, none of it was serious."

Julia looked at Simon questioningly, "How about you Simon? Were you one of the boys that fancied, Lucy?"

"All the boys fancied Lucy back then and yeah, I probably did ask her out at some time, but I never actually took her out so she must have turned me down."

"That's because I told her you were mine," said Susan smiling.

Simon laughed at his wife's comment and retorted, "Is that right!....You ruined my chances with the hottest girl in the school? I want a divorce."

"She wouldn't have been right for you, Si." Then turning to the Inspector again, she continued, "All joking aside Inspector, I think Lucy might have been seeing someone she didn't even tell me about. And if she didn't tell me, then there had to something elicit about it. I thought about it a lot at the time, and since. I think it may have been an older man, maybe even a married man. It had to be something like that or she would never have kept it from me. The night she went missing, she told her parents she was with me and I agreed to cover for her, but even though I asked her where she was really going and who with, she never told me. You won't believe the number of times I've blamed myself for covering for her. If I'd refused that day she might still be alive now."

"What happened to Lucy's not your fault, Susan. It's purely the fault of whoever killed her...no one else," said Roy, seeing the anguish surfacing in her face.

"That's what I keep telling her," said Simon putting an arm around his wife.

"Did you tell the police your suspicions at the time?"

"Yes of course. I was Lucy's closest friend. I was interview several times."

"So what did you think at the time? Did you have suspicions about anybody."

"No....well, only Odd Job," said Susan, fiddling with the hem of her jumper, "but the police checked him out and he had the all clear."

Roy and Julia exchanged glances and Roy asked the question that was on both their lips, "Odd

Job? Who was that?"

"The caretaker. He had a bit of a funny way about him especially with some of the older girls. There was never any trouble or complaints or anything, at least as far as I am aware. It's difficult to put your finger on what it was about him. He just seemed to enjoy the company of the older girls, but you would never see him chatting to any of the boys. He was always chatting to Lucy and me, and some of the others in our year. There were a couple of girls that told stories about him and called him a pervert, but they were girls who didn't know him, ones he didn't chat to, so I think that was just malicious talk. He didn't speak out of turn or anything. He didn't ask us about our sex lives or try to touch us or anything like that. He just used to ask about what music we liked, what we wanted to do when we left school, all innocent stuff like that."

"But you said you suspected him when Lucy went missing. Why was that? If it was all so innocent?"

"I don't know Inspector. We all thought he was a bit strange, but none of us felt threatened by him. He was just different. I don't think we really suspected him of being involved in her disappearance, but Lucy's disappearance was practically the only subject of conversation back then, all sorts of silly theories surfaced."

"What was his name? Can you remember?"

"Yeah, it's just come to me actually, talking about him I suppose. It was Geoffrey....Geoffrey Emerson. We used to think it was a posh name for a caretaker, when we didn't call him Odd Job, we used to call him, Sir Geoffrey."

"And the police cleared him you say?"

"Oh yeah! I remember that as well now. Gosh! I'd forgotten. He had an alibi for the day Lucy went missing. It turned out that he was away in London, on a jolly with some girlfriend or other I think."

"How do you know what his alibi was? Not from the police?"

"No; from him Inspector. Like I said, he used to talk to us all the time. As I told you Inspector, I don't think we really thought he was involved in Lucy's disappearance. It's just that he used to talk to us and he was a bit unusual in his manner; that's all it was. He was a singer by the way. A good one I believe. He belonged to some choir or other and I remember, now, the head tutor used to get him to sing in assembly sometimes; some of the kids thought it was strange but he had a lovely voice as I recall."

"What about Jacob West? What did you make of him?"

"Jacob West?" Susan paused as she brought the man to mind and brushed another hair away, "Lucy used to have piano lessons with him. He used to go to the house, and I had a couple of guitar lessons with him at the school, but not for very long."

"Why did you stop having lessons?"

"Because I was never any good, Inspector. Nothing to do with West. In fact, I only started going to his lessons because there was a boy I was keen on in his class. I'm not terribly musical Inspector, not like Lucy, she was really good."

"OK. Susan, you've been very helpful, we may need to speak to you again though."

"What happened to Lucy Inspector? Was it whoever she was seeing do you think?"

"We're still investigating at the moment Susan, but whatever happened it wasn't your fault."

As Simon showed them to the door they could hear Susan start to cry in the room they had left. "Thank Susan for us," said Roy, "it sounds like she needs you now, we'll be in touch."

"What do you think Guv?" asked Julia, as they left Susan's house and got into their car.

"Well I certainly think our Mr Geoffrey Emerson could be worth interviewing again. Pull him in when we get back, will you."

"Sure thing, Guv. Is that because he liked spending time with the girls?"

"And because he was a singer. Perhaps *he* had a musical themed tie-pin."

Julia cried out, "*Oh! bloody hell!*...of course! *the tie pin*.....Geoffrey Emerson!"

Roy turned and looked at her, puzzled by her sudden excitement. "What's got into you all of a sudden?"

"The music notes on the tiepin......They're a G and an E.....Don't you see? They may not be just random notes. They might be the owners initials.......G and E......Geoffrey Emerson!"

"Christ!.....Why did none of us think of that before now. Of course they could be someone's initials. It's obvious now you say it. If you're going to go to the expense of having something like that made to order for someone, you're definitely going to choose notes that match their initials, if possible."

Chapter 6

Daniel bundled up the last of the police crime scene tape and pushed it into the black bag that Rebecca held open for him, "Well that's the last of it," he said, taking the bag from her; "perhaps we can get back to some kind of normality now."

"I'll ring the conservatory people after we've had a cup of tea," said Rebecca, "it will be easier to put all this behind us when the conservatory is finished."

"Are you sure Roy Darnley said it was alright to go ahead?"

"Yes......They've taken away anything of interest; we need to put this all behind us."

"You might be able to do that, but I can't, not until we prove my Dad didn't kill that poor girl......and are you sure you're going to be alright living here now that a body's been found in the garden? I'd hate to think you had bad feelings about the house now, but if you're not going to be happy here we'll move."

"Don't be silly Daniel, this is your home.....of course I'll be happy here.....it's not as if I believe in ghosts or anything........you don't....do you?"

"No."

"Well then."

She put her arm around him and they walked together into the house. Once inside Rebecca looked about in dismay and fought to hold back the tears. The house was a mess, having been searched from top to bottom by the police.

Daniel looked at her and could see the distress in her face. He grabbed her shoulders and turned her to face him, "Look," he said, "why don't you stay a couple more days with your parents. Aren't you and your mum going to some charity event tomorrow anyway?"

"Yes," she replied, winning her battle against the tears, "but we need to get this place cleaned up.....*just look at it!!*"

"I know," he said, also annoyed that the police had left the place in such a mess. "Listen to me; you stay with your Mum and Dad tonight, get an early start with your Mum tomorrow. You're bound to be back late, so stay tomorrow night as well and by the time you're back here, I'll have the place "ship shape and Bristol fashion," how's that?"

"OK," replied Rebecca, kissing him on the cheek, "I will spend the next two nights with Mum and Dad, but I'm making a start on this lot right now," she continued, stooping down and picking up newspapers and circulars from the hall floor.

"I think I might have a quiet word with Paul," said Daniel. "I know that Inspector Darnley is a friend of his, or a colleague anyway, but I'm astonished that the police should have made so much mess. I'm tempted to put in a formal complaint about the state of the place. They had no right to leave it in this condition."

Rebecca had walked into the kitchen picking up bits and pieces off the floor as she went. As she entered the room she surveyed the scene with horror. The large square widow to the left of the back door was unsecured; somebody must have opened it and then failed to secure it properly when they closed it. Rebecca was dumbstruck; the police had left the window unlatched so that it could just be pulled open from outside!

She called back to Daniel, *"I can't believe it! They've even left a window unlocked in here, anybody could have come in."*

Daniel entered the room to see for himself, "Well that's it.....I'm definitely going to complain......We could easily have come home to find the place cleaned out or overrun with squatters."

Daniel walked over to the window and made sure the handle was located properly to prevent it being opened from outside, wondering to himself why the police would even have needed to open it in the first place.

Two hours later the house was beginning to look more like home again and a somewhat happier Rebecca called up the stairs to Daniel, "I'm going to put the kettle on for a cuppa, Daniel, are you coming down? What are you doing up there?"

A muffled voice floated down to her that sounded as if it was coming from another world. "I'm in the loft; trying to organise the space up here now the police have taken Dad's files. I'll be down in minute I could *murder* a cup of tea.......Oh sorry, unfortunate choice of verb."

Rebecca was standing at the kitchen worktop, stirring the two piping hot mugs of tea when Daniel walked in carrying a small, quite old looking, leather case.

"What on earth have got there, Daniel, I thought we were supposed to be putting things away, not bringing out more rubbish?"

"I know, I'm sorry. The police must have missed this old case when they took away all of Dad's stuff. It was under a piece of insulation in the loft. I recognised it as the case Mum used to keep old family photographs in. It'll be fun to go through it, I haven't seen it for years. Forgotten it existed even."

Rebecca moistened a cloth under the cold tap and handed it to Daniel. "Wipe it over with that," she said, "before you do anything else with it. It's filthy."

Daniel made to place the case on the kitchen table but halted mid-stride when Rebecca shouted at him... "No!....let me but some newspaper down first. Honestly Daniel, we're supposed to be cleaning remember!"

He stood and waited as Rebecca fetched newspaper that she had only just deposited in the recycling box and spread some on the table before him. Suitably admonished, Daniel put the case down on the newspaper and dutifully wiped it all over with the damp cloth, removing years of accumulated dirt and dust and revealing a rather good quality, brown leather attaché case.

"You're not going to go through it now, are you?" asked Rebecca, as Daniel flipped the catches to open the case.

Daniel looked at her a little sheepishly, "I thought I might," he answered cautiously, aware of the fact that he was skating on thin ice, "we've made good progress with the clearing up. If you want to get back to your parents after your tea, I can go through the case and finish the rest of the cleaning tomorrow, no trouble."

Rebecca stared at the contents of the case, which was brimming over with an assortment of old documents, postcards and photographs. She had to admit to herself that if she had found a similar case of old photographs relating to her family, she would be just as anxious to go through them; and she was well aware of the fact that Daniel was still desperately hoping to find something that would prove his father was innocent of poor Lucy's murder.

"OK....if you're sure, there is a film on the box tonight that Mum and I both want to watch, so we could see it together, and that would be nice. Thank you Daniel....I'll leave you to wash the mugs up as well then," she said, draining the last of her tea, "and I'll see you when Mum and I get back tomorrow evening." And with that she embraced him, kissed him passionately enough on the lips to make him regret suggesting that she stay with her parents that night, and was gone.

Despite missing Rebecca within minutes of her departure, Daniel was anxious to go through the contents of the case, and it was going to be a lot easier without Rebecca leaning over his shoulder every five minutes asking, "Who's that?" and, "What relation are they to you?" which he knew she wouldn't have been able to avoid doing.

At 6 o'clock that evening Daniel had been though the entire contents of the case and sorted it into piles on the table. One pile was old letters and documents that he wanted to go through carefully before throwing anything away. Another pile was photographs where he recognised either the location or the year if they were holiday snaps, or who they were of if they were people. The third pile was by far the most interesting. There were some holiday snaps of places that he didn't recognise and others of people he couldn't place or didn't know. He was determined to discover who these people were and put a location and year to the holiday pictures.

The next morning was a Saturday and Daniel woke up at 7am with aches and pains in almost every muscle, having fallen asleep whilst going through photographs on the settee and spent the entire night there. He never bothered to open the music shop before ten o' clock in the morning on a Saturday simply because, even when he used to open at nine, his first customer would seldom appear before ten thirty anyway. So when he looked at his watch and saw that it was still only seven o'clock he couldn't resist having another quick look at the photographs on the table.

There was one picture in particular that caught his eye. It was of his mum and dad at some function or other. It looked as if it had been taken in a club or perhaps a ballroom. They were standing with another two couples and he was sure he had known two of the people when he was younger. Their faces were familiar but he couldn't put a name to them. Gradually, however, he began to remember intriguing bits and pieces about the mysterious pair. They were definitely friends of his parents.....now wait a minute......they were *good* friends.......He could remember they had a house with a long back garden, he could remember being driven there on several occasions and he could remember playing cricket in the back garden with them all, his mum and dad and the woman and her husband. It was a happy memory.

It's funny how the mind works. That game of cricket was now vivid in his memory. He could smell the fresh cut grass of the lawn they'd played on. And he could remember that the couple's house had been in Clevedon. They'd taken a boat out on the boating lake in the afternoon.....It was gradually coming back to him.....The road had a funny name......something way........*Yeo!!! Yeo Way! Clevedon.* Daniel punched the air in triumph. If only he could remember their names but those just wouldn't come.

He wondered if there was any possibility that they could still be living at the same house. To hell with opening the shop today, Daniel was on a mission. He showered, had a quick piece of toast and a cup of tea and was on the road to Clevedon within the hour.

Yeo Way was easy to find. A quick look at a map had sorted that. He drove down the road and soon located the house as well. He recognised it straight away when he saw it because of the large horse-chestnut tree in the front garden. But it was disappointing, although not entirely unexpected, to find that the couple he was looking for no longer lived there.

He enquired of the neighbours who were home, whether they remembered the couple he described. One couple, who had lived opposite in the same house for thirty years, did remember the couple, and thought their name may have been Edwards, but they couldn't be sure.

"I think, *he* was a teacher at the local school," said the woman, "but I don't remember what she did. I have a feeling they split up. Chris and Marge across the road would know. I think they used to be friendly with them, but they're away at their daughter's until next week. number 16 across the way there. Next Saturday they're back; I should call on them if I was you."

Daniel made a note of the names and the address and despite the fact that it would mean having to close the shop for another Saturday, he was determined to call on them that day. On his way home from Clevedon, feeling quite excited about the possibility of identifying the couple in the photo, though not really holding out much hope that it would help in his quest to prove his father innocent of murder. Daniel decided to call into the police station where Paul and Roy Darnley were based, in the centre of Bristol. After telling the desk sergeant who he was and that he wanted to speak to Inspector Darnley, he was told that if he took a seat the Inspector would be down to see him.

Two minutes later Roy Darnley came out of a doorway with his hand outstretched. "Daniel, what can I do for you, or do you have something for me?" he asked expectantly.

"Well," Daniel began, "I've been giving a lot of thought to who would have had access to our house or grounds while we were away on holiday? We had some fish back then and I suppose Mum and Dad would have made arrangements for somebody to come in and feed them, and mow the lawn maybe; that sort of thing. But I was a twelve year old boy Inspector. I wouldn't have taken any interest in that sort of thing. However, I am trying to find a couple that my parents were friendly with back then. They used to live in Yeo Way in Clevedon. I have a feeling they were very close friends in those days and if Mum and Dad had anybody in to feed the fish, they may remember who it was. Well, apparently, the people who may know where they are living now are themselves on holiday at the moment and won't be back until the weekend. I'll contact them then. But whoever it was that buried the girl in the garden, they would only have had to know the house was empty and been able to get into the garden. They wouldn't have needed access to the house itself."

"That's true Daniel, and it does make our task more difficult, so keep delving. Anything you can find out may prove to be useful." Roy could tell there was something else on Daniels mind and looked at him questioningly, "Was there something else Daniel?"

"Yes actually, the real reason for my visit Inspector," he began, "the reason I called in to see you, was to complain about the state my house was left in after you had completed your investigations there. Not only did the place look as if it had been ransacked. But somebody had even left the kitchen window open, so burglars or squatters or anyone could have got in. Rebecca was in tears when she saw it. It's really not good enough."

"Whoa! Hang on Daniel. I was there myself the day everyone finished and I can assure you the place was left tidy. I knew you were a friend of Paul's so I even ensured that they cleaned up any traces of where they had dusted for prints, and I personally made sure the house was secure. Are you saying the place was untidy when you and Rebecca moved back?"

"You bet it was. Well, still is to some extent, I suppose Rebecca's going to kill me. I'm supposed to be cleaning the place up not gallivanting about trying to chase down old friends of Mum and Dad's.

"Are you going back to the house now?"

"Yeah, why?"

"Because I'm coming as well, I swear to you

Daniel, the place was tidy when we left it. If it was a mess when you and Rebecca moved back then somebody has been in there after we left........You've been burgled!"

Daniel just stared at Roy Darnley, nonplussed.

"When you get back to the house, have a check to see if you can identify anything that's missing. I'll be there shortly."

Daniel didn't know what to make of Roy's remarks but ninety minutes later he was making Roy a cup of tea. "Are you sure you won't join us?" he asked Julia White, as she re-entered the kitchen.

"No, really, not for me." Then, turning to Roy, she added, "they said a fingerprint team would be here in a couple of hours, Guv. What do you want me to do now?"

"Well you could just sit down for a minute. It tires me out just watching you. Perhaps you can think of a reason why somebody would want to burgle a crime scene because I can't? Unless we're missing something fundamental here and we missed some vital clue as to who killed Lucy Penrose and the murderer has returned to retrieve it after all this time."

"Oh! Come on Guv. You can't think there is any connection between the two events? Lucy was killed sixteen years ago and our prime suspect is dead! How can a break-in now possibly have any connection?"

"The house had crime scene tape over the door and, according to Daniel, nothing has been taken. Why would anybody break in and not take anything? Did you manage to find how they got in, by the way?"

"I'm not absolutely sure, but the window Daniel said was unlocked is easy to open with a knife," she said, "and there are some new looking marks here if you look,"

Roy walked over to see what Julia was referring to, as she continued, "Once that's open, if you have long arms and are flexible enough, you can just reach the bolt on the back door. Then it's just an old fashioned rim lock and any old back door key would probably open that or, if you're agile enough, you could probably just squeeze through the window itself."

Roy took another sip of his tea. "Suppose the thing the burglar was looking for wasn't here? That would account for the reason nothing was taken."

Julia's brow furrowed, "Guv?"

"We brought a lot of stuff away from the house that hasn't been returned yet. Suppose our friend was looking for something that's amongst that?"

"But that was just old papers and photographs belonging to Mr West, and if you're now thinking that maybe Mr West wasn't the murderer after all, because of this, how could anything amongst that lot be of any interest? It doesn't make any sense, Guv! It was just an opportunist thief who took a chance."

"I know it doesn't make any sense, Julia, but my gut is telling me these things are related. The house is miles away from anywhere. What would an opportunist thief be doing out here and, if it was one; why the hell didn't he take anything? No.....we need to get back to the nick and we need to go through all the stuff we brought away from here again, with fresh eyes."

"Whatever you say, Guv," said Julia frustrated at a possible red-herring to the case.

Roy had picked up on the tone in her voice as she replied and said, "Yes Sergeant, that's right, it is whatever I say."

"Sorry Guv."

"Does this mean you think my father is innocent now?" asked Daniel excitedly.

"Let's just say I've got a more open mind on the subject than I did have, and leave it at that for now Daniel. Don't get your hopes up, Julia could be right."

"I told you he didn't kill anyone," said Daniel.

"We'll see. Come on Julia, we've got work to do."

On the way back Roy asked, "Have we arranged for a second interview with our caretaker? What did Susan call him? "Odd Job," do you want to sit in with me on that one?"

"You bet, Guv."

* * * * * * * * * * * *

Clive Pascoe knocked on Roy's door and announced, "Geoffrey Emerson is in the interview room Guv. Who do you want with you?"

"Sorry Clive, maybe next time, but I want Julia with me on this one. After all, she did make the connection that his initials matched the notes on the tie-pin. What did you make of him?”

“Sure thing Guv.” said Clive, somewhat disappointed. “I only saw him very briefly; I didn’t pick up on anything untoward in his manner, but then I’m not a sixteen year old girl. I can’t believe we didn’t make the connection with initials earlier though. I suppose none of the rest of us read music, but you would have thought that one of us would have asked what notes they were and that would have triggered the thought.”

Clive was about to exit the office when Roy called him back, “Clive.”

Clive turned back to look at the Inspector, “Guv?”

“Don’t feel too bad about not making the connection. There’s at least one other member of the team that reads music and should have made it.”

“Yeah, who’s that Guv?”

“Don’t ask.”

"Oh!"

"Tell Julia I want to speak to her before we see Emerson will you."

"Will do Guv," said Clive politely, as he left the office.

* * * * * * * * * * * *

"Well Julia, tell me what we've got," requested Roy expectantly, as she entered his office a few minutes after Clive had left. "You've been very busy on the phone for the last couple of hours. What have you been up to?"

"Only possibly cracking the case Guv, that's all!"

"Well don't keep it all to yourself, Julia, I'm all ears," said Roy, keen to hear what she had to say.

"Well it goes like this Guv. We've got the recording tapes from the original interview with Geoffrey Emerson. The team back then were keen on him at first because of what the girls at the school said about him, basically what Susan Cooper told us yesterday, about him being a bit strange and liking talking to the older girls but not the boys. Now the reason they let him go was because he had a watertight alibi for the day Lucy went missing."

"What was this alibi?"

"Apparently, he had spent the day in London with a woman friend, one Angela Phillips. They'd taken Angela's car and, when they stopped at services on the way, there was a chap there with a stall set up, etching number plates onto car windows for security reasons. Well it seems that Angela decided to have her car done while she was there and the team managed to trace the man who, of course had a record of the plates he had done and what day and where he had done them. He confirmed that there had been a man and a woman in the car but he couldn't give an accurate description. Angela also managed to produce two ticket stubs for a London show with the appropriate date on them. She swore that it was Geoffrey who was with her that day so the police let him go. They had no reason to doubt his alibi."

"Well, it's not sounding too good for us then, is it if they had no reason to doubt it?"

"They had no reason *then,* to doubt his alibi......but I've got a good reason now, Guv."

Roy perked up, "Well, don't keep me in suspense Julia, how come you doubt it when they didn't?"

"Because his alibi, Angela Phillips, has form now. Back then she was unknown to us. Two years after Lucy went missing, Angela Phillips and her boyfriend, Alan Robbins, were arrested and convicted for a series of robberies on jewellery shops. They would pose as a couple getting married and when the shop assistant had a few trays of rings out they would grab what they could and run. Alan Robbins was a nasty piece of work by all accounts and if it was one of those places where you have to be let out, Angela would grab the gear and he would produce a knife and hold it to the assistant's neck until the door was opened. They were eventually caught when lover-boy held his knife to the neck of an assistant who had spent some time in the Para's and seen service in the

Falkland's.   He was in hospital for a week apparently.....You've got to hand it to those army boys."

"I still don't see how this affects Geoffrey's alibi?"

"Well, when they were convicted, Alan Robbins and Angela Phillips asked for several other offences to be taken into account and one of them was the robbery of a shop on the day that Lucy Penrose went missing, so the whole business of her going to London with Geoffrey Emerson that day was an alibi for her as much as him. Apparently, she and Alan and another couple of villains would often set up alibis for each other, so this other couple must have taken her car to London and obtained the tickets for the show and had the etching done on her car. She and Alan would presumably reciprocate the favour at some other time."

"OK, so this Angela lied about being in London that day, but why did they involve Geoffrey Emerson in it? She could have just said she'd gone to London with her boyfriend. Why would they have bothered to give *him* an alibi?. They didn't need him."

"That I don't know, Guv. We'll have to ask

him.”

“OK, that’s really good work Julia. Let’s go and do just that, shall we?”

Roy Darnley held the interview room door open to allow Julia White to enter behind him and they took up residence on the opposite side of the oak table to Geoffrey Emerson who was looking somewhat bemused by the situation.

“Oh! At last.....Is somebody going to tell me what this is all about?” he asked, annoyed at having been kept waiting.

“Hello Geoffrey, I’m Detective Inspector Roy Darnley and this is Sergeant Julia White. We have a few questions for you but you’re not under arrest or anything like that so you can leave if you’d like to. It’s purely voluntary but, having said that, you’ve no reason not to help us, I hope?”

“Help you with what? When they came for me I thought I was being arrested for something,” replied Geoffrey nervously, “what’s it all about?”

"So you don't mind helping us then, that's great. Just a couple of questions; it shouldn't take very long and then you can go. You don't want a solicitor or anything?"

"What questions?"

"Well....I understand that you know an Angela Phillips, is that right?"

"Angela!...yeah, of course I know Angela. We grew up together. Why? Is this something to do with her?"

"What do mean you grew up together? How was that?"

"We're both orphans, Inspector, Angela and I grew up in the same children's home together. We became friends. Is Angela in some kind of trouble again?"

"Again? Does that mean that Angela's been in trouble before then, Geoffrey? Can you tell us about that?"

"Not until you tell me what sort of trouble she's in now. Where is she? Can I see her?"

"I didn't say that Angela was in any trouble, Geoffrey. You jumped to that conclusion on your own. I just asked if you knew her. When did you see her last?"

"I haven't seen her for a few years. She met some creep and got into trouble with the police. You must know all about that. She and the creep went to prison for a while and I haven't seen her since she got out. She moved away, up north to stay with a girl-friend, I think. The creep had to do a bit longer inside, as I remember, but, like I say, I haven't seen her for years."

"Do you remember a girl called Lucy Penrose?"

"Ah!.....So that's what this is all about. I had a feeling it might be. I saw in the paper that you had found her body and that's why you're asking me about Angela, because she and I were in London that day. We told all this to the police at the time, surely you must know all this?"

"So on the day that Lucy Penrose went missing, you and Angela were in London, is that right?"

"Yes, the police checked it out at the time. They couldn't pin it on me then even though some of them would have liked to, and you can't pin it on me now."

"Oh, I wouldn't be so sure about that if I were you. Now, you told the police that you and Angela went to a show in London....I believe you produced the tickets for it?"

"Yes, that's right."

"Except that Angela wasn't in London that day, at a show or anywhere else....She was in Bath with her boy-friend, Alan Robbins, robbing a jewellery shop."

The colour drained out of Geoffrey's face, "What?"

"We now know that on the day Lucy went missing, Angela was robbing a jewellery shop in Bath with her boy-friend and not in London with you as you claimed at the time. So where were you really Geoffrey?" Roy leaned forward menacingly over the table and stared intensely into Geoffrey's eyes, "Were you with Lucy Penrose?"

"No!!! Oh for Christ sake...no....you can't think that I had anything to do with that. I knew Lucy, of course I did. We chatted sometimes. I chatted to lots of the students....Lucy was a nice girl. I wouldn't hurt her...I wouldn't hurt anyone."

"So where were you the day she disappeared?"

"I don't know....I can't remember...It was a long time ago."

"Oh come on Geoffrey....Are you seriously expecting us to believe that you can't remember what you were doing on a day when you felt you had to concoct an elaborate alibi to conceal whatever it was? We know that you liked Lucy and that you often chatted to her. We know that you lied about where you were on the day she went missing. Why would you do that if you've got nothing to hide? Give me a good reason why I shouldn't charge you with Lucy's abduction and murder right now."

"Because I didn't kill Lucy, that's why," shouted Geoffrey on the edge of despair.

"Then why lie about where you were? You must realise how guilty that makes you look. Tell me now where you were and we can check it out."

"I doubt it."

"Why?"

"Because the place is probably long gone; certainly the person I was with is."

"What place? What person? What's the big secret?"

"Haven't you worked it out yet? Why do you think I would chat to the girls but not want to be seen chatting to the boys? I'm gay, all right Inspector?..I was at a gay bar that evening with my then partner."

"Oh! Come on, Geoffrey...Are you seriously telling me that you would rather be a murder suspect than admit that you're homosexual? I don't believe you."

"Well no! Of course I wouldn't and I didn't

have to did I? Angela covered for me....I thought she was doing me a favour because we were friends but if what you say is right, it looks as if I was doing her one as well. She never mentioned that.”

“So you approached her and asked her to supply you with an alibi for the day, is that what you’re saying? and she agreed to help you out because it would give her an alibi as well, is that right?”

“Yes...the police were interviewing everyone who had any contact with Lucy. I knew I would have to account for my time and I didn’t want everyone to know about my sexual orientation. Some people have a problem with it Inspector, would you believe?”

“What’s the name of this friend you were with then? And what bar?”

“Jeremy Clark. He was a car mechanic. Well probably still is for all I know. We shared a flat for a while but I haven’t seen him for years and I’ve no idea where he is now.”

“And the bar?”

“The Portcullis in Park Street.”

"OK Geoffrey, we'll check it out. Can you think of anything about this Jeremy Clark that might help us to locate him?"

Geoffrey Emerson fidgeted with a button on his shirt cuff. "He's a Bristolian by birth, a car mechanic by trade and a homosexual by nature. That's all I know about him, Inspector," he said, getting more agitated by the minute.

"Well, it was obviously a deep and meaningful relationship you had with him then," said Roy, who had always had a problem with homosexuals and would have preferred to go back to the days when he would have been able to lock them up, "judging by how well you knew him."

Julia gave her Inspector a disapproving glance. "Tell me about Jacob West, Geoffrey," she asked, "you knew him as well didn't you?"

"Jacob West....the music teacher? Yeah I knew him. I used to lock up after his class had finished. Sometimes I got there early and would help him clear away; he was alright."

"So...would you describe Jacob as a friend?"

"Well I never socialised with him or anything, so no. We moved in different circles but we were friendly enough when we met. We used to chat, I like chatting, why?"

"What sort of things did you and Jacob talk about?" asked Julia, "Music, holidays, cinema? What?"

"Well yeah, all those things I guess. We both liked music and film and we both enjoyed going to Italy for our holidays. I think we'd been to some of the same places, Rome and Venice, places like that."

"So you would have known when Jacob was on holiday then?"

"I guess....maybe....I don't know."

"You don't know?"

"I can't remember; it was a long time ago."

"Where was it Jacob lived?"

"I can't remember that either; I'm not sure that I ever knew. Like I said, we never socialised."

“So you’ve never been to his house?”

“No, I’ve never been to his house....Why?”

“You said that you saw in the paper that we had found the body of Lucy Penrose. Did you see the photograph of the tie-pin that was found with her?”

“Yeah I saw it, why?”

“Did you ever own a tie-pin like that, Geoffrey?”

“No.”

“You like music though, don’t you? You sing in a choir or something don’t you?”

“So, lots of people sing in choirs, Inspector, and I expect a lot of them are gay. That doesn’t make them murderers does it?”

“This particular tie-pin had your initials on it. Are you sure you’ve never owned one like it?”

“No, I never owned a tie-pin...with or without my initials on it.....and I never killed anyone....so can I go now....please?”

"OK, I think that's about it for now Geoffrey," said Roy.

"You can go then Geoffrey.....for now," said Julia, "but we'll be wanting to speak to you again, so don't leave the country or anything will you."

Roy and Julia got up and left a now rather frightened Geoffrey Emerson to his thoughts.

"What do think Guv." asked Julia, after they had left the room. "Do you fancy him for it?"

"Yes, I think I do, at least as much as Jacob West now. The fact that he's homosexual doesn't rule him out. The motive may not have been sexual. Maybe she knew about his homosexuality and was threatening to tell everyone. He wouldn't have liked that."

"He wasn't exactly keeping it a secret, Guv. He was sharing a flat with this Jeremy Clark."

"Then there's the fact that he used to chat to Jacob about holidays. He could easily have known when the house was going to be empty. Maybe he even fed Jacob's fish when they were away and then there's the fact that his initials match the notes on the tie-pin; it could well have been his. What about you? Do you fancy him for it?"

"A bit, but my money's still on Jacob, although it would be nice if we could actually prosecute someone for Lucy's murder, so I'd quite like it to be Geoffrey Emerson. But not because he's gay, simply because we would actually have someone to charge."

"You think I'd like it to be him because he's homosexual."

"It's obvious you don't like them Guv. But no, I don't think you'd let that cloud your judgment. You're too good a copper for that. That's not what I meant."

"Good," said Roy, making it sound remarkably like a reprimand.

"I'll see if I can track down Jeremy Clark then Guv," said Julia, as they strolled back to the incident room.

“Good idea.”

On his return from interviewing Geoffrey Emerson, Roy Darnley found Constable Strange, waiting to see him. “Phillip, have you got something for me?” he asked expectantly.

“I have Guv, but whether you’ll view it as good news or not is another question.”

“Well, let me be the judge of that....what is it?”

“Another box of case files has been discovered only partially damaged by the flood,” Phillip began. “They must have been moved out of harm’s way during the attempt to stop the leak and got separated from the rest of the files. Some kind fellow came across them while looking for files for another case. He realised they were in the wrong place and when he tried to replace them he found that the files were in use and that the box must have been missed. Luckily for us he was conscientious enough to find out who had the files and let us know.”

“Good for him....Are they of any significance?”

"I'll say....There is an entire file on Jacob West and it shows that he and his family were on holiday in Italy when Lucy Penrose was murdered. There is a copy of a second interview with him plus confirmation of the holiday from the travel company they booked with and some dated receipts from the hotel in Lake Garda where they stayed. It's all pretty watertight Guv. That's why there's not much about him in the rest of the files we've got. Jacob West didn't do it."

"Thanks Phillip, that's really helpful."

"Sorry Guv."

"No, that's all right, I really do mean it's helpful. I wasn't being sarcastic. Julia still fancies Jacob for it but we've just interviewed Geoffrey Emerson, the caretaker from Lucy's school. The alibi he gave at the time is a load of garbage and he's had to come up with another one. He's beginning to look like a new prime suspect to me."

"Well, Inspector Manley will be happy Guv."

"Yeah, and it might get him off my back a bit, so not all bad news after all Phillip."

* * * * * * * * * * * *

"What have you got for me Reg." Paul asked anxiously, as he tried unsuccessfully to find some more room on his desk.

"Absolute diddlysquat Guv. We've spoken to everyone who lives along the road facing the park where Sid found the silver and nobody saw or heard anything at that time of the morning. The park keeper was working in a different area of the park, so he has no idea whether Sid was there that morning or not, but he did confirm that Sid does often sit there and that he sometimes lets him have a cup of tea and one of his sandwiches. He reckons Sid's not such a bad lot, just down on his luck and he feels sorry for him."

"OK Reg, it was worth a shot anyway. And talking of Sid; we'd better release him. We can hardly charge him with trying to sell gear that he found in rubbish bin. See to it will you."

"Will do Guv. What about our friendly neighbourhood pawn broker? Are we going to charge him with receiving? He knew the gear was stolen."

"No, he said he was about to phone us. A good barrister would have a field day in court."

June Kelly stuck her head round the door and announced, "John Bridgeman is here to see you Guv. I've put him in interview room three."

"Thanks June, did he say what it was he wanted?"

"Only that he wanted to speak to you, Guv. He's got some kind of album with him"

"OK, thank you June." Then turning to Reg. Paul said, "Come with me Reg. let's see what's brought Mr Bridgeman to our door shall we? It sounds like it might be the photograph album you said he picked up from the house when you took him there."

John Bridgeman was sitting at the interview room table when Paul and Reg walked in, sipping a cup of coffee that some kind soul had fetched him.

He immediately got to his feet to greet them when they entered the room. "Inspector Manley, thank you for seeing me, and Sergeant Evans isn't it," he said, shaking hands with both men enthusiastically.

The man looked better than the last time Paul had seen him, but the bags under his eyes said he still wasn't sleeping well and he obviously hadn't shaved that morning.

"Please, sit down," said Paul, indicating the chair John Bridgeman had just risen from, and taking the one opposite him. "What is it you want to see me about?"

Reg remained standing and took up position to one side of the room, leaning casually against the wall. On the table in front of John Bridgman was the photograph album and he had one arm laid across it protectively.

"You said that I should let you know if I thought of anything. Well, I was gathering some clothes from my house, thank you for allowing that by the way, I know you could have refused. Anyway I went into the spare room to get a photograph of Alice to take to the flat, and I started to pick up some photographs that had been scattered on the bed during the burglary, two or three of them had come out of their album you see. Well, I put them back into their albums, but there are two photographs missing. There are two gaps in this album you see, they must have been taken by whoever ransacked the room. Why would the burglar have taken two photographs Inspector? It doesn't make any sense."

John Bridgeman opened the album and turned it so that it was facing Paul on the table. Reg walked over and stood behind Paul so that he could also see what John Bridgeman was talking about. The photographs were held in place by means of self-adhesive corners and it was quite apparent that two had been removed.

"Well, I expect you missed them and they're on the floor, under the bed or somewhere, John. I can't think that they would have been of interest to whoever killed Alice. Not unless they could be used to blackmail you, or maybe Alice's first husband in some way. Perhaps they were removed years ago, John, or maybe Alice left a couple of spaces in the album on purpose in order to put some pictures in at a later date, or, perhaps she removed them to put them somewhere else. There could be all sorts of explanations for the gaps."

"No Inspector, let me explain. Some time ago, when Alice was out of the house one day, I went through all of her old albums, every one of them. Partly because I was curious about her life before she met me and partly because I wanted to see just what she looked like when she was younger and, I suppose, if I'm completely honest, because I was a little jealous of her first husband, I know that sounds rather pathetic."

"No, it doesn't sound pathetic at all John, I think I can understand. Was Alice secretive about her life before she met you?"

"No, she was always open with me about it all, as I was with her about my past, I just had a sudden urge to see pictures of her from back then. The point is Inspector that I know there were no gaps then. If there had been I would have been suspicious, I would have wondered why the pictures had been removed, do you see? I can promise you Inspector, there were no gaps then, but there are two pictures missing now, and whoever burgled my house, he took them!"

"Do you remember what the missing pictures were of?"

"Not specifically," John Bridgeman answered, "but I am sure they were more group shots of these people," he continued, indicating the photographs either side of the two gaps in the album.

Paul examined the two pages he was being shown and realised that John was right. The three photographs before and the two photographs following the gaps were all of the same group of people at some party or other. It was implausible that the two missing pictures would have been of anything other than more shots of the same people.

"Do you know or recognise any of the people in these pictures?"

"No Inspector, I afraid I have no idea who any of them are apart from Alice of course and I think that man there is her first husband," he said, indicating a man in one of pictures with his arm around the late Alice Bridgeman.

Something about the photographs made Paul examine them more thoroughly. One of the couples with Alice Bridgman and her first husband, George Edwards, looked vaguely familiar for some reason, but Paul supposed it was just because he had interviewed George Edwards recently and that made the whole group seem familiar. Nevertheless he knew it was one of those things that would keep nagging at him.

"Can I hang on to this for now John?" asked Paul.

"Yes of course. So you do think it's significant

then?"

"The only reason anyone would steal the pictures, other than for the purpose of blackmail, would be if there was something incriminating in them and, if, as we suspect, they were simply more pictures of the same group, I'm at a loss to think of any reason for the theft, if theft it was, or why they would have selected two and left these behind."

"It was definitely theft Inspector. The man that killed my Alice stole those two photographs, I know he did."

"OK John, leave it with me for now, and thanks. If you think of anything else, let me know."

As John Bridgeman left the station, Paul and Reg exchanged bewildered glances and shrugged their respective shoulders, as if to say, well...what do you make of that? and Paul answered the unspoken question, "Beats me."

* * * * * * * * * * * * * * *

Sid was still angry as he exited the police station and returned to Barton flats. His anger increased when he arrived and discovered that the fencing around them had been repaired and strengthened. There was no way he could get in. No point in trying even and any of his meagre possessions would be gone anyway. He had to find somewhere else to squat. That bastard Michael Tucker has grassed him up. One minute Sid had been looking at more money than he'd seen in his whole life, the next he was penniless and homeless. That bastard owes me, thought Sid; I'll pay him a visit.

Ever since he had left the police station Sid had felt he was being followed and he kept looking around but was unable to shake the feeling off. The impression that that somebody was following him persisted even after he left Barton flats and was with him right up until he entered Michael's shop.

As Sid entered Michael's shop he was almost knocked down by an angry woman on her way out. "You grassed me up you bastard," he called out, seeing Michael behind his counter, "you owe me."

Michael took an instinctive step back when he saw how angry Sid was, even though he was protected behind the grill atop his counter. "Calm down Sid, nobody grassed anyone up, it was just bad timing, the police turning up when they did.”

Sid grabbed hold of the grill and was just about to test its strength when two men entered the shop. Sid turned and stared at them, somehow aware that these were the men whose presence he had felt following him; he was suddenly very afraid but had no idea why.

“What can I do for you?” asked Michael, also on his guard for some intangible reason.

The first man to have entered the shop spoke up, “We'd like a word with you both, in your office I think.” he said pointing.

“We can conduct any business you want out here, my office is private,” said Michael, alarmed when the second man turned the sign on his door to closed and slipped the bolt across.

“You can't just come in here and close my shop because you want a word; a word about what anyway?” asked Michael, discreetly reaching for the panic button behind his counter that would trigger his silent alarm and summon the police.

Noticing Michael's actions, the first man produced a gun from inside his jacket, discouraging

Michael from pressing any buttons and said, "Oh I think we can. Don't do anything stupid. Why don't you open the grill and we can all sit in comfort in your office."

Michael reluctantly withdrew his hand and opened up the flap in his counter after releasing the grill and sliding it to one side. The man with the gun gestured to, a now uncharacteristically quiet, Sid, to follow Michael into the office.

"What's this all about?" asked Michael, trembling.

"We're curious to know what sparked off the raid on Barton flats and you two would seem to be up to your ears in it."

"That bastard grassed me up," cried Sid, pointing an accusing finger, "that's what sparked it off."

The man turned to look at Michael. "Is that right? Michael isn't it? Did you grass Sid up Michael?"

"Look, we had nothing to do with the raid on the flats, I had no idea where Sid was living, the police must have found him some other way."

The first man turned to his colleague and said,

"Looks to me like six of one and half a dozen of the other. I'd say they share the blame, what about you?"

"Oh I concur," agreed the second man. Then turning to Sid and Michael he announced, "We'd like you to come with us....both of you."

"What for? Where are you taking us?" asked Michael, alarmed, "we haven't done anything."

The man with the gun put a finger to his lips, indicating that the chat was over and they should be quiet, he then motioned that they should leave the shop. Outside, a third man was patiently waiting behind the wheel of a black **BMW** with tinted window and Sid and Michael were bundled, protesting, into the back seat.

Chapter 7

When the Saturday arrived, Daniel explained to Rebecca that he was hot on the trail of some friends of his Mum and Dad and was going to track them down rather than open the shop.

"Well, that's up to you Daniel," she could see that he was excited. "I have to take a turn as duty manager at the hotel today and I won't be back until around seven. Give me a ring and let me know if you are going to be later than that. And don't forget to ring Roy Darnley back, remember he left a message that he wants to speak to you. It could be urgent."

"OK," agreed Daniel, giving Rebecca a kiss and setting off on his quest, "I'll ring him later this morning, I promise."

As he drove to Clevedon for the second time in two weeks, he wondered if he was doing the right thing, neglecting his business for another day to go on what would probably turn out to be a fool's errand. Even if he did manage to track down the people in the photographs, the chances that it would somehow, magically, clear his father of the suspicion of being a murderer were pretty remote.

When he reached Clevedon he pulled into a layby and called Inspector Darnley, curious to know what he wanted and to get an update on how the case was going. Unfortunately he was connected to the Inspector's answerphone so he hung up quickly, not wanting to listen to the long list of instructions and alternative telephone numbers before being asked to leave a message. He'd try again later.

As it turned out, Chris and Marge at number sixteen Yeo Way, no longer had contact with the people Daniel was looking for, but they did remember their names, Alice and George Edwards.

"They split up and moved away," explained Marge earnestly, "but wait a minute though, I think I wrote George's new address in our book for some reason. I can't remember why he gave it to us though, we were more friendly with Alice than George, and she never gave us her new address. Just bear with me while I go and have a look," she said and toddled off to get her address book.

Chris stayed on the doorstep chatting to Daniel as Marge went to see if she really did have the eagerly awaited address.

"Here it is," she beamed on her triumphant return a few minutes later, "I thought I still had it, 172 Riverbank Road, in Sand Bay," she hesitated a moment "I hope he won't mind me passing it on to you after all this time."

"I'm sure he won't mind. It's only that I think he might be able to identify some friends of my parents for me, that's all. It's nothing sinister I assure you," Daniel explained, seeing that Marge was suddenly wondering whether she was doing the right thing.

"Would you like me to write it down for you?" enquired Marge, a little more relaxed.

"No, that's fine, I shall remember it," said Daniel, shaking each of their hands in turn, "and thank you ever so much, you've been really helpful."

Once back in his car, Daniel punched the address into his sat-nav and turned on the ignition. The engine turned over but failed to start. Daniel cursed although he was used to this happening. Sometimes when he tried to start the car with a warm engine it would take several attempts to get the engine going. He had mentioned it to the garage when the car was last serviced but, being an intermittent fault that only manifested itself under certain conditions, the garage had failed to find anything wrong. He even paid for a full diagnostic on the vehicle to no avail. The car eventually started after the fourth attempt and he pulled away, determined to have it looked at again. It was a small thing, but it was driving him insane. The drive to Sand Bay was a pleasant one, the autumn sun was shining down from a sky with few clouds, the odd tree here and there was beginning to display its autumn colours and the roads were surprisingly clear, so Daniel arrived at his destination in a little less an hour feeling pretty optimistic. He rang the bell of 172 Riverbank Road, Sand Bay, not knowing what he was going to say to whoever opened it. If the couple in Yeo Way, Clevedon were correct, then the door would be opened by one of the couple he remembered from his childhood, George Edwards. Although there was always the possibility that George had moved on again and the door would be opened by someone who would be annoyed at his turning up on their doorstep unannounced. Daniel put the thought from his mind. Would he recognise George after what must be the best part of seventeen or eighteen years? Would George remember *him*? He almost certainly wouldn't recognise him as the twelve year old boy who once played cricket in his garden.

When the door was eventually opened, it was done so by the much sought after, George Edwards. The two men stared at each other for some time, recognition slowly dawning on Daniel who nervously said, "George.....George Edwards, you probably don't recognise or even remember me, I was probable no more than ten or twelve when we last met. I'm Daniel......Daniel West, Jacob and Florence's boy, do you remember me at all?"

George soon regained his composure after the shock of seeing Daniel on his doorstep. "Daniel!....Yes of course I remember, you look so much like your father. Do come in," he continued, stepping aside to allow Daniel to enter, his mind working overtime. "Well, well, what brings you to my door after all this time? And how on earth did you find me?"

"Well I was lucky to find you actually, I remembered the house you used to live in, in Yeo Way. I remembered the tree at the front of the house and playing cricket on your back lawn with my Mum and Dad. I called on a few neighbours to see if anyone remembered you and knew where you had gone. Where is Alice by the way? Is she still with you? The couple I spoke to thought that you might have split up."

George had taken Daniel through to the lounge where he offered him a seat. "Yes, Alice and I split up years ago I'm afraid. Can I get you anything to drink?....Tea perhaps?"

George's head was spinning. It couldn't just be a coincidence that Daniel had turned up out of the blue like this. It has to be connected to Lucy's body being found at his house. Had Daniel come across the photographs he'd been looking for when he broke into the house? Was Daniel about to turn him in to the police, *or perhaps he intended blackmailing him.* His manner, however, didn't convey any kind of hostility. He seemed friendly, genuinely pleased to have found him. Was something else going on? George needed to keep his wits about him. How much did Daniel know?

"Tea would be good," said Daniel, dropping the small case he was carrying onto one of the red leather easy chairs, "do you mind if I use your bathroom first?"

"Top of the stairs and to the right," said George, noticing the case for the first time, and fearing what it might contain.

Daniel returned from the bathroom, at the same time as George brought two cups of tea and a plate of biscuits into the room on a steel and glass tray, which he placed on a coffee table in front of the sofa. Daniel had expected him to enter with two steaming hot mugs, and was a little taken aback by the two china cups and saucers with their matching sugar bowl and milk jug. He couldn't help feeling it was a slightly effeminate way to serve tea. His mother had always brought biscuits, or sometimes even slices of cake, on a tray when serving guests tea. His Dad would certainly have been a two mugs man.

"So, what made you take the time and effort to look me up Daniel. Is there something I can do for you?" asked George proffering the plate of biscuits.

Daniel declined a biscuit and said, "Well, you must have seen in the papers, or heard on the news, about the girl's body they found at our house."

"Your house! Not the one where your parents lived?"

"Yes, I inherited it when they died and I've never even thought about moving away."

"Good Lord! I've seen about it on the news of course, but I didn't associate it with where Jacob and Florence lived. I realised it must have been near-by of course because the news reports mentioned Congresbury, but not for one minute did I think it could be the same house.   Are you still living there? How awful for you. What is it can I do for you Daniel?"

"Well, because the body was found in Dad's garden, he's the prime suspect in the case. The police think that because this girl's body was found in his garden, then it stands to reason he must have been the one that killed her. So I am trying to establish an alibi for him, seeing as how he's unable to speak in his own defence. The murder took place on the 6th August 1996 and I'm hoping that we were all on holiday abroad somewhere at the time, but there is no record of it that I can find. I'm going through some old photo albums from back then and, although there are a lot of holiday snaps, there is nothing to say when they were taken. I know it's a long shot, but as you were good friends of Mum and Dad, I was wondering if you would look through a couple of albums with me. You might be able to put names to some of the faces I can't, and you might even recognise some of the holiday destinations and narrow down what year we went there. Would you be able to do that for me?"

"Yes of course, Daniel, is that what you have in the case?"

"That's right," said Daniel opening the case and showing the contents to George, who viewed them with interest.

The two men sat side by side on the sofa, drinking the tea George had made and going through the three albums that Daniel had brought with him. George was able to put names to some of the people in the first album, but wasn't as much help as Daniel had hoped with the others, not even being able to identify the other couple in the picture with himself and his first wife Alice. In fact, George tried to turn that particular page a little too quickly and move on, but Daniel insisted he look again. George had said he was willing to help and had with the one album, but he didn't appear to be trying very hard with the next one. Daniel was beginning to think he was wasting his time.

"But you and your wife are in those four pictures, along with Mum and Dad and that other couple, are you sure you don't remember anything about them?" Daniel asked again, frustrated.

"No....I'm sorry Daniel, they look familiar of course, but we may have only just met them on the night."

"And had your photograph taken with them?" queried Daniel, beginning to wonder if George was being deliberately evasive. "It looks in the photo's as if you all know each other quite well, to me."

"No, I'm sorry Daniel, it was all such a long time ago."

Daniel stared at the four pictures again himself. All four were of the same group with a different person missing each time, presumably taking the picture. Daniel suddenly noticed that there was something a little different about George in one of the photo's......There was something about the tie he was wearing.......Yes that was it, in the last one he was wearing a tie-pin, but not in the others. Then Daniel realised that some of the tables in the background were empty in that one as well, as if the people who had been occupying them when the first photographs were taken had left. The last picture he realised, the one where George's tie looked different had obviously been taken later in the evening than the others. Daniel looked closer again.....The tie-pin was quite small in the photograph and difficult to see, but something about it was familiar. He stared harder. All of a sudden his heart skipped a beat and then began beating faster. He would need to check with a magnifying glass to be sure.......*But the tie-pin George was wearing in the last photograph, looked just like the one that had been found with poor Lucy's body.*

Realization struck Daniel like a physical blow. "My God!" he exclaimed, and instinctively looked up at George, who had stood up, and was now looking down at Daniel on the sofa with resignation written all over his face.

"So now you know...the question is Daniel...what are you intending to do about it?"

Daniel was still taking in the full implications of his discovery, "***You*** *killed her!.......*why?....how did you know her? How did she end up in ***our*** garden?"

George was quiet for a moment, as if collecting his thoughts, and then he explained quite calmly, "You were all on holiday Daniel, just as you suspected. Lake Garda I think it was."

"Yes....I remember the holiday in Italy....I remember Lake Garda, it was one of the best....was that then, 1996?"

"Yes, I'm afraid it was Daniel. You were all going to be away a long time; at least three weeks as I remember. I had the keys to your house so that I could feed the fish and mow the lawns while you were away. Your Dad used to do the same for Alice and me if we went away."

"How did you know the girl?" asked Daniel, still finding it difficult to believe what he was hearing.

"Lucy and I were having a, what shall we call it, a relationship and we went to your house after a night out, I'm sure I don't need to tell you what for."

Daniel was horrified, "But why did you kill her?"

"Well I didn't set out to Daniel, I'm not a violent man, but the silly girl had been taking drugs, unbeknown to me, and the whole thing went pear shaped, as they say. I had to bury poor Lucy in the garden. It was just the way events played out Daniel. It wasn't meant to turn out the way it did and it wasn't my fault. It just happened. It wouldn't have been fair if my life had been screwed up because she was stupid enough to take drugs when she had been drinking. So I had to get rid of her somehow, and burying her in the garden seemed to be the perfect solution. *Just that bloody tie-pin.* All those photographs you've got there were taken at Alice's and my twelfth wedding anniversary, and Alice had the bloody thing specially made for me. She gave it to me that night. I always hated the bloody thing! It's gaudy, more like something a rock-star would wear, but I'm afraid Alice didn't have any taste at all."

"But it's picture has been in the paper now," said Daniel, "the photograph was all over the nationals. Surely somebody besides me is going to recognise it.

What about Alice, your wife, she is going to recognise it for sure if she is still alive.....Is she still alive?"

George shrugged his shoulders as if resigning himself to something unfortunate, "Not anymore Daniel...no!" he said in a tone that made Daniel's blood run cold, "and she's the only one that would have recognised it as mine, apart from your Mum and Dad and the other couple in the pictures. But one of them is dead and the other moved to the other side of the world. I only wore the damn thing a couple of times after that party. That's the reason I never missed it after burying Lucy. When I saw a photograph of the accursed thing in the paper, I realised there was a chance your Mum and Dad might have had a copy of the photographs taken that night, but I couldn't find anything when I checked your house out. Then with Alice out of the way, I was beginning to think I was home and dry. Now you've messed all that up........Silly boy. Where was the album, by the way? How come I didn't find it at the house?"

"So it was you that burgled my house?" exclaimed Daniel.

"Yes!...Do try to keep up Daniel. None of that

matters anymore, does it, you've kindly brought me what I was looking for."

A cold shiver ran down Daniels back and only now, because of the cool, casual tone of George's voice, did he feel threatened. George had killed Lucy, and Daniel was beginning to think he may have killed his wife Alice also. If Daniel was now the only person standing between George and a prison cell, what were the chances he would now try to kill him.

Trying to act in as normal a manner as he could, Daniel stood up, but with some difficulty. For some reason his knees felt stiff and slow to function. Fear was making movement difficult. He picked up the albums and started putting them back in the case to leave. The air in the room seemed to have got thicker and it felt as if he was moving through treacle.

"What do you think you're doing, Daniel? Not planning on leaving I hope," said George, stepping menacingly between Daniel and his route to the door. "You must realise that I can't just let you go running to the police with your new knowledge."

George was momentarily distracted by the appearance of both Lucy Penrose and his former wife

Alice, standing together at the back of the room and watching events unfold with interest.

Ganging up on me now are you? he thought, is that how it works? Do the consequences of evil acts build up in the body? gradually increasing in intensity like taking small doses of a poison over a period of time. Well if so, he was also building up an immunity to them. When he had seen Lucy materialise in her grave at the house he had been shocked to his core, it had frightened him half to death and even the next day he'd been nervous and unsettled. This time he was more prepared for the visitation, he'd half expected Lucy to put in another appearance and his heart-rate barely altered. The apparitions stared at him sternly as if he was a naughty child and they the nanny but this time, even though the two of them had come to torment him, he was immune to their devices. They couldn't hurt him or suddenly conjure up a conscience for him when none had existed before. It was as if the first sighting of Lucy, or should he call it haunting, had somehow given him phantom antibodies. He smiled at them and they faded away as quickly as they had come; and this time it was Lucy who looked shocked, not him.

Daniel was about the same size as George, younger and therefore probably fitter as well, although George did look as if he worked out a bit. Daniel had always managed to avoid physical confrontation, apart from the odd schoolboy scrap in the playground. He abhorred violence in any shape or form, but now, he was wishing that he had taken boxing lessons or attended martial arts classes, because it was becoming increasingly obvious that any moment now, he was going to have to defend himself; *to fight for his life in fact.* He knew he needed to act quickly if he was going to get away but his brain was refusing to function like the clever, calculating device that he knew it to be. Eventually, instinct took over, and he threw the case he was holding directly at George's head with all the force he could muster, and made a break for the door, pushing George aside as he did so.

George staggered back, surprised by Daniel's sudden burst of action, but he managed to get his hands up defensively, just in time to protect his face from the impact of the case that now fell at his feet, spilling its incriminating contents across the floor.

If Daniel had run just a little slower to the door rather than at full pelt, he may well have been able to grasp the handle and pull it open, before George caught up with him. As it was, the door opened inwards and Daniel slammed up against it in his haste to escape. He had to stop and take a step backwards in order to open it and that small delay cost him dear. George was behind him in an instant and placing his hand against the back of Daniel's head, pushed it forward with considerable force, slamming his forehead hard against the solid wood of the door. As Daniel staggered backwards, away from the door in a daze, George looked about him for something with which to strike Daniel. Behind the red leather settee was a reproduction sofa table on which sat an alabaster figure of Andromeda chained to the rocks. Snatching the figure from the table, George struck Daniel over the head with it, dispatching him unconscious and bleeding to the floor.

* * * * * * * * * * * * *

As Rebecca pulled her little Renault Cleo onto the drive of The Cedars she noted straight away that

Daniels car wasn't there. She was disappointed. It had been going to be a long day at work for her, but her manager had decided to put in an extra shift, in order to catch up on some outstanding work and, as Rebecca was owed some time off, he had sent her home earlier than expected. She had hoped that Daniel would have completed what he was doing and been there to greet her. She had driven past his shop on the way home to see if he had opened it after trying to find some friends of his parents. The fact that the shop was closed meant that either he was still trying to locate them, or that he had concluded that business and gone home. Maybe he was even ready to surprise her by having a meal ready. After all, she had texted him to let him know what was happening her end. But instead of being home, he was nowhere to be seen and he hadn't let her know where he was going or what time she should expect him. It was unlike Daniel. As soon as she was in the house she rang his mobile again. She had tried an hour earlier to no avail, but she was anxious to find out where he was. She hated not knowing.

He was in the unfortunate habit of allowing the battery to run down on his phone, and it would switch itself off. She could only assume that is what had happened today. He did have a charger in his car but if he didn't realise his phone was dead, he wouldn't think to use it, unlike Rebecca, who connected her phone to a charger whenever she was in the car, whether the battery was low or not. Once again there was no reply from Daniels mobile and Rebecca tossed hers carelessly onto the kitchen worktop in frustration.

She was desperate for a cup of tea, so she filled the kettle and switched it on before going upstairs to change out of her work-shoes and into some more comfortable slippers, before her feet actually did kill her. After making the tea and enjoying the first few satisfying sips, she decided to try Daniel one more time and made up her mind that she would refuse to cook or clean for him again, until he remembered to keep his phone topped up. She was so frustrated at not being able to contact him. She walked over to her bag to retrieve her phone, but was suddenly reminded that she had left it on the worktop when it sprang into life, and produced the satisfying bleeps which announced the arrival of a text message.

"At last!" she said out loud in frustration and

read the incoming message. She read the message over several times wondering what it could possibly mean, *"I'm sorry Bec's. I've found a picture of my dad, wearing the tie-pin that was found in the grave. It was him, after all. I can't believe it. Not sure I can cope with this....need to think....I'm so sorry. Dan."*

"Oh my God!" she cried out loud, thinking.....Poor Daniel, he must have found the picture in the case he brought down from the loft. He must be devastated to discover that his father *was* a murderer after all! But that didn't seem right. How had his Dad kept it a secret from the family? Surly Daniel's Mother had known nothing of the murder. And Daniel had told Paul that he had helped his father with the decking.....It made no sense to her. Daniel was obviously very upset she could tell that from the manner of the text message, it didn't sound like Daniel at all. In fact, in all the time she had known him, she didn't think he had called her Bec's once, not to her face anyway, and even when texting he always signed off as Daniel, never just Dan.

Now she was becoming worried. Surly he wouldn't do anything stupid? She picked up the phone once again and this time rang Paul.

* * * * * * * * * * * * *

Paul's phone rang just as he was about to bite into the first cake, apart from his own wedding cake, which he had eaten in he couldn't remember how long. It took him an agonising moment to decide not to take a bite before answering it because he had a premonition that once he picked up the phone he would be too busy to indulge. Reluctantly, he put the cake down and picked the receiver up.

"Paul Manley."

It was the front desk. "Sorry to bother sir but is your team still interested in Michael Tucker, the pawn broker?"

"Not unless it's of relevance to the murder of Alice Bridgeman. Why?"

"A woman has just phoned in Sir. She said she has just been to Mr Tucker's shop and found it all left open, apparently the closed sign was showing but the shop door was ajar. She went in and the place was empty. There's no sign of Mr Tucker at all or anyone else for that matter. The woman thinks something has happened. Do you want to have a look or shall I leave it to uniform?"

Paul considered the question for a moment. "Leave it to uniform for now. Maybe he was just careless when he went out but tell uniform to let me know when he's located. I don't see why it should be related to our case but you never know. Keep me up to date on it."

"OK Sir, will do."

Chapter 8

When Daniel regained consciousness he was aware of only two things. One, his head felt as if somebody was constantly hitting it with a hammer from inside and two, he was tied-up. As his eyes slowly began to focus he realised that he was still lying on the floor where he had fallen but his hands were now bound uncomfortably behind his back. There was what looked like duct-tape wrapped around his thighs just above his knees and more at his ankles, so he assumed that it was duct-tape that secured his hands as well. He struggled and twisted his hands trying to free them but to no avail. The tape, if that's what is was, held fast. Lying on the floor just a foot from his head was the ornamental figure of a woman who appeared to be tied to same rocks and it briefly crossed his mind that their respective plights were not dissimilar. From what small knowledge he had of Greek mythology he assumed her to be Andromeda, awaiting her fate at the hands of a sea monster, while he was waiting to find out what fate, in the form of George Edwards, had in store for him. All he knew for sure was that he would have to be the means of his own salvation. No Perseus would be coming to his aid.

George entered the room carrying what turned out to be Daniel's mobile phone. He turned one of the easy chairs round so that it faced Daniel, then sat in it and looked at him. The expression on his face was a mixture of sympathy and resignation, rather like that of a doctor who was about to give a patient bad news.

"You may find this hard to believe Daniel," he began, "but I am truly sorry about all of this. If Lucy had been prepared to be reasonable about events, things would have turned out very differently. She certainly wouldn't have needed to die. If Alice had seen the pictures of the tie-pin in the papers there is no doubt she would have taken great pleasure in turning me in to the police, so I had no choice there either and if you hadn't been so intent on clearing your Dad's name there would have been no reason for you to die so young either. None of this wretched business is of my making....You do understand that Daniel, don't you?”

"What are you going to do?" asked Daniel, more scared than he had ever been in his life, tied as he was, and totally vulnerable. He had never been completely at anybody's mercy before and it chilled him to his core. This man was in a position to do whatever he wanted to him. Not only did he have the power of life and death over him, but he was at liberty to select the manner of death as well. Daniel could only hope that, if George didn't suddenly have a rush of conscience and change his mind about killing him, at least he would be merciful and make it quick.

"Well, I've been able to give that quite a bit of thought while you were out of it, and I think I've come up with the perfect solution to my problem. I'm going to send a text message to your partner, Rebecca. I've been looking though the text history on your phone to see what your text speak is like, and I'm pretty sure I can devise a message that she will believe is from you. It goes like this." George began typing a message into Daniels phone, and read it out to Daniel as he went.

"I'm sorry Becs. I've found a picture of my dad wearing the tie-pin that was found in the grave. It was

him, after all, I can't believe it. Not sure I can cope with this....need to think....I'm so sorry. Dan"

"She'll know that wasn't sent by me," said Daniel a little shocked, and then realised that it would actually be a good thing if Rebecca worked out that it wasn't from him. George had made a mistake. In their texts to each other, Rebecca always called him Dan and signed off Bec's but Daniel never called her by anything other than her name, Rebecca, and he always signed off as Daniel, never just Dan. George had got it the wrong way round. However, it seemed unlikely that such a small error on George's part would somehow convey to Rebecca that he had been kidnapped and was about to be murdered. Maybe after the event, after he was dead and his body recovered, maybe in her grief she would question the origin of the text, but that was of no help to him now.

"Maybe.....Maybe not Daniel....But I think the police will. They'll take it as a suicide note. They'll have no reason to think you didn't find a picture of your Dad wearing the tie-pin and that'll wrap their case up for them."

"And just how am I supposed to commit

suicide trussed up like this?" asked Daniel, not sure that he really wanted to have advanced knowledge of the manner of his passing.

"Patience Daniel, all in good time, but take it from me, I've given that a lot of thought as well."

While Daniel had been unconscious, George had formulated a plan that he thought would solve his immediate problem with Daniel and also stop any further problems from arising should the police be over conscientious in their endeavours to find Lucy's killer. George had always loved the coast, and he had a small caravan on a site near Porlock in North Devon, where he spent several weeks each summer, indulging in his hobbies of sailing and bird watching. He knew the North Devon and Somerset coast well and spent hours just walking along the cliff tops with his binoculars and camera. He knew that if you took Hill Road, north west out of Minehead, instead of the usual A39, there was some beautiful scenery to be enjoyed and some wonderful wild walks along the coast. Approximately half way between Minehead and Porlock, there was a fork in the road. If you kept to the left fork, you could follow the road almost to Porlock, although if Porlock was your actual destination, you would have to re-join the A39 at some point. The right fork on the other hand, was little more than a track that actually saw more walkers than vehicles, and there were precious few of those. The only vehicles that used it were those of people staying in one of the remote holiday cottages that could be reached that way, or the odd van delivering goods or groceries there. It took you right up to and along the Devonian Slate and Sandstone cliffs that had been formed some 400 million years before when Devon itself was still under the sea. Those cliffs now stood proud and looked out arrogantly over the Bristol Channel.

A few months earlier, the sea had finally achieved one of its goals, at least in one small section, and had undermined the rocks at sea level, removing any support for the weight of the cliffs above. The inevitable result was that a section of the cliff face had slipped down some thirty or forty feet, taking with it a large section of the track above. Now there was no longer a decision to be made by those travellers confronted by the fork in the road. The fork to the right was closed. Concrete bollards had been erected to stop vehicles using the track and there was a large sign declaring dispassionately, "DANGER! ROAD CLOSED," and a small explanation saying that there had been a land-slip and that the road had gone and the cliff edge was unstable.

George's idea was to drive Daniel to this remote spot, sit him in the driving seat of his own car and send it over the cliff, making it look as if Daniel himself had driven it over in the act of suicide. This would eliminate the one person left who knew of George's dark secret, and when his text to Rebecca was revealed, solving the murder of Lucy Penrose for the police into the bargain. George would be home and dry. It was so perfect that he was almost pleased Daniel had taken the trouble to find him although he knew that carrying out his plan was not without risk. He looked at his watch, 11.30am. It would take the best part of an hour to reach his destination, and a half hour or so to stage the suicide. But then, how was he to get home again with no car? He would have to walk into the nearest village or pub and call a taxi to take him to his caravan. He had a bike stored there and he could cycle into Minehead the next day and get the train home. He had nothing arranged, so nobody was going to miss him if he was gone for a day. It wasn't perfect, but he saw no reason it shouldn't work if he was careful.

That decided, he went into his kitchen and selected the most lethal looking carving knife from the rack and returned to cut the duct-tape that bound Daniels ankles and helped him to his feet. Once Daniel was standing, he indicated to him with a casual wave of the knife that he was to go outside to the car.

"What if I refuse to move?" asked Daniel defiantly, "are you going to carry me?"

George jabbed the knife into the fleshy section of Daniel's upper arm, extracting a cry of pain from him. The resulting wound was not deep enough to cause any great injury or loss of blood but was painful enough for Daniel to comply with the request lest it happen again. Although George had removed the tape from Daniel's ankles he had left it where it bound his legs, just above his knees, forcing Daniel to walk in a somewhat comical manner that made it look as if he was desperate for the toilet. It had an advantage from George's point of view because it meant that Daniel was mobile enough, with a little support, to move under his own steam, but any kind of flight was impossible.

Daniel's car was a four year old Volkswagen traditional four door saloon with a boot and now, with the tape removed from his ankles, he was forced to hobble out to it with the aid of a supporting arm from George and a little encouragement from the blade of the knife. George had removed Daniel's keys from his pocket at the same time as his mobile phone and he now used them to unlock the car and open the boot. There were two guitars in the boot that Daniel had been going to take to his shop. George removed them and placed them on the back seat all the while keeping a watchful eye on his prisoner.

"Get in Daniel," he instructed, indicating the boot of the car and brandishing the knife once again.

Daniel eyed the interior of his car boot with foreboding. He had serious doubts about his ability to fit into such a confined space but the alternative seemed to be to suffer the death of a thousand cuts, courtesy of George and his knife.

"How do you suggest I do that with my arms tied behind my back?" challenged Daniel angrily, "I shall need my hands free to climb in."

All the time since he had regained consciousness Daniels had been trying to work his hands free of the tape that bound them but without success and his wrists were now almost as painful as his throbbing head. The only reason he kept trying was that it must be causing marks that would be noticed at any post-mortem, making it obvious that his wrists had been bound and contradicting any interpretation of suicide. He began trying to think if there was any way that he could do or leave something, *anything*, that would in some way point the finger at his killer. To write his murderers name in blood as it were. They were so good at retrieving DNA now, perhaps he would get the opportunity to scratch George as he was manhandled in and out of the car boot. He couldn't stand the thought of George actually getting away with what he was planning.

"Just lean into the boot and I'll lift your legs in behind you. Stop stalling for time Daniel, the cavalry aren't coming to save you."

"I won't be able to breathe in there."

George pushed Daniel's head down towards the boot, "Your problem.....not mine," he stated, once again using the knife as encouragement to comply with his demands.

Daniel managed to lean into the boot of his car and turn slightly sideways so that he would be resting on his right shoulder, the edge of the boot cutting painfully into his upper thigh as he did so. George lifted Daniels legs up and tucked them in carelessly, heedless of the pain Daniel was enduring. Once lying in the boot Daniel shifted his position as much as he could to try and find a relatively comfortable one, as George cut off another strip of duct-tape and made to apply it to Daniels mouth.

"We don't want you calling out, now do we?" he said.

Daniel turned his head away in an attempt to prevent the tape being fitted and shouted, "I won't be able to breathe in here with that on!" but George grabbed hold of his jaw with one hand and held the knife to Daniels left eye with the other.

"You won't be able to see very well either, with only one eye Daniel so stop being so bloody awkward and you can keep them both for a bit longer."

Daniel held his head still as George applied the tape to his mouth and closed the boot, horrified at the prospect of being stabbed in the eye. With the boot closed he found himself imprisoned in a world full of nothing but darkness and fear.

Daniel was in despair. The boot of the car was cramped, dark and uncomfortable, his head was pounding, and it seemed likely that he was soon to die a violent death at the hands of his captor, and as yet he had failed to do anything to indicate to others who that captor was. He had never been a particularly spiritual or religious person, but in the dark confines of his car boot he began to pray, not because he had any expectation of a useful outcome arising from it, he didn't expect God to personally intervene or send angels to help him escape, but simply because he couldn't think of anything else to do. He could hear George going to and from the house a couple of times and then get into the driving seat and start the engine.

George checked the fuel gauge and was pleased to see it was a little over half full, more than enough to get where they were going and back. Not that there would be a return journey to worry about of course.

He didn't want to risk calling into a filling station with Daniel trussed-up in the boot. Even gagged he could still make a lot of noise by kicking his legs and thrashing about. He knew the route to Minehead like the back of his hand, having made the trip countless times, as well as the roads and tracks along the section of coast between Minehead and Porlock. The site he had in mind saw only a handful of walkers at the best of times and, now that the road had fallen into the sea at one location, he was confident he could get the car over the cliff at that point, totally unobserved.

He normally completed the journey to Minehead from Sand Bay in just under an hour and today was no exception. Under different circumstances he would even have enjoyed the drive, and he wondered whether he should have packed a bag so that he could spend a couple of nights at the caravan but he soon dismissed the idea. Although he was sure there was nothing to connect him to Daniel, he thought it would nevertheless be prudent not to be too close when Daniel and his car were recovered.

It was just after 12.45pm. when he exited Minehead on Hill Road to the north west. After approximately six miles he came to the fork in the road. He slowed the car down to a snail's pace to check that nobody was in sight, either walking or driving, and then manoeuvred the car slowly around the bollards which had been placed there to prevent any unsuspecting, or possibly drunk, drivers from continuing along the track and over the cliff. It wasn't very long before he reached the spot he had in mind and, even though he knew it was there, he still came upon it unexpectedly, suddenly having to break hard lest he drive too far and accompany his intended victim in his plunge to the buffeting sea below.

Wow! That was close, he thought, as he applied the hand-break and turned off the engine, sitting for a moment to gather his thoughts, double check that he was still unobserved and plan his next move carefully. He had always loved this coast. He loved the smell of the sea air and the squawk of gulls on the wing. Sometimes he would just stand and feel the force of the sea breeze against his face, happy to be alive, or, "still looking at the grass from the top," as his father had been fond of saying. It had always amazed him how the savage and violent action of the sea crashing against the base of the cliffs below could produce in him such a relaxed mood.

Back at the house, when he had formulated his plan, it had all seemed quite simple and straightforward. Put Daniel into the driving seat, select second gear, depress the clutch with the walking stick he had brought along for the purpose, start the engine and then slowly release the clutch, allowing Daniel and his car to quietly trundle over the edge to their joint destruction. Now that he was on site as it were and faced with actually carrying out the operation, all sorts of unthought-of, though admittedly minor, difficulties presented themselves. The first of these difficulties involved the transfer of Daniel, from the boot of the car to the driver's seat. He obviously wasn't going to cooperate no matter how many times George encouraged him with the knife. Likewise, it wouldn't be a very convincing suicide if Daniel's body was discovered all trussed up with duct-tape so he would have to be unconscious when George set the car in motion or Daniel would simply steer the car away from the edge and escape. Unfortunately George had failed to bring anything with him with which to knock Daniel out. He cursed himself for his own lack of foresight in the matter.

George got out of the car and looked about him on the ground, hoping to find a large stone to knock Daniel out with, but there was just grass and bracken, with the occasional bush. Damn! Why hadn't he thought it through more thoroughly? After all, he laughed to himself, it wasn't as if he was inexperienced in such matters. Then he had a minor brainwave. There had to be a spare wheel in the car and that meant a jack and probably a tyre-iron. *Perfect.* He would drag Daniel out of the boot and leave him bound on the floor while he searched for the spare wheel and tools. Then he would knock Daniel out, manoeuvre him into the driving seat and then follow the rest of the plan. That decided, he got out of the car and walked towards the boot.

While Daniel had been lying in the boot of his own car being driving to his death by a man who had killed at least once, and possibly twice, before, his mind had not been inactive. Once he had finished praying, he began to think more positively. George had indicated that he was going to make Daniel's death look like a suicide and Daniel wondered how he proposed to achieve it. They had been in the car a good hour or so Daniel calculated, so he thought he was probably being taken somewhere specific. He couldn't see George trying to carry him up to the top of a tall building to throw him off, so unless he intended cutting his wrists and allowing him to bleed to death, it was probable that he was going to use the car in some way. If he was going to shut Daniel in the car with a hosepipe connected to the exhaust and fed into the vehicle, he speculated that he would have been able to find a much closer location so Daniel thought it much more likely that they were heading for cliffs somewhere. But whatever the scenario he had in mind, George would have to get him out of the boot and untie him. It wouldn't be a very convincing suicide if he left him bound and gagged. That is when Daniel would have to make his bid to escape, but how?

Daniel wrestled with the problem and thought to himself. George isn't going to untie me if I'm conscious, that would be too much of a risk, so he is going to have to knock me out again. Daniel's head was still pounding from the first blow it had received, so he certainly wasn't looking forward to enduring a second. He wondered if he could pretend to be unconscious when George opened the boot, but decided that it would be difficult to maintain the pretence whilst being manhandled out of the car, especially if George suspected he was shamming, as he almost certainly would, seeing as he was fully conscious when put into the boot. But what was the alternative? Perhaps, when George was lifting him out of the car boot, he could contrive to knock his head on something nearby, maybe the boot lid itself, not too hard, but hard enough to convince George that he had been knocked unconscious again. It would be painful, and still difficult to be convincing, but the alternative seemed to be to allow George to bash him over the head again for real and that held very little appeal. Also Daniel realised, if that happened, he would never see the light of day again.

No sooner had Daniel made up his mind about what he had to do than the car drew to a stop and the engine was switched off. Daniel's heart was pounding in his chest and every beat of his heart was answered by a pulse of pain in his head. He was close to tears but he had to pull himself together if he was to stand any chance of surviving the next half hour or maybe less. After a little while, when Daniel thought he could hear George pacing around outside the car, his small enclosed world was flooded with light as the car boot was opened.

At first Daniel found it difficult to make anything out, the light was blinding after the darkness of the last hour. George towered over him, a dark menacing and featureless figure surrounded by a bright halo of light. He couldn't see details, only the dark shapes of George and the open boot lid with the central catch hanging down at its centre like a solitary tooth.

"Time to get out now," said George, reaching in and grabbing hold of Daniels legs, "Swing your legs out and over the lip."

Daniel did as he was instructed and with George's help managed to get his bound legs over the back of the car so that his feet were dangling just a little way off the ground. George then reached further into the boot and stretched his arms around either side of Daniel's shoulders.

"Up you come," he said, pulling on Daniel with some difficulty. Daniel thought it would have been quite difficult for George to achieve his end if he had resisted and fought back and for a brief moment he considered kicking out towards George's bowed head, but decided that even if he made firm contact, it would only give him a brief respite. He stood no chance against the man while he was trussed up the way he was. Instead, he cooperated, and allowed George to pull his torso up so that his feet made contact with the ground. He then stood straight up, pushing George away as if making a break for freedom, and making sure that his own head impacted with the boot catch, causing himself a great deal of extra pain. He cried out and fell forwards onto the ground. With his hands firmly secured behind his back he had no way of breaking his fall and only just managed to avoid falling flat on his face by turning slightly sideways and landing instead on his left shoulder. The impact with the ground was only slightly cushioned by the fact that he landed in a small gorse bush, but the extra pain in his head and now his shoulder was considerable and it took more willpower than he realised he had to prevent a scream of agony but, somehow, he had to play dead and convince George that he was unconscious.

As George was lifting Daniel out of the car, he wondered, for a moment, why Daniel seemed to be cooperating. He had expected him to resist but then all of a sudden Daniel managed to get his feet on the ground and gain some leverage. He stood up forcibly and shoved George to one side, obviously in a vain bid for freedom, but he had knocked his head, quite hard it seemed, against the underside of the boot lid and fallen to the ground unconscious.

George marvelled at the way things had turned out. A minute ago he'd been wondering what he was going to use to render Daniel unconscious and now Daniel himself had obliged and accomplished the deed himself. Funny how things turn out, he thought. Perhaps the gods had decided to smile on him for a change rather than putting obstacles to happiness in his path all the time. Now, as he looked at the prone body before him, he pondered over whether it would be easier to manoeuvre it into the driving seat of the car before or after untying it, and decided to get it into position first. Easier not to have limbs flopping about all over the place he conjectured.

It actually took quite a while to drag the limp body to the front of the car and then physically hoist it up into the driving seat, tuck the legs into the foot-well and sit it upright behind the wheel. Once it was done, George had to sit on the grass at the side of the car to regain his breath, conscious of the fact that Daniel could come round at any minute.

Daniel was screaming internally. His head was pounding so badly he was finding it difficult to keep still and silent and now his left shoulder felt as it was on fire where he had fallen on it. He wondered whether he had actually broken something in his fall, the pain was so bad, but George appeared to be completely convinced that he was unconscious and that was good. Once he was behind the wheel of his car, he risked opening his eyes very slightly and noticed that the car keys had been left in the ignition. However, Daniel knew his car well and remembered that one of its many little idiosyncrasies of late was that it was sometimes difficult to start when the engine was still hot, frequently taking several attempts to start. If he managed to push George away when he freed him of his restraints, and close and lock the car door even, he still couldn't be sure his car wouldn't let him down and if it did, it would give George valuable time to fight back. Smash the window maybe and regain the upper hand. It wouldn't be difficult to do with him in such a weakened state.

George felt that he couldn't wait any longer. Although the place was deserted and the track closed, there was always the danger that a dog walker or bird watcher might happen by, or of course Daniel could come round. He retrieved the knife that he had prodded Daniel with from the driving door glove pocket, reached into the car and cut through the duck-tape that secured Daniels legs. He then removed the tape completely, not wanting any trace of it to be found. Microscopic examination would no doubt uncover traces of it but, if the suicide was believed, there would be no reason for such close inspection. He then leaned Daniel forward against the steering wheel and cut the tape securing his arms and wrists.

What happened next came as a complete surprise.

Daniel elbowed him in the stomach with some force then lashed out with his fist, catching him painfully on the bridge of his nose. George staggered backwards away from the car and his right heel caught on clump of thick gorse causing him to fall backward and land painfully, striking the back of his head on the ground.

Daniel watched with some satisfaction as George fell and briefly contemplated trying to start the engine, knowing that if successful he would have no trouble getting away. But instinctively he knew his car would let him down and be difficult to start. In his weakened and pain wracked condition, he knew that he would be no match for George in a physical struggle, so instead, he grabbed the keys from the ignition and took flight on foot. He had no idea which way to run, other than away from the cliffs. Was civilisation to his left or his right? He had no idea where he was, he tried to think as he ran. They hadn't been on the road all that long, an hour or two at most he surmised. It was unlikely that George would risk having to stop and pay a bridge toll, so South Wales seemed unlikely and the sun was more to his right then his left, that indicated that he was probably running south away from the coast. North Devon or Somerset then, he reasoned. This new knowledge was of little help to him but the thought process helped him to concentrate and keep his mind off the pains he was suffering. He ran as fast as he was able but each time his foot connected with the ground it sent bolts of pain through his head and shoulder.   He glanced behind and saw that, even though George had regained his feet, he had nevertheless managed to put some distance between the two of them. The ground under foot was uneven and difficult to run on and he wondered how much longer he could keep going but was urged on by the knowledge that he was fleeing for his life and he was given extra incentive when he sighted a small cottage or farmhouse in the near distance.

Despite his condition, Daniel had put a good distance between himself and George by the time he reached, and banged heavily on, the front door of the cottage.   There was no reply and close up the property looked deserted except for the fact that the small garden was obviously well cared for and had been tended recently. Daniel staggered more than walked to the rear of the building, looking for some sign of life or means of entry. There was a small metal box on the side of the building, just under the roof line, proudly announcing the fact that the property was fitted with an alarm. Daniel kicked hard at the back door hoping to at least set the alarm off, but it showed no sign of giving in to his assault, so he turned his attention to what appeared to be a small barn some yards away from the main building. Here, Daniel had more luck. Although the large double doors were secured by a substantial padlock through an equally generous hasp and staple, somebody had been very careless in their approach to security. Behind a nearby pile of expertly cut logs was the long handled axe that had been used to cut them. Whoever had sweated over the task of cutting the logs had either intended returning to cut some more and been side-tracked, or had carried some to the house and simply forgotten that they had left the axe outside. Whichever scenario was correct, it was good news for Daniel, who now used the axe, swinging it high over his head despite the pain in his shoulder, and landing two substantial blows behind the hasp and staple and dislodging them. The heavy double doors creaked open a few inches under their own weight once the lock was no longer fulfilling its role and Daniel pulled them open further.

He had no idea what he would find inside. Although a large, armed police officer would have been his first choice, he would happily settle for a car, or some other form of transport that would eliminate the need for more running. Wielding the axe had used almost the last of his energy. When he actually looked inside the barn he almost laughed out loud. The transport that confronted him was a bright red, sit-on lawn mower, hardly the quickest of get-away vehicles. Daniel noted straight away that the keys were in the ignition so he climbed aboard, praying there was fuel in the tank, and started it up. He had also noted that the front of the mower projected beyond the front wheels with a robust looking front end that resembled that of a tractor. At least he now had a battering-ram with which to open the back door of the house. Daniel was quite familiar with mowers of the type. The lawns at The Cedars were considerable and took a long time to cut, so Daniel had long ago invested in one himself. In no time at all he managed to manoeuvre it into position and drive it straight into the back door of the cottage, smashing it open but still failing to set off any alarm. Daniel assumed the alarm was either turned off for some reason or maybe just a dummy to deter burglars. Not bothering to reverse clear, he clambered over the top of the mower and entered the house, spotting George out of the corner of his eye nearing the garden as he did so.

Once inside, Daniel looked about for two things, a telephone with which to summon help, and a weapon with which to defeat his assailant. He cursed himself for not having the forethought to bring along the axe, even though the thought of wielding it against a fellow human being, even a killer of schoolgirls, filled him with revulsion. Daniel found himself in the kitchen of the property, a large room that obviously served as a dining room as well. The room had a modern slate tiled floor and the furniture consisted of a large pine kitchen table around which were six Windsor style chairs and a pine dresser that occupied the greater part of the wall to his left. Daniel opened each of the three dresser drawers in turn and found the first full of general kitchen utensils and table mats. The second, however, contained an array of cutlery including several large carving knives, and Daniel selected the largest and most lethal looking of them with some satisfaction. He held the knife firmly in his right hand, steadying himself against the dresser with his left and scanning the rest of the room, expecting George to come crashing in at any moment. The only other door into the kitchen was the one leading off the entrance hall and this stood open to Daniels right, through which he could see a small octagonal table, on top of which sat the welcome sight of a telephone.

* * * * * * * * * * *

When Daniel had attacked George so suddenly after he released his arms, it had been both a painful and an unexpected experience for him, and George cursed himself for being so gullible, realising that Daniel had probably only pretended to knock himself out. He watched as Daniel took flight, wondering why he hadn't elected to take the car, seeing as how the keys were in the ignition. As he got to his feet, holding his nose, which he was convinced was broken, he looked into the car and noted unhappily, that the keys were no longer in there, and that he would have to pursue his prey on foot. The blade of his knife glinted in the rays of the autumn sun, which was now beginning its descent towards the horizon. He retrieved it from where it had fallen and set off in pursuit of his quarry. It must have taken longer than he thought to recover from the blows he had received because, George noted with dismay, Daniel appeared to have already put some distance between them.

George had been able to observe Daniel's flight ahead of him right up until the time he disappeared behind the house. Both men had stumbled and fallen several times in their race over the uneven ground and either of them could have easily broken a leg, which would have almost certainly resulted in death for Daniel or prison for George. George had been unable to close the gap between them over the difficult terrain. In fact, it was even possible that he had lost ground to the younger man despite his injuries. Panting and out of breath, he entered the garden of the house, which he knew to be a holiday home owned by some wealthy couple from London. As he did so, he heard what sounded like a lawn mower engine being started, followed shortly by a terrible crashing sound coming from the rear of the house and he realised that Daniel must have somehow gained access to the property. As he reached the building itself, he noticed that there were wires running down the exterior of the property and entering a small grey plastic box on the outside of the house. He recognised them as telephone wires straight away and knowing that a telephone was the first thing Daniel would search for, he used the knife he clasped in his hand to sever them, denying Daniel his lifeline. Then, rushing to the rear of the property, he clambered over the lawn mower that blocked the doorway and followed Daniel into the house, finally confronting him as he stood at the small table in the hall, unsuccessfully trying to dial out. He raised the knife in his hand, indicating to his prey why the phone wasn't working, and feeling just a little sorry for Daniel as he saw the look of total dejection on his face.

Daniel dropped the receiver, which smashed open on the tiled floor with a sound that seemed out of all proportion to the size of the event and echoed through the whole house. Startled, first by George's sudden appearance and then by the sound of the telephone receiver hitting the floor, Daniel lifted the knife he was holding and held it out in front of himself at shoulder height threateningly, as if this gesture alone would fend off his pursuer.

The two men stood facing each other like gunfighters on the streets of Dodge City, not knowing what to do next, neither of them relishing the idea of being involved in a knife-fight. Daniel's instinct, as always, was for flight, even though he now wished that he had stood his ground back in George's lounge, what seemed like a lifetime ago, and fought the man then, when he'd been fit and uninjured. Now, he knew he stood little chance in a physical confrontation even armed as he was. Escape still seemed his best chance of survival but he was unsure where to go. The front door of the house was secured and there was no key in the lock so the only options were the other door off the hall that probably led to some kind of lounge, or upstairs to the bedrooms. Neither of those options offered an easy escape route so the only way was back through the kitchen again but, that way, he would have to get past George and his knife.

George was also in a turmoil of indecision. Daniel was now armed with a knife as well and, even if he managed to be victorious, his intention had been to make Daniel's death look like a suicide. Even now he was still harbouring hopes that he could achieve that, even though he realised that it would be far less convincing now a house had been broken into. He still wanted to overpower Daniel, however, not stab him to death.

Daniel was the first to make up his mind what to do. He grabbed hold of the small table the telephone was on, dropping the knife so that he could grab hold of its top with both hands, then lifting it with the legs sticking out away from him, the way a lion tamer would hold a chair, and sending the telephone crashing to the floor where it suffered the same fate as its receiver. Without a moment's hesitation, he ran at George as fast as he could, causing him to back away and bring his arms up to defend himself against the onslaught of the table legs. Unable to get out of the way in time, George took the full impact of two of the four legs, one on his left upper arm and one to the right hand side of his abdomen, causing him some considerable pain and knocking him to the floor, dropping the knife.

Had Daniel been a military man, or trained in combat in some aspect or another, he would no doubt have pressed home his advantage and overpowered George before he could recover from the fall, a sharp karate chop to the throat perhaps or a blow to the head. Daniel, as always, opted to run instead and made haste once again over the lawn mower, which, from the doorway, had remained an impartial observer of the confrontation, and out of the back door. He realised that he still had the keys of the car in his pocket and that, now the engine was cold, it would start without too much persuasion so he headed back in the direction he had come.

Having escaped from the house and with another head start on his would-be assassin, Daniel felt more confident than he had in a while, especially with the keys to the car in his pocket and adrenalin now driving him on. The scales seemed, for the moment at least, to have tipped in Daniel's favour but the fates are fickle.   George had fallen onto his back under the impact of the table with Daniel's weight behind it, and now, from his prone position on the floor, he spotted something of interest. Underneath the dresser was a long oak box with brass corners and escutcheon. George recognised it straight away as a gun case. He reached out and pulled it towards him, surprised to find it unlocked and delighted to discover it housing a double barrelled shotgun with all it accoutrements. George had done a little bit of clay pigeon shooting when he was younger and had no difficulty assembling the gun, which turned out to be a comparatively modern over and under gun with two barrels, one above the other, both of which were fired independently by a single trigger. George was familiar with the type of weapon, knowing that the first pull on the trigger would fire one barrel and that the recoil from that would then cock the gun again so that, the next time the trigger was pulled, it would unleash the fury of the second. George ransacked the dresser and quickly found a couple of boxes of cartridges, one of which was half empty. Whoever owned the gun was remarkably casual about its security. He would be likely to lose his licence if the police ever discovered how lax he was at keeping it under lock and key. He quickly loaded the gun, abandoning any thought now that he could still fake Daniels suicide, stuffed half a dozen cartridges into his pocket and once again set off in pursuit of Daniel who, for the second time that day, had established a not inconsiderable head start on him.

Daniel was exhausted and found himself stumbling more and more, once or twice actually falling and having to pick himself up and set off again. He kept looking back to see how close his pursuer was, which also delayed him, and it was obvious that George was gaining ground this time.

Now that he had finally abandoned all thought of faking a convincing suicide after all that had happened, George decided that, if he had to shoot Daniel, he would simply put the gun in the front of the car with him, after wiping off his prints and substituting Daniel's, and let the police make of it what they would. Even though the police would dismiss any thoughts that Daniel had shot himself, especially if George was forced to shoot him in the back, as seemed likely, the evidence would be confusing at best.   Suicide might still be considered a possibility of course if Daniels body was washed out to sea and never recovered, even with the obvious involvement of a third party at the cottage and especially after the text he had sent on Daniel's phone. But whatever happened and whatever conclusions the police came to, he thought, there would be nothing to point an incriminating finger at him.

George was running various plans of action through his mind as he continued the pursuit and decided that shooting Daniel too far from the car would be counterproductive, simply because he would then have to drag him the rest of the way, or go and get the car and bring it down for him, always assuming that Daniel had the keys on him and hadn't thrown them away somewhere, a scenario that seemed unlikely. From the direction he was running, there seemed little doubt that the car was Daniels goal and that would indicate that he was still in possession of them. By far the best plan however, would be to wait until he was almost at the car, and shoot him then. He was, after all, gaining on poor Daniel all the time now.

Daniel turned to look over his shoulder one more time. George appeared to be carrying something in his right hand, a stick perhaps, but he couldn't see very well. Although George had almost caught up and it was going to be close, Daniel was convinced that he would be able to get into the car and lock the doors before George could stop him. He could then start the engine and make good his escape. He had hope for the first time in hours.

All of Daniels hopes vanished in an instant however, when he was taken completely by surprise by a loud bang behind him and a terrible burning sensation in his lower back and legs. It felt as if he had been struck from behind by several bull-whips in unison and he fell to the ground. His lower back, buttocks and legs felt as if they were on fire and he realised that he had probably been shot. The thing in George's hand must have been a shotgun which could only have come from the house. Daniel was done for at last. The fates had conspired against him. He had been struck on the head, fallen heavily to the ground on several occasions badly injuring his shoulder, and now it seemed he'd been shot. There was no longer any resistance left in him, he was beaten.

When George caught up he easily dragged Daniel the short distance to the car and sat him in the driver's seat. Even though Daniel was semi-conscious, he was totally unable to resist, the fight was gone out of him.

After he managed to get Daniel into the driving seat he wiped the gun clean of fingerprints with the tail of his shirt and pressed the gun into Daniels hands so that his prints would be on there should it ever be recovered. It wasn't that he was trying to stage a particular series of events for the police any more, or force them to a particular conclusion, he was simply trying to muddy the waters. He searched Daniels pockets, retrieving the car keys and replacing them with Daniel's phone, also wiped clean of his prints and replaced with Daniel's. All this time Daniel sat only semi-conscious in the driving seat offering no resistance whatsoever. George leaned across Daniel and put the car into second gear, depressed the clutch with the shotgun, which he held with his handkerchief, and started the engine. Slowly releasing the clutch, he set the car in motion, threw the gun across to the passenger side and attempted to slam shut the driver's door, but the car was gaining momentum and the door swung open again. George, fearing that Daniel would fall out, watched with some satisfaction as the car finally went over the cliff edge carrying Daniel along with it.

George sat on the ground, drained both of energy and emotion. He wondered what the police would make of the conflicting evidence. A farmhouse broken into, Daniels finger prints on the lawn mower that was used to break in the back door and on the phone, the wires of which had been cut. There were signs of a struggle and an empty shotgun case and there was the missing shotgun itself, which may or may not be found in Daniel's car with his fingerprints on it. In truth, George had no idea whether Daniel's car would ever be recovered, let alone his body or the other items in it. There would be the text message from Daniel to Rebecca implicating Daniel's father in Lucy's murder. The police would have to assume a third party was involved in some way or another if they did recover his body, simply because there was no way Daniel could have managed to shoot himself in the back. The evidence would certainly tax their minds to come up with a series of events that would explain everything. Perhaps, if Sherlock Holmes and Poirot put their heads together, maybe they could explain it, but not the local plods. But no matter what the police come up with, he thought, there was nothing to lead them to him, he was certain of that. All things considered, George felt he was home and dry.

What now? He had achieved his main goal of disposing of the last person who could identify him as the owner of the tie-pin maybe not as cleanly as he would have hoped, but at least it was done. He had intended to walk back to Porlock and get a taxi to his caravan but he was far too fatigued for that now. He remembered that there was a nice little country pub not far from the fork in the road where it joined the cliff track. The Smugglers Rest, or something, it was called, so he determined to call a taxi from there. He picked himself up with some effort and set off. A pint of beer would go down rather well, he thought.

* * * * * * * * * * * * * * *

The phone on Paul's desk rang for the umpteenth time that morning and before answering it he made a wish that this time, it would be the break they were all hoping for.

It turned out to be Reg calling from another part of the building, "Hi Reg what have you got for me?" asked Paul expectantly.

"You wanted uniform to let you know when they located Michael Tucker, Guv."

"Yes that's right, have they found him?"

"Both him and Sid together Guv."

"Michael and Sid together," repeated Paul, confused. "Where?"

"On some waste ground along-side Barton flats."

"On waste ground!...I don't understand, what happened?....Are they alright?"

"No, they're not alright Guv, they've both been shot through the head. It looks as if Michael was interrogated before he was shot as well; there are some cigarette burns on his arm. Do you think it's anything to do with our case?"

Paul thought for a moment, trying to piece

together what might have happened. "No, it's not related, I suspect it's more to do with the raid on Barton flats, that's why the bodies were dumped there, as a message to someone. Better let the Met boys know, it sounds as if the two gunmen we arrested had some equally nasty friends. They must have targeted Michael and Sid as punishment for the raid, but why they should have thought Michael was involved is a mystery. But it's a mystery for others to sort out Reg not us. We've got our own mysteries."

Paul hung up his phone, saddened by the news. Nether Sid nor Michael Tucker deserved what had happened to them, but in his line of work he saw lots of innocent people suffer, he didn't have the time to grieve for them all.

Chapter 9

It was late in the afternoon when Paul received an unexpected call from Rebecca.

"Hi Paul," she said when he answered, "I'm sorry to bother you at work but I'm really worried about Daniel. He was going off today on the trail of some friends of his Dad's, trying to establish an alibi for him the day of the murder, but he's not home yet. I have no idea where he is or where he went even and I've had this really strange text message from him."

"What message?"

Rebecca forwarded Daniels text on to Paul's phone so that he could see it first-hand.

After reading it through a couple of times Paul said, "I agree that it sounds a little unusual, and I'm as surprised as you to discover that it was his Dad after all, but Daniel's not the sort to do anything silly. Keep trying him on his mobile, I'm sure he'll turn up soon and you can give him a right dressing down."

"I know you'll think I'm being stupid Paul, but I am beginning to wonder if it was even Daniel that sent the text. It doesn't sound anything like him....he never calls me Bec's and he never signs off as Dan."

"Have you no idea at all where he was going?"

"None, all I know is that he found some old photographs in the loft and was determined to trace a couple that were in one of them."

"Look, I shall be off duty soon, I'll call in on my way home. Try not to worry, I'm sure he's fine and just unable to get in touch. You said yourself that his phone could be flat."

"Thank you Paul, I know you are probably right, but I'm just so worried."

Rebecca put down the phone and waited anxiously for Paul's arrival.

Before leaving to see Rebecca, Paul called in to see Roy Darnley to ask if there was any news and to inform him of Daniel's text.

"Hello Roy," said Paul as he entered the incident room and looked round.

"Paul, I'm glad you called in, I've been trying to contact Daniel. I've got some news I think he'll be pleased to hear."

"Oh yeah, what news is that?" asked Paul expectantly.

"We've ruled his father out as a suspect in Lucy's murder. Some new files have come to light, along with evidence that he and his family were out of the country at the time Lucy went missing."

"Wow! That's strange. Daniel will be over the moon, of course, but I've just had a very distressed Rebecca on the phone. She can't find Daniel anywhere and can't contact him by phone, but she has had a strange text from him, saying that he has found a photograph showing his Dad wearing the tie-pin that was found in the grave with Lucy Penrose. Have you heard any of this?"

Paul took out his phone and showed Roy the text.

Roy read it with a furrowed brow and replied, "No, and I'm surprised about the photograph because, as I said, we've just discovered evidence that puts the Wests in Italy at the time of Lucy's murder. It was either a different tie-pin in the photograph or the photograph was so bad that Daniel has mistaken someone else for his dad."

"Did you say that you've also been trying to contact Daniel? Did you leave a message at all?"

"Only that I wanted to speak to him, not what it was about, why?"

"I'm worried that he hasn't returned your call because I'm sure he would have done if he got your message. What kind of evidence have you got?"

"We've located another box of files from the original investigation and it contains the interview with Jacob West. He states that at the time of Lucy's disappearance, he and his family were on holiday in Italy, and there appears to be a statement from the travel agent confirming it. That's obviously why Jacob didn't feature as a suspect at the time. It also makes any photograph showing him wearing the tie-pin somewhat unlikely, unless it didn't belong to the killer after all. I suppose it's just possible it could have belonged to Jacob and he lost the tie-pin in his garden, and it just happened to get buried along with Lucy. But it seems a bit unlikely."

"I agree.....I can't make top nor tail of any of this, Roy, can you?"

"It's peculiar to say the least. We need to get in touch with Daniel and see this photograph for ourselves."

"I suppose it's just possible," speculated Paul, "that if the murderer was a friend of Jacob West, that he may have lent it to Jacob for some reason and Jacob just happened to be photographed while he was wearing it."

"Maybe it's as simple as that."

Paul glanced casually at the photographs on the notice board to his left and focused on those of Daniel and Rebecca, alongside which were pictures of Daniel's parents, Jacob and Florence West. The picture of Jacob West had been taken with him standing proudly in front of an old Ford Consul and Paul supposed it was probably the one he had been driving when he and his wife were killed. The picture had a big blue circle draw around it and, prime suspect, written above.

Paul walked up to the notice board to get a better look.....there was something about it. He'd seen a picture of Jacob before, but something about this one......All of a sudden he cried out, *"Bloody hell! It's Jacob West."*

"Well of course it's Jacob West, Paul," said Roy somewhat confused by the outburst, "until an hour or so ago he was our prime suspect, you know that."

"Yes...yes, I know.....just a minute.... Let me get my head round something a second."

Paul held up one hand to indicate that he didn't want anyone to speak while he was thinking, but eventually said, "Listen...and hear me out, I think our two cases are related, I think......"

"Oh come on Paul, get a grip.....How do you make that out," interrupted Roy.

"Just hear me out Roy....The husband of my murder victim, John Bridgeman, brought in a photograph album, from which he is convinced his wife's killer took two pictures. We think the missing pictures were two of a group of photographs taken of three couples at some kind of function, one of the couples being my victim, Alice Bridgeman, and her first husband, George. Now, I thought that there was something familiar about one of the other couples and I've just realised what it is.......*One of the couples with Alice and George Edwards.....was Jacob and Florence West.*"

"Wait a minute....did you say, George Edwards," asked Julia.

"Yes, that's right, he's my victim's first husband....Why?"

"Oh Christ, I've been so wrapped up in making the connection between the notes on the tie-pin and Geoffrey Emerson, that I completely missed the fact that I had already interviewed someone with the same initials....George Edwards, he used to teach at Lucy's school."

Paul stared at Julia intently, "My George Edwards used to be a teacher as well. Where does your Edwards live?" asked Paul, "not Riverbank Road in Sand Bay by any chance."

"You've got it, Sir. The very same."

"Well, this whole thing seems to hinge around photographs of Jacob West, for some reason," said Paul. "First he turns up in a picture with George Edwards and then Daniel says he found a picture showing him wearing the tie-pin, which we don't think can be right."

"Oh bloody hell! And there's more," said Roy. "Daniel and Rebecca's house was burgled just after we finished there, but nothing seems to have been stolen. We think whoever did it might have been looking for something we removed.......It could easily have been a photograph he was after."

"Then this whole thing is definitely to do with photographs," said Paul, "but what bloody photographs, surely not just one of Jacob West with some couples at that party? And not one of him with the tie-pin if he didn't kill Lucy, so what are we missing?"

"Wait a minute!" shouted Julia, "Photographs, you say it all seems to be about photographs....well....Your victim, what's her name, Alice Bridgeman, was killed two days after Lucy's body was found."

"That's right, why?"

"Because that's the day the nationals carried the photographs of the tie-pin that was found with Lucy's body, it's another photograph connection."

"That's got to be it!" said Paul excitedly, "Lucy's murderer sees the picture of his tie-pin in the papers and realises that he is not the only one that will recognise it, so if he's ever been photographed wearing it, say at a function with friends, then he has to try and retrieve any copies that are likely to still be knocking around somewhere."

"Yes," said Julia, "and the person who commissioned it to be made would certainly recognise it, especially if that person happens to be his ex-wife."

"Then he'd have to make damn sure she kept her mouth shut," finished Paul.

"Wait...wait, Let me get this straight," said a somewhat bemused Roy Darnley, "You two are saying that George Edwards, for some reason we don't know about, killed Lucy Penrose, and because he was friendly with Jacob and Florence West, he knew their house would be empty. Maybe he even had access to it for some reason, mowing the lawn say."

"Maybe he even killed her at the house," said Paul.

"OK, then sixteen years later," continued Roy, "when Lucy's body is discovered, he sees the photograph of his long lost tie-pin in the paper and realises that his ex-wife will recognise it, so he goes to her house, kills her and stages a robbery. Then he presumably, remembers that Jacob and Florence had a copy of the picture of him wearing it at this party and burgles Daniels house in an attempt to find it.

"Christ!!" exclaimed Paul, "the picture Daniel found and the picture George was looking for could be the same one.....Maybe Daniel has gone looking for George and took the picture to confront him with it or something.......Daniel could be in real danger if he finds George Edwards......We need to get hold of Edwards now.....before he hurts Daniel...Come on."

Paul, Roy Darnley and Julia White left the incident room in a hurry together, "Julia, you drive," cried Paul, "I'll ring Rebecca and let her know that I'm tied up and won't be able to call in after all.....Roy, can you ring the nearest police station to Sand Bay and get them to send someone straight away, they'll get there quicker than we can. Tell them to arrest Edwards."

Julia jumped into the front of the car and started the engine as Roy got into the passenger seat beside her and Paul slid into the back, both on their respective mobiles. Julia, a keen driver and racing enthusiast, had once spent two weeks of her annual leave doing an advanced driving and pursuit course at her own expense; she completed the journey to Sand

Bay in record time giving both Roy and Paul cause to reassess their opinion of her driving skills.

When they arrived at 172 Riverbank Road, a local Sergeant was waiting for them outside the front door, "There's no reply from the house Sir," he said, looking at the two men as they got out of the car and trying to figure out which of them was the senior officer, "but there's a car in the garage and the neighbours tell me it belongs to the owner and that it's his only vehicle Sir."

"That's all right Sergeant, that's good work. Force an entry for us would you," said Paul, mater-of-factly.

The sergeant look uncertain until Roy said, "This is Inspector Paul Manley and I'm Inspector Roy Darnley of Avon and Somerset Constabulary. We have reason to believe a crime is being committed at this address. We need to get inside at once."

"Yes Sir," the sergeant replied, much relieved and now a little excited at the prospect of barging in on a crime in progress with two Inspectors. He quickly retrieved a battering ram from the boot of his car and had the door open in the blink of an eye.

As they all entered the house, Julia White looked at the sergeant and whispered, "Sergeant Julia White, my Inspector forgot to introduce us....you are?"

"Peter Wainwright, nice to be working with you Julia," he replied smiling and thinking that Julia looked just his type.

"It's Sergeant White, Sergeant," replied Julia, wiping the smile from his face.

Inside the house, they quickly established that there had been a struggle of some sort. There was blood on the inside of the lounge door as if someone had hit their head against it, and a statue on the floor, also with traces of blood on it. Paul's heart sank, wondering how he was going to break the news to Rebecca that, not only had he not found Daniel, but thought it likely that he had been abducted by a killer.

"Sorry Paul," said Roy, "it looks as if we are too late and George Edwards has taken Daniel somewhere." Then turning to Julia and the Sergeant who had knocked in the door he said, "check out the garage you two, we'll get **SOCO** in straight away, see if they can come up with anything useful and obviously check the blood for a match."

Paul was already on his phone once again, "Reg, get as much information as you can on our victim's first husband, George Edwards. It looks as if he's not only Alice's murderer, but that he killed Lucy Penrose as well, and now it seems he may have abducted Daniel West with the intention of killing him. We have to get to him before he harms Daniel. Find out if he has another house anywhere, a holiday home, static caravan, lock-up, anything. Tell June to wait for me at the station and she can drive me to Rebecca and Daniel's house. Perhaps Daniel has left a clue there. Get an alert put out to find Daniel's car. I think George may have kidnapped Daniel in it."

"There's nothing more we can do here Paul," said Roy, as Julia returned from the garage shaking her head. "We'll leave it to SOCO and the local boys. Let's get back and organise things from there, and you have to break the news to Rebecca."

* * * * * * * * * * * * *

Daniel was barely conscious as his car took itself over the edge of the cliff. He was aware of two things only, firstly that he was in pain, more pain than he had ever known in his life, more than he thought he could bear, he was hurting from head to toe, and secondly, he knew that he was about to die. Part of him was prepared to eccept the latter, simply because it would mean the end of the former. But there was another part of him, the stronger part, the part that loved Rebecca and desperately wanted to see her again, that part of him wanted justice for his father and vengeance for himself, that part was determined not to meet the grim reaper just yet.

George had failed to shut the car door properly after setting it in motion and it now swung open. Daniel wasn't strapped in so, in an act of sheer desperation, he used every ounce of what little strength he had left to push himself out of the door, crying out as he did so, both from the extra pain his exertions had caused him and also from the sudden, devastating knowledge that his actions were too late.

As he exited the vehicle, he was aware that the car had already begun to plummet to its destruction on the rocks below and that, although he was now miraculously outside the car, he was falling alongside it, to certain death.

Something strange started happening to time itself. Perhaps Einstein would have been able to explain to him why everything was happening so slowly. He certainly didn't understand it. It was as if he had somehow been suspended in space and time and his fall had been almost halted so that he was able to look around and observe what was happening about him. His car had nosedived over the edge of the cliff just as he had exited and it was now about to hit a ledge, some thirty feet below it. The ledge had once been part of the cliff top itself, but that had all changed dramatically when the face of the cliff had slipped down towards the sea, taking part of the coastal track with it. The front of Daniel's car struck the ledge, but momentum kept it going and caused the vehicle to somersault over its front edge and continue its descent to the rocks below, where the sea accepted its new toy with open arms, and began playing with it immediately, pulling it out away from the rocks one minute, only to throw it crashing back against them the next, moulding and reshaping it until it bore almost no resemblance to its former self.

Fortunately for Daniel, he fell a little to the right of where his car had impacted, and his already abused and broken body refused to bounce, or do anything even remotely resembling a somersault. So *his* landing, although culminating in broken bones and blissful unconsciousness, resulted in him remaining exactly where he fell, a new, if somewhat insignificant, detail in the landscape and an item of curiosity for the passing gulls.

About a mile off the coast from where Daniel's car was about to perform its impressive dive, Jack Eastman, a forty year old trawler hand from Porlock, had just finished stowing away the last of the gear after another, less than successful days fishing. He was looking forward to a hot bath and a few bevvies at his local inn, where he would often entertain holiday makers with, somewhat exaggerated, tales of his time at sea before the drink had him boring them with his life story, telling them of when he owned his own boat and how the government failed to protect the fishing industry resulting in him having the sell his boat to pay off his debts. Jack Eastman was a good man, but a chip on the shoulder never earned anybody any friends.

Right now, his back was aching something wicked, and he stretched to try and ease the stiffness a little. as he did so, something caught his eye on the top of the cliff. At first he thought he was seeing things, but his eyes were those of a man half his age and there could be no mistake......*It was a car! Going over the cliff!.......and......did someone fall out?* He replayed what he had seen over again in his head. He'd seen it alright. a car had gone over the cliff and cartwheeled off the new ledge that had been formed after the landslip, plummeting to the sea below, *in spectacular fashion.* As it had gone over, but before it had hit the ledge, a man had fallen out of the driver's side door, also landing on the ledge, but unlike the car, he had stayed were he fell. He must be trapped up there, thought Jack, and probably badly injured, if not dead.

He ran to the boat's small wheelhouse and rapped hard on the door to attract his skipper's attention, *"Bloody hell, Jo! Did you see that?"* he shouted, "A car.......over there," he said, pointing, "I swear...a bloody car went over the cliff, someone fell out....I think they're stuck on the ledge up there."

"Yeah, yeah, alright, what's the punch line? I'll bite."

"For God's sake Jo, I'm not bullshitting you, I really did see a car go over."

His skipper stared at him, trying to determine whether he was the victim of a wind-up or not. "Are you sure? The lights not too good now.....It could just have been a large bird or something, swooping over the edge, or maybe another bit of the cliff face has come away, it's pretty unstable up there."

"It wasn't a bloody bird!......And it wasn't part of the bloody cliff.....credit me a bit of sense will you.....It was a car I tell you...and somebody fell out as it went over.....They're stuck on the ledge!......*Now for God's sake....call the coastguard!*"

"You'd better be right about this Jack. If I call the coastguard and tell them a car's gone over they're going to call out the lifeboat, mountain rescue and probably a bloody chopper as well. There'll be hell to pay if you're wrong. How sure are you?"

"Just bloody well do it will you! I'll take the flack...... I know what I bloody saw! Call the F.....ing, coastguard."

Chapter 10

The Smugglers Inn was having a quiet night. The usual locals were all there but most of the townies from the caravans and holiday homes in the area had gone home early because of the, to say the least, inclement weather they'd been enjoying. The last couple of days hadn't been too bad, but generally it had been a poor summer and autumn wasn't expected to be much better. There were a couple of holidaying families in the dining room having a meal, the children out of control as always and running about, but there were only the usual few locals in the bar.

The stranger who came through the door, looking around warily as if he was entering some kind of hostile environment, looked somewhat bedraggled and bruised, as if he had been in a fight, or even a car accident. There was blood on his forehead and nose, and mud on his clothes. Everyone turned to look at the new arrival as he approached the bar.

Seeing that he was the centre of attention, he said, as much to the clientele as the landlord, "I took a bit of a tumble just up the road, tripped on something and went down like a sack of spuds, I could do with a pint of your best and the number for a local taxi."

Mary, the landlord's wife and hardworking barmaid gave him the once over, trying to ascertain whether he was going to be any trouble or not.

Deciding that he was harmless, she greeted him by saying, "You take a seat over there love," and pointed to a table near the fireplace. "I'll bring your pint over, you look as if you've been in the wars and no mistake."

"Thank you," said George, taking up residence in a seat next to the unlit and rather cold looking stone fireplace. It was almost large enough to walk into and it showed signs that it was in regular use but there were no holiday makers in the bar that night, and presumably it wasn't worth lighting it, just for the locals, until winter made it essential.

No sooner had he sat down than the wished for pint of beer was delivered by the rather concerned looking Mary, who placed the glass on the table together with the business card of a local taxi firm. "There you are," she said, "you get that down you. Do you have a phone to call the taxi?”

George smiled reassuringly at her, pleased by the hospitality, and said, “Yes, thank you, that’s very kind of you. What do I owe you for the pint?”

“Oh, that one’s on the house love but, as you’re not driving, I’ll be expecting you to buy the next one,” she said, giving him a friendly wink. “Do you want anything to eat with that, a pasty perhaps or a toasted sandwich?”

The question made George realise that he hadn’t eaten in a while. He had been intending to make himself something when Daniel had called and upset all his plans.

“A hot pasty would be very welcome,” replied George, smiling for the first time in ages, and Mary went off to fetch him one.

As George took the first sip of his beer he began to relax a little. He found himself wondering if the inn had any rooms. Certainly it was tempting to stay there the night and get a taxi in the morning but he really wanted to be away from the area when Daniel’s car was discovered, and there was no way of knowing when, or indeed if, that would be.

The man behind the bar, six foot four at least, sporting a beard that Father Christmas would have been proud of, and whom George took to be the landlord, answered a phone that that had been ringing behind the bar for a good thirty seconds.

After talking briefly to whoever was on the other end of the line, he looked towards a group of locals who were sitting in the room's only booth, and announced in a loud booming voice "That was the coastguard on the blower guys. They need mountain rescue up at lighthouse view where the cliff path has slipped. They've had a call to say a car has gone over the cliff and they think the driver may have fallen out and is trapped on the ledge up there."

Four of the six men who had been drinking in the booth stood up and started to leave. One of them replied to the landlord as he headed for the door, "Ring Dave and Henry, would you, Frank? Tell them to bring the gear in the Land Rover and that we'll see them up there," and then to one of his companions, "Pete, you've had the least to drink out of the four of us, we'll all go in yours."

George watched the four of them leave, cursing

his luck and thinking rapidly. Why didn't he strap Daniel in? that was a stupid mistake. Well, it was too late to do anything about that now, what's done is done. It was that bloody moving finger again. Even if Daniel did get out of the car, he thought, he's obviously fallen some distance and may be dead anyway. But if not, all of George's efforts could have been in vain. If Daniel is able to tell his story, George would be arrested and charged with murder. *He had to do something.*

After the men had left and the landlord had made the requested phone calls, George went up to the bar and ordered another pint. Mary passed him the pasty he had ordered and the smell of it made him feel twice as hungry.

"I couldn't help overhearing all the commotion just now. Do you very often get calls like that? It sounds like someone's in even more trouble than me," he stated as he started to devour the pasty.

"The boys who left are all members of our local cliff rescue squad, nice lads," said Mary proudly, "they've been called out by the coastguard because they think somebody drove over the cliffs and may be trapped."

"What will they do, do you think? And where will they take whoever it is, if they're still alive?"

"Well, the boys will get him up off the ledge if that's where he is. They're a good team, and they get a fair bit of practice round here in the summer. As to where they'll take the poor chap, or lassie of course, that'll depend on how badly he's hurt. There's an accident and emergency unit in Minehead but it's not that big. My guess would be that the coastguard will have called out the chopper and, if that's the case, they'll take him straight to Barnstaple. They've got a major trauma unit there and the helicopter can land in the grounds. That's where they take most of them."

George knew that if they brought Daniel up alive, he would certainly be in need of considerable help. After all, he'd been beaten over the head more than once, shot in the back and driven over a cliff. The chances were that he was dead, but George couldn't afford to take that for granted. He downed his second pint, finished off the remains of his pasty and rang for a taxi.

He checked to see how much cash he had in his wallet. Twenty five pounds; not enough incentive to persuade a taxi driver to take him all the way to Barnstaple, he thought.

He smiled at the landlord and asked, "Excuse me....Do you give cash-back?"

"No sir, I'm sorry," said the Landlord who didn't seem anywhere near as outgoing as Mary.

"Look, I'm going to need a lot more money than I have on me at the moment, is there a cash machine near-by?"

Again the landlord replied in the negative, but George persisted, "Look, suppose you take £250 off my card and let me have £200 out of the till, that way you get fifty quid for nothing...what do you say?"

The landlord, who was never one to pass up an opportunity, held his hand out for George's card by way of a reply. George ordered some more food to eat as he took the money and his card back from the now more amenable landlord. He returned to his seat by the fireplace to wait for the taxi. It was nearly twenty minutes before his ride turned up, giving him the opportunity to visit the toilet and clean the blood off his face and a little of the mud from his clothes. When the taxi finally arrived George was pleased to see that it was driven by what looked like a young family man, who was also an owner driver and would probably be pleased to earn some extra cash.

The driver stepped out of the car and stood by his door looking over the roof at George, "Are you the one that ordered a taxi," he enquired.

"That's me," said George smiling back at the young man, "I really need to get to Barnstaple A and E as quickly as possible."

The driver looked George up and down, noticing the fresh looking cut on his forehead and the somewhat scruffy appearance of his clothes, "Barnstaple! They've got a decent A and E in Minehead, that's far closer. They can sort you out there easy enough," he said, assuming that the man wanted his really quite minor looking injury attended to.

"No......I have to get to Barnstaple.....Will you take me?"

"If that's where you want to go I'll take you, but it will be expensive on the meter and I'll need some more on top. It will take me a long time to get back and pick up any more fares...you understand," said the driver, suddenly realising he could be on a decent earner.

"How much do you want to get me there?.....You say a price."

The driver thought for a moment, wondering how much he could go to. It was the best part of forty miles to Barnstaple from where they were. It would probably cost the chap sixty or seventy quid, but he seemed desperate to get there, and quickly. He thought he might as well go in high, see what the chap's reaction would be, and take it from there.

"It's going to cost you a couple of hundred mate. If I take you I'm going to miss out on a load of local shouts when the boozers close. I'm only allowed to drive for so many hours, and it's going to be at least one hour there and an hour back, plus messing about while we're there, and......"

He was prepared to keep making his point a bit longer before accepting a lesser offer, but he stopped when he saw that George had taken his wallet out of his pocket and was counting out two hundred pounds in cash. He couldn't believe his luck.

George passed the money across the roof of the car to the driver, opened the rear door and got in. The young man looked at the money closely as he quickly counted it, and then slipped it into his pocket and they were on their way. The driver, whose name turned out to be Chris, wanted to interrogate George, to find out how he had come to be in such a dishevelled state and why he was so anxious to get to Barnstaple A and E rather than Minehead, but he was sensitive enough to the atmosphere in the car to realise that his passenger was in no mood for explanations, so the journey was conducted in silence.

As George sat in the back of the car he had a hundred possible scenarios running through his mind. He still thought that the most likely outcome was that Daniel was dead and that the men he had seen in The Smugglers Rest and comprised half of the local cliff rescue team, would soon be retrieving a lifeless body. However, if Daniel had somehow survived, he would certainly be in need of major medical assistance, and if Mary was right in her assumptions, Daniel would be airlifted to Barnstaple. George tried to work out some kind of timetable for events. He assumed it would take the cliff rescue team half an hour or so to get to the scene and erect whatever equipment they would need to lower a man down. If Daniel was alive, he would probably have some treatment in situ, say another fifteen minutes, then maybe another fifteen to raise him up the cliff, possibly more treatment at the top, then a transfer to the helicopter and a trip to the hospital. He was guessing at a timeframe of course, but he was reasonably sure that if Daniel was still alive it would be an absolute minimum of two hours after the team leaving the pub, before there was any possibility of Daniel arriving at hospital, but it would probably be longer. He would be there in plenty of time to find out where they would take him initially. What he would do then, if and when Daniel arrived, was another question altogether. What could he do? Daniel would be surrounded by doctors and nurses. He would just have to hang around and take his chance if one presented itself. Anyway, the first thing was to get there. He sat back and tried to rest and recuperate a little himself. After all, he hadn't come out of his confrontation with Daniel, unscathed. He closed his eyes and tried to sleep.

It was only a few minutes after the four men from The Smugglers Rest arrived at the point where Daniel's car went over the cliff, that the Land Rover with the rest of the cliff rescue team turned up. The six men who comprised the team were all from different walks of life, four local lads who had grown up in the area and two previous city dwellers who now worked in the local tourist industry, but they all had one thing in common, a love of climbing. Derrick was the oldest but one in the group and by far the most experienced climber amongst them. Derrick had climbed virtually everything. He'd been up Everest twice and had climbed The Old Man of Hoy when he was seventeen, totally against his parents express wishes. At forty two years of age, he had thirty three years of climbing experience behind him, during which time he had rescued almost as many souls. The team trusted him completely and, after he had taken charge of it six years before, he had introduced a rigorous training schedule that that ensured they all knew exactly what to do in all situations, and exactly what everyone else in the team was doing at any one time. As soon as the first four arrived, they visually inspected the cliff edge from a safe distance to determine exactly where the car had gone over and picked out a safe and secure spot where they could erect the A-frame when it arrived. They were all acutely aware of the fact that the cliff face had slipped, creating the ledge on which the subject of their rescue now rested and the fact that it would probably still be unstable.

Within a very short time, Derrick was edging cautiously towards the cliff edge, wearing a harness and roped to Tony, the biggest and strongest member of the team, so that he could look over the edge and, hopefully, determine where exactly the casualty was, and if it was safe to go down to him from where they were. By the time he had done this and indicated to the team that he could see the casualty, the required A-frame was in place and John and Peter were finishing off the last of the securing points.

The comparative quiet of the cliff-top was broken by the arrival of a paramedic on a motorbike with a police car just behind him. The senior of the two officers in the car alighted from the vehicle and announced to everyone with obvious pleasure,

"There's a chopper on its way. What's the situation here?"

The sun was very low in the sky when Derrick returned from his reconnaissance of the cliff edge and announced, "I'm just about to go down to the casualty. If the cliff stays put, it should be easy enough to bring him up on our stretcher. I'll go down alone first to determine if there is any sign of life because I have to report that, so far, I haven't seen any movement at all. If he's alive, Peter can join me and help to get him onto a spinal board, then we can bring him up the cliff between us. But I need everybody else to keep well away from the edge, it could be quite unstable."

Both police officers and the paramedic took an involuntary step back as Derrick voiced his concerns about the state of the edge, something that brought smiles to the faces of the rest of the team.

Derrick continued, "John....can you and Tony get the generator and the lights set up? We're going to lose the daylight soon and I don't want to be groping about in the dark up here with you lot. God knows what I might grab hold of."

John and Tony exchanged amused glances and Tony replied, "I'll get the lights set up for you, then I'll keep an eye out for the chopper, make sure it's got somewhere safe to put down."

It wasn't long then before Derrick, wearing a throat mike for communication, was checking Daniel for a pulse and announced with concern, "His breathing is very shallow and his pulse is weak, there are obvious broken bones and there are probably internal problems as well. I think we need to get this young man onto a spinal board and to a hospital ASAP or we're going to lose him. How long before the chopper.....oh never mind I can hear it," he said, as the distinctive whirr and hum of the helicopter reached his ears, "Get Peter down here with the spinal board and stretcher. We need to move fast."

As Derrick and Peter struggled to get Daniel onto the stretcher and up the newly created cliff face, the police occupied their time helping Tony pick a clear spot nearby for the helicopter to land and watching as he directed it in.

It was a struggle manoeuvring Daniel carefully onto the spinal board within the confines of the narrow ledge, but the hours of training proved their worth and he was soon topside and being examined by two waiting paramedics, the one that had arrived on his motorbike and a second from the helicopter that had finally found a convenient area to land not too far away. Daniel showed no sign of regaining consciousness so, after he was rigged up to various monitors and his airway secured, he was loaded into the helicopter and everybody started to pack up and leave, the police to make their reports, the paramedic on his bike to answer another call and the cliff rescue team to continue their drinking, promising to ring Barnstaple Hospital later in the evening to check on the new arrival.

After being transferred to the waiting helicopter, Daniel was off on the most important journey of his life, one that would ultimately determine whether he lived or died. As he was whisked away on his voyage, he was oblivious to the ministrations of the highly trained paramedic who constantly monitored his condition, and kept in constant contact with the team of specialists that would be there to meet them at Barnstable Hospital.

The air ambulance landing area at Barnstaple Hospital was only a short distance from the accident and emergency entrance, which had been specially built to accept patients who arrived by helicopter, so Daniel, still totally unaware of the trouble everyone had gone to, was soon being wheeled into the treatment room, surrounded by a doctor and a nurse as well as the helicopter paramedic and two hospital porters.

After the skilled team of doctors and nurses had carried out their various examinations and determined that he was not about to die on them in the next few minutes, Daniel was taken for a series of X-rays and a scan of his head. While waiting for the X-rays, the consultant in charge walked outside to speak to the two police officers who had arrived by car at the same time as his patient.

"Anything for us, Doc? Was he over the limit or not?" asked the senior of the two men.

"I don't think your man had been drinking at all officer, but there are things about him that might interest you."

All of the sudden the two officers stopped

looking quite so bored. "How do mean Doc? What is it that might interest us?"

"Well, he's been shot for a start."

"Bloody hell! Shot? shot where?....how?....have you taken the bullet out?"

"Pellets, Sergeant, not a bullet.....He's been shot in the back with a shotgun by the look of it, from a little way off I would say, fortunately for him. The shotgun wounds would have been painful but not life threatening. Although there are some near the spinal column, they're not too deeply embedded, but if the shooter had been any closer he could have been in trouble. Whoever shot him hit him in the lower back and buttocks mostly, but there are some pellets in his thighs and a couple higher up his back as well. Thankfully we managed to get them all out relatively easily."

"What about his other injuries? Were they all from the crash?"

"Almost certainly, although he does have wounds to both the back and front of his head, which is unusual. It's normally one or the other, but it's not unheard-of. He's broken both his legs, one arm and several ribs. He's also concussed and we believe there may be some internal damage, but we're still checking for that. All in all, he's in a bad way, but as long as there is no major damage to any internal organs and there is no brain damage he should make a full recovery in time."

"Did he have any identification on him?"

"Wallet and mobile phone. They're in a tray for you at the reception desk."

"Thanks Doc. I'd better call this in and get a senior officer down here. We just had a report that someone had driven his car over a cliff. Nobody said anything about a shooting."

The conversation that had taken place between the two police officers and the consultant in charge of A and E that evening had been observed, though not overheard. The taxi had dropped George off at the hospital almost an hour earlier, some twenty minutes before the helicopter had arrived, and he had taken the time to find a toilet where he could wash his hands and face again and get some more of the dirt off his clothes so that he looked a little less conspicuous. After doing that he had walked into the reception area of A and E and strolled casually up to the smartly dressed and not unattractive receptionist who looked to be in her mid to late forties.

"Good evening," he said, "my name's Stephen Pearce. I'm a free-lance journalist down here on holiday with the family and bored out of my skin."

The receptionist eyed him with suspicion, he looked more like a bum than a journalist and she got all sorts in there in the evenings, although it was still a bit early for the weirdoes to start turning up.

"The family are all back at the hotel watching some cabaret," George continued, "so I thought I'd pop along here and see if anything interesting has been going on, I could do with a good story. I thought I might write a piece about the workings of a busy A and E department on a Saturday night. Have you got the time for a little chat and can I publish your name if my editors are interested?"

The possibility of having her name published in the paper somehow made the stranger look a lot less like a bum. She'd heard somewhere that journalists were notoriously scruffy dressers.

"Wow...I've never spoken to a journalist before. My name is Sue...Susan Northgate. Which paper do you write for?" she asked.

"I'm freelance, so I can sell my stories to any paper that will pay for it. I mostly publish in the big nationals. So what's been happening tonight Susan? Anything interesting?"

"Well," said Sue, "It's been pretty quiet for a Saturday night so far but that will all change when the pubs close. Then we'll have a stream of drunks in, either because they've fallen over or been involved in a fight or just made themselves ill with too much booze. We'll have the police all over the place because there will be a lot of fights in town and we'll probably have a knife wound or two to deal with. You'd be amazed how many young people carry knives with them when they go out these days. The waiting room will start to smell of sick. We keep a cleaner on all night, because if you don't stay on top of it you get toilets blocking up and all sorts. It's appalling in here some nights. People are disgusting when they drink too much and it breaks my heart when I see the state of some of the girls that come in, sixteen and seventeen year olds sometimes, out of their heads on booze. Think of the risk they're taking, not just because the alcohol will destroy their livers eventually, but they're prey to anyone that wants to take advantage of them. Lots of them end up pregnant with no idea who the father is. It wasn't like that in my day I can tell you."

After George had cleaned himself up earlier, he'd had a search around to familiarise himself with the hospital layout and had located an unlocked stationery cupboard, from which he had taken a notepad and pen, intending to make notes about where things were in the hospital. He had no idea how things were going to pan out and he didn't want to have to go searching for particular departments if he found himself in a hurry. Whilst Sue had been telling him her views on the evils of drink, he had been taking notes so as to reinforce his role as a journalist.

"Oh....you might be interested in this," continued Sue, "there was a helicopter here earlier on, well only fifty minutes ago actually, you just missed it in fact. Cliff rescue have saved some chap who drove his car over the cliffs up near Porlock. The doc's are working on him now. What's the betting he'd been drinking. They're all the same, they cost the NHS a fortune. I think they should be made to pay for the treatment they receive. You could write an article about that."

"How badly is he injured, this driver, do you know?" asked George, hoping there was still a chance Daniel could die of his injuries and negate the need for him take any further action.

Trying to kill somebody who is in hospital would not be easy, especially with police hanging around.

"He must be bad I suppose, for the helicopter to bring him in, and they were working on him for a while before he went to X-ray and that's not a good sign, but I don't really know....Oh hang on there's some more police just turned up, I'll bet they've come about him; you sit over there," Sue said, indicating a small waiting area by the door, "I'll see what I can find out for you. Do you want me to tell them you're a journalist?"

"No, don't mention me at all, I'll get all my information through you if that's all right, it's easier if I just have the one source," said George, giving her a conspiratorial wink, and taking a seat by the window as suggested, where he hoped he would be able to overhear any conversation concerning Daniel.

The new arrivals, one in uniform and two in plain clothes, introduced themselves to Sue and showed her their warrant cards, "I'm Inspector Davidson, Barnstaple CID and this is Sergeant Cartwright and Constable," he looked at the uniformed officer, obviously unaware of his name, and the man volunteered that his name was, Morse. "Constable Morse," the Inspector continued, "We're here to find out about the man who was brought in by air ambulance, what details have you got? Oh, and I would like to speak to the doctor in charge as well. Could you get him for me?"

Sue was resisting the urge to smile, and thinking that it would have been better if, Morse had been the Inspector's name rather than the Constable's, but she replied, "I'll see if the doctor can see you, but the only information we have about the man is here," she said, handing the Inspector a blue plastic tray that contained the contents of Daniel's pockets.

"Thank you," he glanced at her name badge, "Sue."

Sue picked up her phone and after a moment George heard her say, "I'm sorry to bother you Doctor, but there is an Inspector," she almost said Morse for the sheer hell of it but resisted, "Davidson, here and he would like to speak to you if you're not too busy....That's right....I'll tell him." She put the phone down and looking up at the Inspector said, "Doctor Castle said he will come and see you in a moment. Do you want to take a seat?"

The Inspector looked about him. The reception desk where Sue was sitting was to the left of the main A and E entrance doors and to the right of the entrance were double doors that required a pass number or swipe card to get through. There were a few seats to the left of Sue's desk with their backs to the large plate glass window but a man was occupying one of them and he really wanted to wait for the Doctor somewhere a bit more private.

"Is there somewhere more private we can wait?" he asked.

Sue pointed down the corridor to the right of her desk and said, "If you go down there, past the main waiting area and through the blue double doors, there's a family room on the right. If that's occupied, there is a small prayer room opposite it. There's hardly ever anyone in there."

The party of police thanked her and moved off down the corridor. Once through the double doors they entered the little prayer room without bothering to check on the emptiness or otherwise of the family room.

The three sat down and after putting on plastic gloves the Inspector handed Daniel's phone to his Sergeant saying, "See if there's anything interesting in the log. Find out what the phone's number is and who was called or texted last."

The Inspector then opened Daniel's wallet and pulled out one of a small packet of business cards. "Daniel West, Guitar Manufacturer and Music Dealer," he read out loud, "home telephone number is Weston-super-Mare, I think, and the business one is definitely Bristol."

He took out his own mobile phone and dialled Daniel's home number, "Well Daniel, what have you been up to that has made somebody want to shoot you, I wonder?" he said out loud as he was dialling.

Chapter 11

Rebecca was waiting for Paul to call in, pacing up and down and occasionally trying Daniel's phone which was still switched off. She thought Paul would have been with her by now. He must have realised how worried she was. She contemplated ringing her Mum and Dad, but was reluctant to worry them, especially if Paul was right and there was nothing to worry about. She felt so helpless.

When her phone rang she nearly jumped out of her skin. She snatched up the phone to answer it, "Daniel!"

"It's Paul, Rebecca. I take it you still haven't heard from Daniel?"

"No...and I'm really worried. Are you on your way?"

"I'm sorry Rebecca, something's come up and I'm not going to be able to get there for a while. Why don't you ring your mum and dad and tell them what's happened? It's better than being on your own if you're worried."

"Yeah, OK Paul....perhaps I'll do that," she said, sensing that there was something Paul wasn't telling her. "You are coming later though, aren't you?"

"I promise I'll be there as soon as I can, Rebecca. Call your Mum and Dad....yeah?"

"OK, Paul....I will...I promise."

If Paul really thought there was no need to worry why had he suggested that she ring her parents? She was sure Paul knew something that he wasn't telling her.

Richard and Elizabeth Drake picked up fish and chips for the three of them on their way to Rebecca's and, after they had eaten and tried to ring Daniel for the umpteenth time, they sat and talked. Although they tried to be positive for Rebecca's sake, she could tell that they shared her concerns.

It was nearly three hours later when Paul finally turned up with Constable June Kelly in tow and Rebecca asked him anxiously, "What's going on Paul?"

Paul was pleased to see that Rebecca had taken his advice and rung her parents, "Elizabeth....Richard,

I'm glad you're here...Let's all sit down, please," he said, gesturing towards the suite, "and I'll tell you what I know, which I warn you isn't much."

"Daniel's been in an accident...hasn't he?" stated Rebecca.

Elizabeth put an arm around her daughter as Paul told them, "We don't know where Daniel is I'm afraid Rebecca, but we suspect that the friend of his dad that he was trying to contact is a George Edwards. We now have reason to think that this George Edwards is the man who killed Lucy Penrose and buried her in the garden. I can only suppose that Daniel was unaware of that fact or I am sure he would have come to me, rather than try to confront the man alone."

"Oh my God!" exclaimed Rebecca, "You think Daniel has gone to meet the man who killed the girl in our garden?"

"I sorry Rebecca; we don't know for sure, but it is a possibility. We have been to Mr Edward's house and he's not there, but his car is, so at the moment we are working on the assumption that they are somewhere in Daniel's car together."

The three of them just sat and listened to Paul

in silence, trying to take it all in, so it was a minute before Rebecca asked, "Do you think that Daniel is in danger then Paul? Is that what you're saying? Do you think this George Edwards has kidnapped or killed Daniel?" she asked, fighting to hold back the tears, "You don't think that Daniel has just gone somewhere with this man voluntarily?"

"We don't know Rebecca...We only know that we can't find either of them.....so it's possible.....yes," Paul conceded reluctantly.

Rebecca broke down and was wracked by bouts of uncontrollable sobbing. Richard looked at Paul accusingly and said, "Break it to us gently, why don't you, Paul."

"I'm sorry Richard, I'm trying to be honest with you. We are concerned about Daniel and we are trying our best to find him."

"I know Paul," said Richard apologetically, "I'm just concerned about my daughter....and, Daniel,....I wasn't having a go at you."

Paul's phone rang and everybody looked on anxiously as he answered it, "Paul Manley," he barked, "well done, get some men over there right away and let me know as soon as you're there." He turned to Rebecca and her parents who were looking on anxiously, "That was Reg. Apparently George Edwards has a caravan near Porlock. Men are on their way there as we speak and they'll let me know if they find anything."

Rebecca split her time between pacing up and down the room and sitting on the sofa, hugging her mother, and Elizabeth could do nothing to console her. They all felt helpless, Paul most of all, as he knew they would all be looking to him for answers.

Thirty five minutes later Reg rang again, "Sorry Paul," he reported, "the local boys got there pretty quick and they say that there is no sign that anyone has been near the caravan for weeks and that was confirmed by the site owners. I've asked them to keep an eye on it and they've assured me they will keep the van under surveillance for twenty four hours."

"Thanks Reg. No news on the car yet?"

"Negative Guv.....We're all trying."

"Sorry Rebecca," said Paul sadly, explaining what Reg had said, "I was hoping he may have gone to the caravan, and he still may of course, but we're watching it now. He's bound to turn up somewhere soon."

"I know.....but will that be before or after he's killed Daniel?" she cried.

Later in the evening Margaret turned up. Richard and Elisabeth had looked after Margaret after her parents had died and she and Rebecca had become very close and she had met and married Paul less than a year ago. She was sitting talking to Rebecca when the house phone rang and Rebecca rushed to answer it.

"Hello, Rebecca Drake," she almost screamed into the mouthpiece.

The voice on the other end was matter-of-fact. "Hello Rebecca, I'm Inspector Davidson of Devon and Cornwell Police, I believe you may know a Daniel West, is that right?"

"Daniel! Yes! is he alright?......Has he been injured at all?.....Tell me how he is?......He's not dead is he? Tell me he's not dead," prattled Rebecca, finding it difficult to control her words.

"Wow! Slow down Rebecca......Tell me how you know Daniel....Are you family?" the man asked.

"He's my partner, we live together. Tell me how he is....please!"

"Daniel's not dead Rebecca."

"Oh!....thank God."

"But he has been involved in an incident, he has been injured and he's in hospital."

"Which hospital? How badly is he injured?"

"He's in North Devon district hospital in Barnstaple. If you are coming down to see him I would very much like to talk to you Rebecca. We need to find out what happened to Daniel."

"Of course I'm coming down to see him...I'm coming now....straight away."

Paul had been standing by Rebecca's side listening to the conversation and now interrupted, "Let me speak to him Rebecca," and she handed Paul the phone.

"Hello...Inspector Davidson, is that right?" began Paul.

"That's right...who am I speaking to now?"

"I'm Inspector Paul Manley, Avon and Somerset. Have you arrested anybody in connection with Daniel's accident?"

"No.....should I have done?....Is there something I should know Inspector? Because I have an awful lot of questions concerning what's happened here. I would be grateful if you could shed some light on events for me if you know anything."

"Oh, I know the whole story Inspector, but it's actually quite complicated. I think it would be easier if we met. I believe Daniel to be in some danger and I would be grateful if you could spare a man to stay with him until I get there. Could you do that for me?"

"OK, Inspector, I'll arrange that, but when can we get together?"

"I'll come down with Rebecca tonight."

"All right, that sounds good. I'll leave a man at the hospital with Daniel until you get here. I'll let you have my mobile number and you can ring me when you arrive. I'll come and see you at the hospital and you can fill me in," said Inspector Davidson, hanging up the phone and thinking it was going to be a long night all round.

* * * * * * * * * * * * * *

Richard and Elizabeth drove their daughter to Barnstaple hospital in Richard's car and Paul followed in his with Constable Kelly driving.

"You really didn't need to come you know," Paul said to her, "I am capable of driving."

"Nonsense Guv you can't go investigating on your own. Suppose you have to interview someone, you're lousy at taking notes and it's a long drive at this time of the day. You need someone to share the driving with you, you look fatigued already. It's all right for the Drakes, they're going to book in somewhere and stay over so they don't have to drive back."

Paul didn't argue with her, he was actually quite pleased to have the company and June had proved a useful person to have around and bounce ideas off.

When Paul and June arrived at the hospital they found Richard and Elizabeth waiting for them in reception.

"Paul," said Richard, as he saw them come through the doors, "Rebecca's in with Daniel now. He's in a bad way I'm afraid, he's broken both legs and his left arm, and he's got a couple of broken ribs. His internal organs seem to have escaped thank God, but he's had a nasty bang to the head that they are a bit worried about. So far he hasn't regained consciousness. He's in the high dependency unit. Rebecca's in pieces."

"I'll bet she is, I'm so sorry Richard," he said, as Elizabeth gave him a hug.

Paul had contacted Inspector Davidson with his estimated time of arrival and he and his sergeant came through the doors just as Richard finished filling Paul in on Daniel's condition.

Inspector Davidson stood two inches taller than Paul's six foot one and his height made him look painfully thin; at forty two years of age he was nine years older than Paul but looked more. His face was lined and his eyes dark and hooded. Paul suspected that he would not age well. They took themselves off to the little prayer room with June and Sergeant Cartwright so as to be alone, leaving Richard and Elizabeth in the family room with only out of date magazines for company.

Paul updated Inspector Davidson with what had happened and the fact that they thought Daniel had probably been kidnapped by George Edwards with a view to killing him.

"What actually happened to Daniel, Inspector?" asked Paul.

"Well, what you've told me kind of fits with what we've got Inspector. Since I spoke to you earlier we have discovered that a holiday home near where Daniel apparently had his accident has been broken into, literally broken into. Somebody drove a sit-on lawn mower into the back door. There are signs of a struggle in the house and it looks as if a shotgun was taken from the premises, because there is an empty gun case on the floor and that ties in with the fact that your Daniel has been shot in the back by a shotgun."

"Daniel's been shot!....I had no idea."

"No...I'm sorry....I didn't mention it before because I didn't want to alarm the young lady any more than she already is. He was shot at some distance so the injuries from that are not life threatening at all, though they must have been painful. It would then appear that he was placed in a car that was driven over the cliffs."

"Bloody hell! How did he survive that?"

"Quite.....Fortunately for your friend, he

appears to have fallen, or managed somehow to jump out of the car and ended up on a ledge. Cliff recue managed to get him up and he was brought here in a chopper. And that Inspector, is the full extent of my knowledge. We stand next to no chance of recovering any of the car, it's far too risky to try and get a boat near those cliffs at the best of times, but now the face has slipped it would stupid to try. The car will be smashed to pieces anyway. By the way, do know whose car it was?"

"Edwards car is still at his house so it must have been Daniel's. I think the idea must have been to make it look like a suicide. That would account for the somewhat ambiguous text that Rebecca received and something must have gone wrong. Have you considered the possibility that Edwards might have been in the car when it went over?"

"The coastguard are keeping an eye on that section of the coast just in case a body turns up because, of course, we had no idea how many people were in the car when it went over, it could have been full for all we knew."

"So you haven't seen hide nor hair of our Mr

Edwards."

"Nothing at all. If he wasn't in the car and he saw Daniel go over the cliff, he probably thinks he's succeeded in killing him and has gone home. Why would he hang about here?"

"That's a possibility of course, but we've got people watching for him and there's no sign yet. We have to assume that he has no transport so where would he have headed for after leaving the crash site?"

"He'd have had a bit of a walk according to men at the scene. My guess is he would have tried to get a taxi to pick him up from somewhere unless he had a bike in the car when they got there and took it out before the car went over. Either way, it's too much of a trek for him to get home if he lives up your way."

"Well he must know the area because he owns a caravan near Porlock and knew where he could drive a car over the cliffs, but as I said, we're watching both his house and his caravan."

"Train from Minehead in the morning maybe."

"Yeah, good call...Can you keep an eye out for him at the station?"

"I think we can do that for you."

"What if he somehow knows that Daniel survived the car going over and has been brought here? He may decide to have another go."

"He wouldn't have hung about at the scene for long so I doubt that he knows of Daniel's survival, but we'll keep an eye on him while he's in here."

Paul and June returned to reception to find Richard and Elizabeth in conversation with a very worried looking Rebecca.

"Ah....Paul," said Richard, "Rebecca has made arrangements to stay at the hospital tonight. They've apparently got a room next to ICU where relatives can stay. I've booked three rooms at a hotel nearby in case you and June are staying, if not I can cancel two of them."

Paul looked at June, "It would be better to stay here tonight and go back tomorrow. Davidson is keeping an eye on the train stations in case Edwards tries to get home that way and I'd like to be here if that happens. Are you OK to stay?"

"A free night in a hotel?.....have they got a spa?"

Richard smiled at June, "I think the lady said something about a pool."

"OK.....as long as I can buy a toothbrush somewhere. Is it too late for dinner?"

"That's settled then," said Richard.

The next morning Richard and Elizabeth were enjoying breakfast with Paul and June in the dining room of the Holiday Inn, when Richard's phone rang.

"Good morning Rebecca," he answered, "how's Daniel? Oh that's great news!" he said excitedly, giving Elizabeth a thumbs-up sign, "your mother and I will be over as soon as we've finished breakfast. Have you eaten anything?"

When Richard hung up the phone all eyes were on him for news. "The good news is that Daniel regained consciousness during the night and they are talking about moving him to a proper ward today as he's out of danger. Rebecca has spoken to the doctor this morning and he is optimistic that Daniel will make a full recovery." Richard turned to look at Paul, "The down side from your point of view Paul, is that Daniel has no recollection whatsoever of the accident or any of the events leading up to it. The last thing he recalls is leaving his house that morning on his way to do something important but he has no idea what it was."

"Damn!....That is a blow....I was counting on Daniel filling us in on what happened and explaining about the photograph and the text to Rebecca. Without his testimony we've got next to nothing. Whatever it was that Daniel found connecting Edwards to Lucy's murder will be long gone. In fact, it is only supposition on our part that there was anything. We have no evidence linking Edwards to the murder and only circumstantial evidence linking him to what has happened to Daniel."

"You mean if Daniel can't remember what happened this George Edwards is going to get away with it,....that poor girl's murder and everything?" asked Elizabeth.

"Unless we get some more evidence....it's possible, but I think Daniel's probably suffering from, what I think they call, traumatic amnesia. I'm sure his memory of events will come back eventually."

"This looks as if it could be new evidence coming in now," said June, who had just spotted Inspector Davidson and Sergeant Cartwright entering the dining room and waved them over. The four of them were sitting at one of the many round tables that had been laid for breakfast. As the two new arrivals approached they picked up a chair each from unoccupied tables and joined the four guests, who now shuffled their chairs round to accommodate them.

"I was hoping we would catch you here before you left for the hospital," the Inspector said.

"Why here?" asked Paul, curious,

"I haven't had time for breakfast yet," came the reply as he eyed their plates, "has no one kept a sausage for me? I'm starving."

"I'll go and get some seconds," said Elizabeth smiling, "what would you like Inspector?....and what about you Sergeant can I get you anything?"

"A couple of sausages and a fried egg would be nice, and maybe a hash-brown," said John Davidson, as his Sergeant nodded in agreement.

Sergeant Cartwright turned and took two cups off the table behind him, placing one in front of himself and the other in front of his inspector. "Any more tea in the pot?" he enquired as Elizabeth returned with the required items from the breakfast buffet.

Paul forced himself to wait while the two policemen devoured a sausage each before enquiring, "Any news?"

Between bouts of mastication Inspector Davidson revealed, "There's an inn called The Smugglers Rest not too far from our crash site apparently, well within a ninety minute walk anyway, and the landlord reckons he had a stranger in at about the right time, who looked somewhat bedraggled. Well, this stranger was in the pub at the same time that the call came through for the cliff rescue team, apparently it's they're watering hole. Not long after the team left, the stranger finished his pint and called a local taxi."

"Where did the taxi take him?" asked June.

"We're tracing the driver now and I'm expecting the call any minute."

Richard stood up, "Right, well Liz and I are off to the hospital. We'll leave you professionals to your work."

Paul shook Richard's hand and gave Elizabeth a kiss as they left, and said, "Let me know if Daniel remembers anything....no matter how small...anything at all, and tell Rebecca I'll be over in a bit to see him myself."

Inspector Davidson finished the last of his purloined breakfast to the ringing tone of his mobile phone. As he listened he looked more and more concerned, "OK...get some uniform over there now...I'm on my way."

Paul looked at him anxiously as Inspector Davidson stood and said, "Come on...we have to get to the hospital now!"

"What is it?" asked Paul, as he and June prepared to follow.

"The taxi that the stranger took from The Smugglers Rest....it dropped him at Barnstaple hospital....the A and E department!"

* * * * * * * * * * *

George left the little hospital canteen feeling decidedly more human than he had when he'd gone in. He hadn't realised just how hungry and dehydrated he had become. There had been some activity concerning Daniel during the night but Susan Northgate, the receptionist who was his main source of information the evening before wasn't due back on duty until nine. He was on his way to see her now but he had to be careful, there seemed to be an awful lot of police about, one of whom was sat outside ICU where Daniel was being treated and he was scrutinizing everyone who went in. He couldn't be sure that the extra police activity meant that they were looking for him, after all, not even Daniel knew of his involvement until he was at his house, but he saw no reason to be complacent either. It would be prudent to keep his head down.

Fortunately there were no police in reception when he got there and Sue was back on duty. "Good morning Sue," he said, "how is our friend doing; the one who drove over the cliff."

Sue was pleased to see him, "Good morning Mr Pearce.....Stephen isn't it? Well I've just spoken to Mary in ICU and she said he regained consciousness during the night so the doctors are hopeful that he'll make a full recovery."

George groaned inwardly, "So has he told them

what happened?.....Had he been drinking?"

"No.....the thing is....he can't remember a thing about it....He's got this, traumatic amnesia thingy, happens all the time in these sorts of cases," she said knowingly, "I've seen it before but they usually get their memory back in the end......more's the pity in a lot of cases. I remember this one time...a young girl it......."

"Sorry Sue, there are a lot of policemen milling around, do you know what that's all about?"

"You're right...there do seem to be a lot. They've only just arrived though; I'll ring round and see what I can find out."

George took a seat and waited. There was nothing else he could do with a uniformed policeman sitting outside Daniel's room, and now with the added complication of all the extra police about, he was beginning to despair.

Sue eventually beckoned him over and said, "Nobody seems to know why all the police are here, but I've found out that Daniel West is being moved to a ward sometime today. The doctors must be pleased with his progress. I expect they'll put him in ward sixteen, that's the main orthopaedic ward and, now he's regained consciousness, it's only broken bones they're treating him for. Except that Mary said, and you'll be interested in this, apparently he's been shot in the back....so it's not drink driving after all....If you want my opinion.....it's beginning to look gang related to me," she informed him with authority.

George thanked her and went off to find ward sixteen, which turned out to be on the second floor. Like the doors on all the wards, you needed to have a swipe card or know a number to be able to get in. The only other way to gain access was at visiting time between two and three thirty in the afternoon and between six and eight in the evening when the doors were left open for visitors. He had to come up with a plan and he had to do it quick before Daniel regained his memory and started shouting his mouth off to the police. He went back to reception to speak to Sue again, only to discover that she was on a break and had gone to the canteen for coffee and a cake. He caught up with her there.

The canteen was on the fourth floor and was surprisingly pleasant, much better than the one on the ground floor that he had visited earlier and which run by volunteers who seemed to specialise in sandwiches that were just about to go out of date. He had expected it to be like an old fashioned works canteen with grumpy staff and dirty cutlery, whereas it was in fact, clean, well-managed and had a varied and well balanced menu. He wondered why the hospital seemed intent on keeping it a secret from the general public. The NHS was supposed to be short of money and here was a potential money spinner hidden away on the fourth floor; it was inexplicable.

"Mind if I join you," he asked, finding Sue sitting at one of the tables near an impossibly long window that overlooked one of the hospital's five car parks.

"Stephen...no, of course not, sit down....I haven't learnt any more I'm afraid."

"That's all right, I have," he lied.

Sue was intrigued, "Do tell then," she said.

"Well I've spoken to a couple of the nationals and they are very interested in getting the full story on this Daniel West now they know he's been shot, and they will pay good money for an exclusive interview with him."

"Wow...that's great.......isn't it?" she asked, seeing his somewhat pessimistic expression, "oh, but of course, he can't remember what happened can he, that's frustrating."

"Well I might be able to jog his memory a bit, and in any case I can get background on him, if only the police would let me interview him, but they won't. The only way I'm going to be able to do it is secretly. If I split the fee with you, do you think you could help me get to see him on my own?"

"How?" she asked, wondering what she was getting into.

"Well I think the best way would be for me to pose as a doctor and get to see him on the ward. I'll need a white coat and a stethoscope to look the part and a swipe card or number to get onto the ward outside visiting hours. Can you help with any of that?"

"Oh! I don't know.....I would probably lose my job if anyone found out. That's asking a lot. How much will the fee be?"

"Well that depends on how good the story turns out to be, but your share will be at least five hundred pounds I would think, but who knows.....it could be a few grand....it all depends. Obviously if I get rumbled I'll keep you out of it.....we journalists never reveal our sources."

"Well, OK, if you promise to keep me out of it I'll see what I can do. Come and see me at mid-day, I have my lunch then. I'll see you in here, is that OK?"

"That's fabulous Sue, I'll make sure you get a good deal out of it, I promise."

Sue was worried about the possibility of losing her job, but she was so excited by the prospect of secretly helping an undercover journalist that she would have risked almost anything. She was sure he would keep his word about not revealing his sources, she had heard of journalists being prosecuted rather than do that. She couldn't wait to see the story in print and be able to tell all her friends about her involvement in acquiring it.

As George left the canteen he decided it would be a good opportunity to hire a car from somewhere so, back at reception again, he borrowed a phone book and rang a local car hire firm. He managed to arrange for a car to be brought to the hospital and for him to be able to return it to a garage in Weston-super-Mare. He was slowly beginning to feel in control of his own future once again. A solution to his problems was edging ever closer.

The Ford Focus that arrived was an inconspicuous dark blue and, after sorting out the paperwork and payment, George managed to find a space for it in the main car park. He was looking forward to getting home and having a nice warm bath and putting all this unpleasantness behind him once and for all.

When mid-day arrived he went back to the canteen for his meeting with Sue. This time she was sitting a little further along the window wall just next to a fire-escape, a single glass door with a quick release bar so that it could only be opened from the inside in an emergency. It led out onto a steel fire-escape that went down the outside of the building onto a small grass area opposite one of the hospital car parks.

"What have you got for me?" he asked as he sat facing her.

"Everything you asked for," she replied, "a white coat, a stethoscope and a swipe card that will get you into ward sixteen. Daniel West was moved onto the ward about an hour ago, but I'm told there is a policeman sitting by his bed. Either he's under arrest or the police think he's still in some danger. Perhaps he witnessed a gangland killing or something and the mob tried to eliminate him. Do you think that's why the newspapers are so interested?"

George put one finger up to touch the side of his nose, to indicate that he couldn't divulge what he knew, and said, "Thanks Sue, you've been marvellous, enjoy your lunch. I have to go, where's the stuff?"

Sue handed him a supermarket carrier bag that had been sitting under the table, "It's in here," she said conspiratorially, "you will let me have it all back when you're done, won't you?"

"Of course I will, don't worry, just don't tell anyone and I'll make sure you get everything back with a nice fat fee," he replied reassuringly.

Once outside the canteen George donned the white coat and hung the stethoscope around his neck. He examined the swipe card Sue had supplied and discovered that it belonged to a nurse by the name of Elaine Stewart. He briefly wondered how Sue had come by it but decided that such things were irrelevant.

The important thing was that he could now get into Daniels ward and put an end to the threat that was hanging over him.

Earlier on, he had given some thought as to how he was actually going to kill Daniel, on what he supposed would be a crowded ward. He had decided that he needed a weapon and a knife was the obvious choice, it would be quicker and easier than trying to hold a pillow over his head. So, after taking possession of the car and before his meeting with Sue, he had located the hospital kitchen. He had stood outside the doors for what had seemed an eternity, peering in whenever the opportunity arose. A little before mid-day an opportunity presented itself and he took it. When everyone's attention was distracted by the clatter of falling pans from the far end of the kitchen, he quickly slipped in through the doors and took a carving knife from one of the racks. The knife was now in his trouser pocket with the blade swathed in toilet tissue and his handkerchief as a make-shift scabbard to prevent it cutting his leg as he walked.

Now armed and ready, he made his way to ward sixteen. He had intended to wait until after visiting time, which is why he required the swipe card, but when he got to the ward he saw the nurses were doing their best to keep out of the way, presumably wanting to avoid getting embroiled in conversation with patient's families. One of the beds at the far end of the ward had the curtains pulled round it and he supposed that would make it less conspicuous when he pulled the ones around Daniels bed. Daniel was about halfway along the ward, almost opposite the nurse's station, but this was unoccupied at the moment and there was nobody at Daniel's bedside besides the expected constable. He doubted that he would have a better opportunity to carry out his gruesome task, so he walked up the ward trying to look like a confident doctor, whilst avoiding eye contact with anyone.

The constable sat up and looked at George as he approached Daniels bed. "Hello Daniel, Constable," said George, as he began to pull the curtains around the bed and smiled at the little notice on them saying, Please respect Patient's Privacy. "I'm going to be with Daniel for ten or fifteen minutes constable, if you want to take the opportunity to get yourself a coffee."

"I'm not supposed to leave his side Doc. I'll be just outside the curtains."

Daniel looked at the Doctor, thinking his face was familiar, but not sure when or where he had seen him before, "I've seen you before Doctor....haven't I?" he said.

"Yes you have Daniel, I saw you when you first arrived.....Is your memory still giving you some trouble?"

The Constable looked from Daniel to the doctor and back again, appearing to be making his mind up about something, "So you've seen this Doctor before then Daniel?" he asked. "Well in that case Doc." he continued, "I will take the opportunity to stretch my legs and grab a coffee, I'd appreciate it if you didn't leave until I get back though. I'll grab a drink from the nearest machine and bring it back here, ten minutes tops, is that OK?"

"Take your time Constable. Daniel and I will be fine," replied George, gaining confidence by the second.

The young constable left Daniel to the ministrations of the Doctor, hoping that he wouldn't be in too much trouble if his Sergeant found out he'd left his post. After all, it wasn't as if he had left his charge alone.

* * * * * * * * * * * *

Richard and Elizabeth Drake were saying goodbye to their daughter and Richard handed her the keys of the car he had hired for her to use while in Devon, "Now remember," he said to her, "any problems you just ring and let me know, and I'll take care of the hotel when you're finished. I don't think it will be long and we can get Daniel transferred nearer home. Maybe he can even finish his convalescence with us."

"Thanks Dad, you've both been great, it would have been ten times worse if I'd been on my own," she said and kissed her parents goodbye.

"We're off now as well, Rebecca," said Paul, who was standing behind her with June Kelly, "I'm just going to pop up and see Daniel before we go." Then turning to June he said, "Give Davidson a ring and let him know, will you?"

"OK Guv, you go on, I'll join you on the ward in a moment."

"I'll come up with you then," said Rebecca as they headed for the lift, "how much danger do you think Daniel is in, Paul?"

"I don't really know Rebecca but we're bound to get a line on George Edwards whereabouts soon, he can't stay hidden for long, and until then Daniel has got a man with him night and day. I'm pushing to have him transferred to Bristol as soon as possible so our people can keep an eye on him so try not to worry, we're going to look after him as if he was royalty."

As they entered the ward a Doctor was pulling the curtains around Daniels bed.

"Why are they pulling the curtains round Daniel?" asked an anxious Rebecca, "He's already seen the Doctor, do you think something has happened?"

Just as they arrived at the bed the constable who had been saitting with Daniel emerged from the other side of the curtains saying something about a coffee to the doctor.

Rebecca pulled the curtains to one side and stuck her head through, anxious to make sure Daniel was **OK**, and was astonished to see the doctor unwrapping what appeared to be a *carving knife.*

"*What the hell's going on,*" she screamed at the top of her voice, as Paul now pulled the curtains aside and surveyed the scene before him.

Paul recognised George Edwards straight away and, seeing the knife in his hand, shouted to Rebecca, **"Stand back Rebecca."**

Rebecca was too worried about Daniel to take any notice and grabbed for the knife in George's right hand but missed as George raised his hand up in the air. Paul was hampered in his attempt to intervene because Rebecca was between George and himself, so he made to grab Rebecca's arm and pull her out of the way, but George beat him to it. He grabbed Rebecca around her body with his left arm and brought the knife up to her throat with his right.

Daniel, with one leg in traction and an arm in plaster could only lie in his bed and watch the drama unfold, shouting, "Leave her alone....what are you doing...Paul...help her!" as Paul backed off now that George had Rebecca as a hostage.

"Give it up George," said Paul, "we know

everything. You can't get away."

"Keep your distance or I'll cut her throat, so help me I will," said George, as he began to back away from them towards the ward entrance, dragging a terrified Rebecca along with him. Daniel watched in horror from his bed, unable to do anything to help as Rebecca was dragged away from him.

"Where are you going to go, George?" asked Paul, "What are you going to do? You can't go home because we've got men there waiting for you. Same thing at your caravan, we've got it covered. Give yourself up now, you know we're going to get you, running isn't going to achieve anything, you're only making things worse."

George didn't appear to be listening. He just kept walking backwards towards the ward entrance pulling Rebecca along with him and telling them to keep their distance, which they did. Once outside the ward he headed down the corridor towards the lifts with Rebecca still in tow, the knife constantly at her throat.

As Paul exited the ward following them, he briefly turned and indicated to the constable behind him to stay out of sight and to contact Inspector Davidson and update him on the current situation.

When George and Rebecca reached the lifts, none of the four were on that floor, and George swung Rebecca around so that she was facing them.

"Press the buttons to call the lifts," he demanded, and Rebecca had no option but to comply, after which George swung her back again so that they were facing Paul, who was still cautiously keeping his distance.

Rebecca was staring at Paul, her eyes pleading for him to do something, but Paul was helpless. He knew that the slightest hostile move on his part could result in George panicking and cutting Rebecca's throat. He had never felt so powerless or so scared. The three of them stood motionless as they waited for the lift to arrive. Paul, who was still several feet away, ready to spring at George should he ever take the knife away from Rebecca's precious throat. There was a ding behind them as the lift arrived and a whoosh as the doors opened.

George began to drag Rebecca back into the lift, completely unaware of the fact that June Kelly was already inside, having come up to collect Paul and say goodbye to Daniel.

June was very quick to assess the situation as George stepped backwards and almost collided with her in the lift. He was still holding Rebecca around her body with his left arm and had the knife in his right hand held against her throat, causing his right elbow to be stuck out. June, although a few inches shorter than George, nevertheless managed to quickly slot her left arm down though the gap between Rebecca's neck and Georges elbow as she ran past him on his right hand side, catching him completely by surprise and wrenching his arm forward and to the right away from Rebecca's neck. She managed to straighten his arm and lock it between her arm and her body, grabbing his right wrist with her right hand at the same time. George, although caught completely off guard by June's manoeuvre, nevertheless managed to twirl Rebecca backwards into the lift with his left arm, whilst shoving June hard up against the inside wall of the lift.

The impact as June hit the inside of the lift with George's weight behind it, caused her to lose the hold she had on his arm and wrist and, as he freed himself, he swung wildly at her with the knife, catching her left arm that she had raised instinctively in defence and cutting a deep slash from midway up her arm, down almost to her wrist, narrowly missing arteries.

Paul had watched from a distance as George had dragged Rebecca into the lift, prepared to run for the stairs as soon as he determined whether it was going up or down. He had however, been completely unprepared for what had ensued. As soon as he realised that a struggle was taking place he had started towards the lift but someone must have called the lift from another floor and the doors closed on him just as he got there. He had seen June slammed against the lift wall and George lash out with the knife but could only guess at what was happening inside the closed lift as it began its ascent upwards.

As soon as it was clear that the lift was on its way up he made for the stairway and was joined by Inspector Davidson and three other officers rushing up from the first floor.

"He's in the lift going up," Paul shouted to them, "and he's got Rebecca and June Kelly with him...There's been a struggle and I think June is hurt."

All five men ran up the stairs as fast as they could but by the time they reached the next floor the lift had passed on its way to the fourth, so they resumed their ascent.

Inside the lift, as Rebecca was flung backwards, she stared in horror as June was slammed against the wall. She watched June raise her arm in defence, only to have it slashed as George swung the knife at her. Rebecca got to her feet and dragged the bleeding policewoman away from her assailant, who now stood with his back to the door holding the knife out as a warning to the two women not to attempt anything foolish. Rebecca looked about in vain for something to staunch the bleeding from June's arm; but in the end they resorted to just holding the sides of the cut together with their hands as they sat together on the lift floor, staring at George.

George allowed the lift to ascend to the fourth floor where earlier in the day he had met with Sue in the canteen, and where he had spotted the fire-escape which he now hoped would serve as his escape route. When the lift came to a stop and the doors opened, he made a dash for the canteen alone, no longer wanting or needing the burden of a hostage.

When Paul and the other officers reach the fourth floor they were just in time to see George disappear around a corner at the end of the corridor and a heavily bleeding June Kelly emerge from the lift supported by Rebecca. Two nurses who had been in the corridor waiting for the lift rushed to June's aid and Paul felt such a sense of relief at seeing the two women alive that he almost burst into tears.

Paul hurried over to June whilst pointing his hand in the direction of the fleeing George and shouting, "Get him!" at the top of his voice, and watched as his colleagues continued the pursuit.

The atmosphere in the canteen was one of peace and serenity. All of the twenty odd diners were busy eating, apart from the three standing in line with trays at the self-serve counter, and most of them sat alone, which accounted for the almost total lack of conversation in the room. The sense of calmness was enhanced by the sound of Mantovani playing quietly in the background.

The calmness and serenity where rudely interrupted however, when George came crashing through the door wielding his knife. In his haste to get to the fire-escape he collided with two tables, tipping one of them over, and sending a woman, who had just risen from her chair, tumbling to the floor. When people saw that the man who had entered their world so abruptly and noisily was armed with a carving knife, there was general panic, especially amongst those who appeared to be in his intended path. Women screamed and got up abruptly from their tables, running for the very same door through which the source of their fear had entered, and adding to the general mayhem.

When Inspector Davidson and the other officers entered the room they were greeted by a mass of people fleeing in the opposite direction which hampered their progress. George's lead on them was increasing by the minute. When he arrived at the bottom of the fire-escape he realised that he was on the opposite side of the building to the car park where his hire vehicle was parked. Behind him were the administration offices for the hospital and he noticed that one of the windows was half open. Seizing the opportunity that was presented to him, he climbed in through the open window, clambering over the desk of a, now very alarmed, woman who had been working at it. As soon as George had started to enter her office the woman had risen from her chair and stood back rigid against the side wall, from where she watched in terror as he slid across her desk, cascading all her paperwork and her telephone to the floor.

George threw open the door of the poor woman's office and found himself in a corridor that he recognised. Confident that he knew where he was and that he had a good lead over the men chasing him, he discarded the knife in an attempt to look less conspicuous. The time he had spent exploring when he first arrived, looking for somewhere to clean himself up, was now proving its worth, as he was quite familiar with the layout of the ground floor. He knew exactly which way to go, to emerge from the building near the required car-park.

John Davidson and the three officers with him

reached the bottom of the fire-escape and looked about them, expecting to see George still running; but he was nowhere to be seen.

Davidson, looked this way and that in frustration and yelled at the top of his voice, "Where the hell is he!"

"He must have made it to the car-park over there Sir," replied one of the constables, pointing, "he must be hiding amongst the cars."

"Well check it out.....what are you waiting for," came the frustrated response. "Damn!!!"

"Hello! You there!" came a call from behind him.

Inspector Davidson turned, and saw a woman gesticulating out of a nearby window, "Over here," she called, "he came through my window."

After recalling his men from the car park, John Davidson climbed through the window just as George had done and out of the woman's office into the corridor where he discovered George's discarded knife, still with traces of June's blood on the blade. Realising that his quarry had eluded them, he ordered the hospital grounds to be sealed so that any vehicle leaving could be checked, little knowing that his order would be implemented just too late to prevent George and his hire car making their escape.

An hour later he and Paul were sitting drinking coffee in the hospital canteen. "How are June and Rebecca?" asked John.

"Rebecca's fine, just a little shaken up, I've managed to persuade her and Daniel that George is long gone and that there is no point in him killing Daniel anymore anyway, because we all know he's Lucy's killer now, not just Daniel. June is a bit peeved that she didn't manage to overpower George and save the day completely but I pointed out to her that her quick thinking probably saved Rebecca. If she hadn't done what she did, George would undoubtedly have panicked when he discovered she was in the lift and there's no telling what he might have done. Her arm is badly cut and she'll be off work for a bit, but it's not as badly hurt as her pride, I'm afraid. Is there any sign of George yet?"

"Not yet, but every uniform in the south west is looking out for him just in case he got hold of a vehicle somehow, although none have been reported stolen from here.”

Just as John finished speaking, his phone rang and after a brief conversation he reported, “The bastard hired a car and had it delivered to the hospital, he’s certainly a slippery customer. It’s a dark blue Ford Focus. We’ve got everyone alerted but he’s got quite a start on us if he had it here waiting.”

“Hire cars don’t usually turn up with much in the tank, it might be an idea to check the local fuel stations.”

“Already being done. We might as well have another coffee until he’s located; he could have gone anywhere.”

Ten minutes later John’s phone rang again, “They’ve got him! He’s on the A361 probably heading to pick up the motorway past Tiverton. Come on, I’ve arranged a little treat for you. Do you think June Kelly would like to come?”

“Come where?...what sort of little treat?”

“Either of you ever chased a suspect in a chopper before?”

“No....and June will love it....I’ll ring her.”

"Tell her to meet us at the helicopter landing pad. Our ride is on its way in now."

Paul had to help June climb into the helicopter because her arm was in a collar and cuff and heavily bandaged, but nothing was going to stop her being there when they finally captured George Edwards. As the ground dropped away below them June felt like she was on a holiday adventure more than a man hunt and she was having the time of her life, despite the nagging ache in her arm.

"Not scared of heights or anything are you June?" asked John Davidson, somewhat condescendingly.

"Me...no...I've done a bit of sky-diving in my time," she lied, a little amused.

Paul looked at her sideways and smiled, knowing that June would no more throw herself out of an aircraft than he would.

The pilot suddenly announced, "That's your man, just up ahead with two police cars right behind him."

"Why don't they pull him over," asked June.

"If the driver won't stop voluntarily in a high speed pursuit, the policy is not to push him but to follow at a safe distance until it's safe to stop him or he runs out of fuel or abandons the vehicle."

"Do we know how much fuel he's got?" asked Paul.

"We think he filled up before we located him, so he could have a full tank."

"Wait a minute....he's slowing down." It was the driver in the first pursuit car who spoke over the radio, "I think he might be going to stop."

"He's probably realised the futility of running. He's got nowhere to go," said John, "I'm surprised it's taken him this long to figure it out."

The pursuit drivers voice could be heard again, "No....hang on....he's not stopping, he's turning off......where the hell's he going?....I think he might be cutting across to the A396."

"He's heading up to Minehead," said John, "why would he do that?"

"Don't forget he's got a caravan up that way," said Paul turning to June. "Have we still got someone there at his caravan?"

"Not now Guv. but we can get them back there."

"There's no need," interrupted John, "he can't get away from us while we're in the chopper."

"You're right....what the hell's he playing at?" queried Paul, puzzled.

* * * * * * * * * * *

George opened the door of his hire car with an immense sense of relief. He couldn't believe that he had managed to evade his pursuers so easily after they virtually had him in their hands. Once out of the hospital grounds he headed out of Barnstaple on the A361 and filled up with petrol at the first opportunity. It wasn't until he was nearing Tiverton that he realised there were two police cars behind him. What was he to do? There was no point in going back to his house, the police would surely be waiting to arrest him there. Similarly they were bound to know about his caravan and have men waiting there as well. If he didn't want to be arrested he would have to go on the run, but he had no doubt that the authorities would freeze his bank account and leave him penniless with nowhere to live. Life would be intolerable. He wasn't equipped for a life on the run. He slowed the car; he might just as well give up and get it over with.

But then, what would be the result of that? He had no doubt that he would receive a life sentence. A life sentence convicted of killing your wife was one thing, a life sentence convicted of killing a sixteen year old school girl was another. What would life in prison hold in store for him? If you believed the films and television dramas he would be subjected to all kinds of beatings and barbaric assaults. *He couldn't, he wouldn't face that.*

He knew the turning that was coming up on the left and, suddenly, *he knew what to do as well.* He speeded up again and took the turning, driving at speed again now so that the police who were following wouldn't risk trying to stop him. The road was a narrow one, just barely the width of two cars and not even that in some stretches. There were passing places at intervals along the narrower sections, but he knew that if he was to meet a car coming the other way it would be difficult to avoid a collision. The police cars had once again dropped back to a safe distance. After three or four miles of twisting and turning, the road came to an end at a T-junction with the A396. He almost crashed the car turning left towards Minehead and sped on. He was calm and relaxed now, realising that fate had left him no option. He couldn't undo the things he'd done. The moving finger had moved on and there was no calling it back. He glanced in the rear-view mirror and wasn't at all surprised to see Lucy and Alice sat in the back seat smiling at him, not in any malicious or angry way this time, it was more friendly and benevolent than that, it was as if they knew what he was planning and were in some way confirming that they approved of his actions for a change.

* * * * * * * * * * * * *

There was a lot of speculation, both in the helicopter and the pursuit cars on the ground, as to just what George was intending to do, but when he exited Minehead to the north west heading towards the coast, June commented, "Wasn't it around here somewhere that he tried to kill Daniel?"

"Oh Jesus!......that's right," said Paul, "we have to try to stop the car."

From the helicopter it was easy to see where the car was heading. Climbing higher they could survey the whole landscape. There was a fork in the road and high up it was possible to see how the track leading off to the right used to follow the cliff but now there was a large segment missing. From the air it looked as if some huge sea monster had risen from the depths and sunk its teeth into the cliffs, biting away a large chunk.

George, for a second time, manoeuvred his car around the bollards that blocked the right hand fork of the road and drove on at speed along the rough track.

"We have to stop him," cried Paul.

"I'm not going to put my men at risk to save a killer, but I will tell them of the driver's intention," said John Davidson as he held the radio to his lips.

"Be aware that the track you are on takes you straight over the cliffs.....I repeat, the road you are on has collapsed into the sea and we believe the driver's intention is to commit suicide. If you feel you can stop him without undue risk to yourselves, that's your decision, I leave it up to you. We will advise when we think you are too close to the cliff edge. I repeat...do not put yourselves at risk."

The police car immediately behind George attempted to overtake him but he speeded up and kept ahead of them. The cars were now fast approaching the cliff edge, getting closer by the minute and Inspector Davidson was afraid that from ground level the police driver would not realise how close they were.

"Abort!" he cried into the radio, "Abort....you're too close....Abort now!"

The spectators in the helicopter watched with mixed feelings as the two police cars came to a screeching halt. The helicopter overtook them and circled out over the sea facing back towards the coastline.

The blue Ford Focus continued on course until it parted company with the ground, sailing out into emptiness. For a moment it seemed to defy gravity, but inevitably Newton's discovery proved too strong for it and it began its inexorable plunge to the waiting rocks and the sea below, where it was swallowed up by the sea with the eagerness of a hungry predator. The observers in the helicopter watched the spectacle in total silence and the pilot turned back for home, there was nothing he could do and he was reluctant to deplete his fuel any further.

Neither the car, nor George's body were recovered. Daniel made a slow but steady recovery from his many injuries, and piece by piece he began to remember the events which led to his stay in hospital. Much of his early convalescence was done at the home of Richard and Elizabeth Drake, where he and Rebecca stayed for six weeks. June Kelly also made a full recovery, apart from a very impressive scar, and received a bravery award for her part in confronting an armed killer. Two months later there was a joint memorial service at Bristol Cathedral to remember the lives of Alice Bridgman and Lucy Penrose, who both enjoyed the service, watching unobserved from the rear of the Cathedral before melting into the shaft of sunlight that was streaming through one of the many stain-glass windows.

The End

Other books by Colin Holcombe

First Time Hard

ISBN: 978 1787233362

www.ingramcontent.com/pod-product-compliance
Lightning Source LLC
Chambersburg PA
CBHW071143100726
47908CB00002B/229